A DARK STEEL DEATH

A DARK STEEL DEATH

Chris Nickson

**SEVERN
HOUSE**

First world edition published in Great Britain and the USA in 2022
by Severn House, an imprint of Canongate Books Ltd,
14 High Street, Edinburgh EH1 1TE.

Trade paperback edition first published in Great Britain and the USA in 2023
by Severn House, an imprint of Canongate Books Ltd.

severnhouse.com

British Library Cataloguing-in-Publication Data
A CIP catalogue record for this title is available from the British Library.

ISBN-13: 978-0-7278-5047-8 (cased)
ISBN-13: 978-1-4483-0763-0 (trade paper)
ISBN-13: 978-1-4483-0762-3 (e-book)

All Severn House titles are printed on acid-free paper.

FSC
www.fsc.org

MIX
Paper from
responsible sources
FSC® C013056

Typeset by Palimpsest Book Production Ltd.,
Falkirk, Stirlingshire, Scotland.
Printed and bound in Great Britain by
TJ Books, Padstow, Cornwall.

To Norma Waterson, 1939 – 2022
The Queen of Song

Leeds, 5 December, 1916

The car slid quickly through the streets. Deputy Chief Constable Tom Harper stared out of the window. Leeds was black, a wartime winter-darkness, barely a single thin sliver of light showing through the blackout. A quarter of an hour before, he'd been comfortably asleep in bed, until he was torn out of a dream by the telephone bell. As he hurried to answer, he wondered if it was finally happening: the Zeppelins had come to attack Leeds.

No. This was worse. Far worse.

He could see the fire from half a mile away. Flames licked high into the sky. A moment later he smelled the hard, overwhelming stink of cordite.

'Duty sergeant, sir.' He'd had to press the receiver against his good ear to make out the words. The man's voice was flat, empty of expression. 'Our officers at Filling Station Number One rang in. There's been an explosion. A car is on its way for you.'

Filling Station Number One. Everyone around here knew it by a different name – Barnbow. The huge munitions factory had been completed in Crossgates just the year before, thousands of women working three shifts a day, manufacturing millions of shells for the artillery. War work. Women's work.

One of the wooden huts had been completely destroyed. All that remained were some splinters and boards, tossed far and wide across the ground. Shed 42. The charred sign lay near his feet. In the flickering light he could make out broken bodies thrown over what had once been the floor.

All Harper could do was stand back and stare as crews fought the blaze. The noise of the burning and the heat pushed him away. He watched the women from the Barnbow fire crew work hoses next to men from the neighbouring brigades.

He'd seen fires before, plenty of them, but rarely anything quite like this. He felt as if he'd walked into the middle of hell. God only knew how many were dead. Injured? It was impossible to guess. It would be daylight at least before they could come up with any kind of tally. Only one certainty: too many. Too, too many.

'Do you know what happened?' He turned to the camp superintendent, a tall colonel who stood with a look of disbelief and horror on his face.

'It could have been anything. It happened a little after ten, so the third shift had just clocked on.' His words halted and he shook his head. 'My God, so many of them in there . . .'

'How many?'

'Dozens,' was all he could answer. 'Dozens of them.'

Harper walked, another ghost moving through the darkness. Two women sat on the ground, arms tight about each other. Once was covered in blood, crying and shivering uncontrollably as the other tried to comfort her.

A little further. A woman stood alone, still as stone as she stared into the flames. Her uniform was torn; the sleeves were just shreds of fabric, her skin stained with dried blood. Her lips kept moving. She never noticed Harper as he came close enough to make out what she was saying. Two words, over and over: 'Edith's gone, Edith's gone.'

Ambulance drivers moved around, calm and professional as they carried away the broken and the dead.

Harper tried to cough the stench out of his mouth. It was impossible.

Gradually the fire was damped down, beams still smouldering, metal hot and twisted, as grim women returned to work in the neighbouring huts. Production had to go on. Everywhere was mud and soot, filled with a bitter perfume.

At the gates he talked to the policemen who stood guard in their heavy winter capes.

'We checked all the fences earlier this evening, sir,' a sergeant told him. 'Everything was solid and the barbed wire was intact above it. No one was getting over that.'

'Just the two entrances?'

'That's right, sir. All secure.' He shook his head. 'Them poor lasses in there.'

It was close to three in the morning when he left. The flames had subsided, the wreckage smoking, embers still glowing red-hot. The same woman stood muttering 'Edith's gone' until someone eventually led her away. Harper could hear singing from the other huts, belting out the music hall songs as they worked. Anything to raise their spirits. The only miracle was that it hadn't been worse.

The camp superintendent was still dazed, struggling to understand.

'Was it an accident, do you think?' Harper asked.

'What?' The man turned to face him. His mouth opened, his eyes widened. 'It had to be. Surely . . . wasn't it?'

Christ, Harper thought as the driver pulled away. He hoped it was.

ONE

Leeds, January 1917

He was starting to believe that he lived in a world made of paper. It never ended: the correspondence from the War Office, the Home Office, the watch committee, divisional heads . . . the minutes of all the meetings. It was probably all important. But Tom Harper felt as if it had nothing to do with coppering. He'd cleared his desk yesterday, starting the week with good intentions. Now it was Tuesday morning and he knew he'd be buried under another blizzard of paper.

For the last month things had been worse: Chief Constable Parker had been on sick leave with pneumonia. A week in hospital, but now he was recovering. It was a slow process; he wasn't likely to return before March. And that meant Harper was stuck with two jobs.

He pulled out his watch and opened the cover. Quarter to seven. Hardly light yet outside. With luck, he'd have the next fifteen minutes to himself. It might be all he'd manage in the days that began and ended while it was still dark.

Then the telephone rang.

'We have trouble, sir.' Superintendent Ash. His voice was immediately recognizable, even turned hard and metallic on the line.

Harper tensed. 'Why? What's happened? Is something wrong at Millgarth?'

'Not here, sir. It's the army clothing depot. You remember they took over the old tram sheds and the King's Mill next door to it back in 1914?'

Harper felt the shiver of fear crawl up his spine. 'Yes, of course.' He'd been part of the group invited to tour the buildings before they opened. Ton after ton of garments sorted, inspected and bundled every week before they were sent off to the soldiers. A gigantic operation.

'Two hours ago, the night watchman was making his final round at the mill.' Ash paused, considering his words. 'He thought he heard someone dashing off, then he found a box of matches and some torn-up newspaper in a corner. Came straight outside and reported it to the bobby on guard. His sergeant started the constables searching, then he rang me.'

Christ Almighty, someone starting a fire in a place like that, filled with clothes . . . the place would be an inferno before anyone could stop it.

'I've had men going through the place from top to bottom, sir,' Ash continued.

'What have they found?' He was gripping the instrument so tight that his knuckles had turned white.

'Nothing, sir. I've had them search that other depot on Park Row with a nit comb, too. It's clean. That's where I am right now.'

Sabotage. It couldn't be anything else. The thoughts roared through his head, hammering hard against his skull.

'I'll be there in five minutes.'

'Yes, sir. I haven't informed the army yet.'

'Leave that to me,' Harper promised. 'I want someone vetting the records of everyone who works in those places,' Harper said.

'Walsh is already on it. One of the new detective constables is helping him.'

He thanked God that Walsh was too old to go and fight. Twice he'd tried to join up; both times he'd been turned away at the recruiting station. Just as well; they needed experienced men like him to stay in the force.

His secretary was hanging up her coat as he rushed out. 'You have Inspector Collins at eight,' Miss Sharp told him.

'Tell him I'll try to be back by nine.'

His mouth was dry and his heart beating a terrified tattoo in his chest as he dashed down Park Row. Another raw winter's day, coming on dawn, the morning sky pale and mottled with high clouds and a thin north wind. He could have been a businessman hurrying down the street to his office, buried in his overcoat and hat. But he had more important things on his mind than profit and loss. Barnbow last month, and they didn't know the cause yet. Now this.

Leeds had a saboteur.

And the police needed to stop him.

Ash was waiting outside the warehouse. He was still a big, brawny man, but with the years he'd acquired plenty of padding. His belly jutted under the waistcoat and his neck had grown thick and fleshy. With his white hair and lined face, and the spectacles perched on his nose, he'd come to look like an old, wise man. Time had left its mark on him, but it had on them all. By rights, he and Harper should both have been put out to grass by now. But with so many good men, younger men, gone to war, they were needed. And they were working longer, harder hours than ever before.

'The army will be here in a moment,' Harper said, and nodded at the staff car racing along the road.

Brigadier Fox looked too young for his rank – barely forty – but Harper knew he'd earned it, gunned down twice in no man's land and patched up before going back to the trenches. Now permanently back in England after a third wound left him needing a stick to walk. These days he supervised the garrison at Carlton Barracks and was in charge of security at the facilities in Leeds. A war hero and his men loved him for it.

'Brian,' Harper said as they shook hands. 'This is Superintendent Ash. You can trust him with your life. I have.'

A nod and a smile, then Fox's expression turned grim. 'What are we going to do about this? We need to discover who's behind it before he has the chance to do any damage.'

'Increase the patrols every night,' Ash suggested. 'Vary the times, so there's no routine.'

'Nobody in or out without proper identification,' Harper added. 'Search everyone. No matches or cigarette lighters allowed inside.'

The brigadier opened his mouth as if to object, then stopped. 'Yes,' he agreed. 'All sensible. We'll do that. I'll post a couple of armed sentries at each of the other places.' He gave a sad, twisted smile. 'A rifle and a bayonet can scare people off very effectively.'

The staff car took them to the clothing depot on Swinegate. The building was faceless, anonymous, the stone black with decades of soot. *Royal Army Clothing Depot* was stencilled across the wide double gates, the letters beginning to fade.

The old watchman, a worried, defensive fellow with patches of white stubble on his cheeks, stared down at his boots as he told his story once again.

Harper stood close, straining to listen, his weak ear trying to catch every nuance in the man's words. 'Are you absolutely positive you heard someone running before you found the matches and torn paper?' he asked once the man had finished.

'Yes, sir.' But there had been that tiny moment of hesitation before he spoke. A speck of doubt. Harper flicked a glance at Ash. He'd caught it, too, frowning under his heavy moustache.

More questions, but the watchman wasn't going to change his tale now he'd told it to the police. Harper dismissed him.

'Well?' Fox asked. 'What did you think?'

'Something happened, that's certain. He found the paper and matches,' Ash replied after a second. 'I'm not sure it was exactly the way he said, but the gist of it is probably true enough.'

'Then . . .'

'Then we have someone who wants to hurt the war effort,' Harper said.

'Why?' Fox's face crumpled: he simply couldn't understand that anyone would do that.

'I couldn't even begin to tell you, Brian. But we're going to have our work cut out finding him.'

More patrols, increased guards on the gas works and electrical stations, any place someone could strike. It didn't feel like enough, but it was a start. It was one thing they could do.

Ash's men were digging into the staff at the depot; soon they'd start asking questions. But so much would depend on luck or the saboteur making a mistake, Harper thought as he walked back to the town hall.

His head was beginning to ache, pressure building behind his right eye, and his neck felt stiff and painful. By the time he climbed the marble stairs to his office on the first floor, all he wanted was an hour in a darkened room. Fat chance of that happening.

At least Miss Sharp brought him a cup of tea as he started to go through the papers on his desk.

'No biscuits today. Shortage.' She rolled her eyes. 'Can't find any for love nor money. And I've given up looking for chocolate, it's nowhere to be found.' She placed the small pile of letters on his blotter. 'These are the ones you need to deal with yourself.'

'Thank you.'

'Chief Inspector Collins is outside. He wants to bring you up to date on the specials and Voluntary Women's Patrols.'

Very quietly, Harper groaned. He knew it was necessary, but it didn't seem vital. Not now.

'Send him in.'

*   *   *

He approved Collins's plans without question. The specials to take over point duty, directing the traffic, and walking the beats in the quieter suburban neighbourhoods. It would free up the real coppers for the tougher work, and there was never any shortage of that. The special constables were all too old or had medical problems that kept them out of the armed forces. But to Harper every one of them was worth his weight in bright, shiny gold. Plenty of the police had been in the army reserves, called up as soon as war was declared. More had chosen to join, until many of the experienced officers had gone. Half of those who remained were like him, past their prime. At least the specials could keep order.

'Final point, sir,' Collins said. He'd spent a long time going all round the houses. 'The Voluntary Women's Patrols are still having a good effect. We need to continue them.'

'That's fine.'

'Your daughter, sir. Mary . . .'

'What about her?' Harper's voice was harsher than he'd intended; he saw the other man flinch.

'Just to tell you I've had excellent reports about her work, sir. Very professional.'

Quickly, Collins gathered his papers, stood and left.

Mary had joined the patrols last September, a week after the news arrived from France. Len, her fiancé, had been killed. He'd queued up to become a soldier the day after the prime minister announced the war against the Boche. Wounded twice, neither injury bad enough to bring him a Blighty. He'd survived the first, deadly day of the Somme, when it seemed as if most of the young men from Leeds had been mown down.

As time passed, they'd allowed themselves to be lulled into thinking he might come through it all, that he had the charm of life surrounding him. But hope was so dangerous, so brutal and banal. The news had arrived on a Sunday night. As soon as they saw Len's father, they knew. He thrust the telegram into Harper's hand, then stalked away with his shoulders slumped, only the husk of himself left. What was there to say? Mary was already screaming.

But the next day she went to work, refusing to talk about it. She worked longer, harder than before at running her secretarial agency. When that wasn't enough to blot out the pain that was drowning her, she joined the Patrol. Two nights a week at first, then three. Driving herself, trying to keep memories and thoughts away.

Harper understood. In her place he might have done exactly the same. But he ached for her. She was his daughter; he wanted to take away all her pain and keep her safe. But nobody could; not even Annabelle, her mother, could touch that. There was no safety in the world any more. Not for any of them.

He'd snapped at Collins. Stupid and pointless; he'd send the man an apology.

Too much on his plate.

And now he had to find a traitor.

Ash was a superb bobby; he really had trusted the man with his life. Before the war, his squad had been the best in Leeds. Now, though, they were dispersed; only Walsh was left. Sissons and Galt had joined up, even though he'd hated to lose them. Sissons was safe, working behind the lines in an intelligence battalion. Galt had died at Ypres in 1914. A little over two years and already it felt like a different age.

Harper knew he needed to be the one to lead this. And he had to succeed.

'Yes, sir. Thank you.'

He replaced the receiver. Chief Constable Parker still sounded a little breathless and dazed. But he was willing to take on some of the load from home.

'This case is more important than anything else, Tom,' he said. 'We're still waiting for the result of the inquiry into Barnbow, too, although I'm told they think it was an accident. Nothing malicious.' He paused to catch his breath. 'I could probably handle most of the routine daily paperwork here. Just send it over with a driver.'

Harper let out a quiet sigh of relief. That would make his job easier.

'Do whatever you have to do,' Parker said, 'but get this man.'

'I will, sir.'

'Make sure you do it fast.'

'I'll be back a little later,' he told Miss Sharp.

'But—' she began, then closed her mouth as she saw his expression. 'I'll cancel your appointments.'

'Redirect all the routine correspondence to the chief constable at home. For now, only pass it to me if it's urgent.'

She nodded, knowing better than to ask. No need, really. Word about the incident at the depot would spread swiftly enough; too many people already knew. But he could try to slow it. At least the papers would print nothing.

At Millgarth, Inspector Walsh had boxes of files sitting by his desk. His head was down, reading.

'Anyone suspicious?' Harper asked.

'Not yet, sir.' He sighed. 'But there are too many for just the two of us to examine properly.' He indicated the man sitting across from him. Cross? Cork? Something like that. A young face, blinking through thick glasses. Cross, he remembered now. Joined as a special, then some bright spark saw his potential and bumped him into plain clothes.

'How many do you need?'

'We could use another couple of men. More if you can, sir. Give me those and we'll whizz through them all today.'

'You'll have them,' he promised.

Ash sat in his office, working through the February rota.

'Apart from Walsh, who are the three best detectives on the force?' Harper asked.

The superintendent pursed his lips together as he thought. 'Probably Fenton and Dixon in C division,' he answered. 'And Bob Larkin over in Hunslet is always on the money.'

'Do you mind if I use your telephone?'

Two minutes and he'd arranged for them all to be transferred to a new squad working out of the town hall.

'I'm taking Walsh for it, as well,' Harper said, 'and you're going to head it up.'

'But sir—' Ash's face dropped as he looked around. Harper knew what the man was thinking: what would happen without him running things at Millgarth?

'Inspector Wills can handle it.' He was in charge of the uniforms. He could look after the entire division; it would do him good to stretch himself. 'It won't be for long. I want you both there in an hour. Bring the files with you.'

It won't be for long. Pray God that was the truth. But how often had they heard those words? It will all be over by Christmas, by Easter, by summer . . .

He'd commandeered the chief constable's office for the squad. It was the only room large enough to house them all. As council

workers in brown shop coats carried in desks and chairs, Harper
took the watch from his waistcoat and flicked open the lid. Half
past nine and they were almost ready to go.

All the men would have their different ways of doing things. He
had to trust that they were quick and professional enough to work
together. And that Ash could guide them. He ran a finger around
his shirt collar, feeling the sweat.

Time was tugging hard.

TWO

H arper watched the faces as Ash addressed the men. Will
Fenton had his head down, scribbling everything in his
notebook. He was a tall, gangling man, curly hair turning
grey and receding. Spectacles with metal frames that caught the
light and an ink smudge on his shirt cuff.

Bob Larkin sat with his elbows planted on the table, hands cupping
his chin and absently chewing on his bottom lip as he listened. He'd
been in CID since just after the start of the century – experienced,
intelligent, and happily free of the ambition to ever be more than
a sergeant.

Before the war, Dan Dixon had been on the beat in Wortley. A
member of the reserves, he'd been among the first wave of the
Expeditionary Force shipped over to fight. In a little more than two
months he was back, missing his left hand after an attack on enemy
lines. He couldn't return to uniform, but he'd proved to be effective
in plain clothes, a man with an acute memory for detail and a quick
ear for a lie.

Along with Walsh, and under Ash's command, he felt certain
they'd find the traitor. But this was going to be *his* investigation.
He needed to impress that on them.

'The superintendent will give you your assignments,' Harper said
once Ash had finished. 'I wanted you here because you're the best
in Leeds. You can think on your feet. You're going to need to do
that.' He paused and drew in a breath. 'We don't know each other
yet, but I daresay we will by the time this is done.' Wry smiles
from everyone. 'You all have different skills. Use them. Cooperate.

I'm going to expect a lot of you, and I'm sure you'll do everything you can. But remember, time is vital. We have to catch this man before he can destroy everything. I know you're the ones who can do that.'

Fenton stopped writing and cocked his head. 'How hush-hush is all this, sir?'

'Very.' Harper's voice was grave. 'The people down at the depot were told not to breathe a word, but . . .' He shrugged. They'd gossip. It was inevitable. 'People will hear. I can promise that the papers won't print a word. We don't want a panic.'

'Where do we start?' Dixon asked.

Harper nodded at Walsh. 'The inspector can tell you. But please understand, I'm relying on you. And I'll be doing what I can, too.'

The town hall clock rang eleven as he marched down the steps and across the Headrow. They'd made a start. Fine detectives on the job. Show me what you can do, those had been his final words to them. With one man to find in a city the size of Leeds, they'd need to be good. And lucky.

Back down at the clothing depot, Harper began to ask questions. All around him people were busy. Women sat at tables, checking bales into the warehouse to be examined while others loaded weighty bundles on to lorries. Old men who looked too decrepit for the task steered overloaded trolleys around. Some were singing, others concentrating, faces fierce as they added columns of figures.

'I gave your officer a list of everyone who was here last night.'

The civilian in charge of the depot looked worn, with the kind of deep circles under his eyes that might never leave. Clipboards stuffed with paper hung from the plywood walls of his office. Nothing here looked permanent.

'I know,' Harper answered, 'and I appreciate it. I need to talk to anyone who's here right now who was also working during the night.'

'Got a couple on double shifts,' the man said. 'We have a big order to go out to Dover. Gladys,' he yelled, and a young woman with a merry, beaming face appeared in the doorway.

'What do you need, Mr Hardy?' she asked.

'Deputy Chief Constable Harper wants to talk to Ronnie Owen and David Fisher.'

'Of course.' A smile. 'Come with me, please.'

She led the way through the maze, corridors of bulging bags rising high overhead.

'I hope you don't mind me asking,' Gladys said, 'but are you related to Mary Harper at all?'

'She's my daughter,' he told her with pride. 'Why? Do you know her?'

'I studied at her secretarial school. This is my first job.' She pointed to an alcove with a desk and two chairs. 'Do you want them together or separate, sir?'

'Separate, please.'

Small world, he thought as he settled. Or maybe that was just because it was Leeds. The city was like a spider's web. Everything was connected.

Ronnie Owen was a timid soul, starting and fearful at the slightest unexpected sound. Shell shock. Harper had seen it before. Men who returned from the front, discharged from hospital and the army, still wandering through the horror and the mud, their minds locked in a place no one else could reach.

His answers were slow, vague. If he'd noticed anything, it was still lurking in the fog at the back of his head. He fidgeted, played with a paper clip from the desk, concentrating with curious desperation as he twisted the metal into different shapes.

Harper tried different approaches, but there was little to learn. He thanked the man and watched him amble away.

David Fisher was very different. In his fifties, short, with a good eye, a sharp memory, and happy to talk.

'I wasn't over in that area much. We had a delivery and they kept me busy unloading it.'

No joy, Harper thought.

Then the man said, 'Mind you, I went by there a couple of times.' A glint appeared in his eye. 'On me way outside for a quick smoke. Need that every so often to get me through.'

'Did you see anything?'

'Now you mention it, I suppose I did,' the man answered after a few moments. At first, Fisher seemed hesitant to say more. Harper was about to prod him when the man continued, 'A man. I can't say I really paid him any mind. I was desperate for that fag. But he looked like he had dark hair.' Another pause. 'Thin. I've no idea what makes me think that.' He shook his head. 'Sorry, that's it.'

Harper's throat was dry and his voice raspy from all the tiny pieces of fabric in the air. But suddenly he had that feeling of anticipation. Had Fisher just given him the first glimpse of the saboteur? It was possible. Not one single scrap of proof, not a tiny bloody shred of it. But still, it was there in his gut. Maybe the start of something. Or did he simply want to believe that?

'Had you seen him before?'

'I don't know. Honest, I don't. I don't even think I registered his face. I was just passing and my mind was on other things.'

Harper spent another quarter of an hour pressing him with questions, trying every tack he could imagine. Fisher hadn't noticed enough. A glance as he went by. Still, it was a start, he thought as he watched the man hurrying towards the back door and reaching into his jacket for a packet of Park Drive.

'Any luck, Mr Harper?'

He looked up to see Gladys's smiling face.

'Maybe a little.' Harper stood, stretched, and walked behind her towards the door out to Swinegate. 'My men will be back tonight to interview the others who were working.'

'I hope you can find him quickly.'

'Do you have someone over there?'

'My chap's in the navy.' Another quick smile, but this one was fearful. 'I've no idea where he is at the moment.'

'I hope he comes home safe and sound.'

Outside, the day was still cold. He breathed deep and coughed, barking the dust of the warehouse from his lungs, then started back to the town hall.

'We have four possibilities from the files, sir,' Ash told him after Harper explained what he'd discovered at Swinegate. 'The men have gone to talk to them. I paired Larkin with Fenton, and Walsh is with Dixon.'

'Any of the names seem worthwhile?'

The superintendent shrugged. 'Too early to tell, sir.'

'Maybe we'll have a suspect later. Someone who doesn't report for his shift tonight.'

'It's possible.' Ash sounded doubtful. 'It could have been someone coming in off the street. A driver, anyone. We've been going through the logs. If he's there, we'll find him, sir.'

'Soon,' Harper reminded him. 'It has to be soon. Do you need any bobbies to help?'

God alone knew where he'd find them. Even with more than two thousand specials, Leeds was stretched. There was plenty of crime – black market, deserters – but not enough officers to stop much of it. Still, whatever Ash needed, he'd find it somewhere. This was the only vital investigation at the moment.

'We're fine for now, thank you, sir.'

He felt relief trickle through his body. He wouldn't need to perform a juggling act just yet. Harper stopped at his own office, picking up the important messages from Miss Sharp. One from a reporter on the *Evening Post* who'd had a tip about the clothing depot.

'You can't use the story,' Harper told him when the man answered the telephone.

'Why not?'

'Defence of the Realm Act. National security.' He hated the words. They were glib, far too easy to say, used to stop awkward, embarrassing questions. But this time it was absolutely true.

'All right.'

'Anything you hear about it, I need to know.'

'That big?'

'Yes. Don't even publish any hints, leave the topic alone.'

The rasp of a match on the other end of the line.

'Understood,' the man agreed with reluctance. 'When it's all over, you can tell me about it.'

'I will,' Harper promised. If this bloody war ever ended.

No joy with the men his squad checked; all of them were clean. Time for supper in the canteen, the six of them gathered together round a table. Harper sat back and watched. They talked together easily enough, laughing with a copper's black humour. Between them, they had the common bond of years on the force. It would work. It had to. As they left for Swinegate to check everyone had shown up for work, he buttoned up his overcoat and walked towards Briggate.

Worry gnawed at his stomach. They had to find this saboteur. There could be no failure.

He'd given up his official car at the beginning of the war. He'd never felt comfortable with it, and it was a way to save petrol. The tram was much more his style. A conductress took his fare, flirting as she worked. With the men gone, women had taken over their jobs, from clippies to machinists, fitting in without a problem. They could escape from being servants or mill hands, earn better money and have more freedom. War work was far more than filling shells at Barnbow or Newlay and the other plants. And they were needed, every single one a part of the effort. As he alighted, he could hear the sounds of the factories across Sheepscar still working. Three shifts a day, busy for the cause.

The Victoria was dark. Public houses were open fewer hours these days, shutting even earlier if they ran out of beer. Dan the barman had gone home, and Harper moved around the pub, careful not to bump against a table or chair. Up the stairs and through the door. Home at last.

Lights burned. A fire in the grate. On the settee, talking quietly in Flemish, the Belgian refugees they'd taken in at the start of 1915. It was Annabelle's decision; without a doubt it was one of the best she'd ever made.

Jacobus Palmaers, Johanna and their son Jef. Jacobus had quickly become Jaak, helping Dan behind the bar, with a strong, hard body for shifting the barrels and an easy, open manner the customers enjoyed. Jef was eight, a stocky little lad who was going to the primary school two hundred yards up Roundhay Road. He was picking up English at a terrifying rate and passing it on to his parents.

And Johanna . . . she looked after Annabelle. The year before the war the doctor had given his wife the verdict: in her early fifties, she was starting to go senile. So early, a heartbreaking sentence that was impossible to halt or reverse. The disease would move ahead at its own pace, and all the consultants in their stiff collars refused to say how quick that might be. They didn't know and they wouldn't predict.

Almost four years had passed since then. Slowly, inch by inch, she kept slipping away from the world. Annabelle still had plenty of good days when the fire sparked in her eyes, her tongue had an edge to it and her mind was crisp. But very gradually they were being outweighed, and that was when she truly needed help.

Johanna had proved her worth ten times over. More than that. She was patient, warm. Still young, in her thirties, plump and always smiling, she seemed to possess the wisdom of a much older woman. Most importantly, Annabelle liked her. She trusted her. Harper could leave for work and know his wife was in safe hands.

'Annabelle has gone to bed,' Johanna told him with a smile. It had taken a few months before he could understand her guttural accent. Now it sounded as natural to him as if she'd grown up around the corner.

In the kitchen he placed the kettle on the range. 'How was she?'

'She was fine,' Johanna answered with caution. 'But two times her balance was not good. I had to hold her or she would have . . .' she searched for the right word.

'Fallen?'

'Yes. That's it. But tonight she says, "We'll go shopping tomorrow, Johanna. We need a few things." I don't know if she will remember in the morning, though.'

All too often she didn't. Annabelle knew what was happening to her, how she was gradually drifting away from the life she'd known. Seeing that pain of knowledge in her eyes only made it harder. At times she cried bitter, angry tears. She shouted. She screamed with frustration and fear. He stood and waited, let her roar and crash around him then held her tight. There were moments when he wanted to go where nobody would hear him, out in the middle of nowhere, then yell and yell until his throat was raw. But in a world where millions were dying, at least she was still here.

'What about Mary?' he asked.

'Patrol night.'

Of course; it was difficult to keep track. He drank his tea and made small talk. Gossip from Jaak about the lunchtime customers. The ordinary pieces of life, reminders that something existed beyond war and illness.

He said goodnight and disappeared into the bedroom. At the edge of his poor hearing he could just make out the soft, even rhythm of Annabelle's breathing. In bed, he stroked the tips of her hair. Coarser now, grey. The sheet was cold, only warming gradually, until sleep consumed him.

The telephone hadn't rung overnight; obviously nothing to report. Harper frowned as he shaved. This was urgent; they needed a quick arrest, a trial out of the public eye and a conviction. Every hour without that felt like failure.

'You're away with the fairies,' Annabelle said as they sat at the breakfast table. Just the three of them; the Palmaers stayed tactfully out of the way.

'Work,' he told her. This would be a good day; he could see it in her interested, lively expression. 'Something big.'

Mary gave him a sharp look. Her face had grown thin, hollowed out by the grief she refused to discuss.

'Nothing to do with the patrols,' Harper assured her. 'How's business?'

'Hectic.' And for a tiny moment, a smile crossed her clouded face.

'Are you making money?' Annabelle asked.

'Hand over fist. Even put a little into those war savings certificates. I'm having to turn clients away.' Mary shook her head in wonder. 'Who knew a secretarial agency could do so well?'

'You did,' her mother said. 'That's why you started one, clever clogs.' She turned to Harper. 'I'm going shopping later. One of those meatless days today. Anything you fancy for your tea? Not that they'll have it, mind, but . . .'

She'd remembered. A few minutes of chatter then he buttoned up his overcoat and tapped his hat down on his head.

Mary was waiting on Roundhay Road. She wore the black wool coat she'd bought the year before the war. The fox fur collar was threadbare and ratty now. A small black hat perched on the crown of her head. Skirt four inches above the ground, the style that had come in a few years ago. She looked ordinary, like a woman not wanting to draw attention to herself. Dowdy. Widow's weeds. Then he tried to recall the last time he'd seen her or Annabelle in a good, bright frock. It was far too long. The spark seemed to have vanished from them both.

'I can't tell you what it is,' Harper said before she could speak. 'You know that.'

'Come on, I'm in the patrol, Da.'

'Weren't they talking about it last night?'

She shook her head. 'We had to go straight out. A report of a fight up on Woodhouse Moor and then we were hopping around until the end of shift.'

'I'm sure you'll hear next time you're in.'

'Da.' He heard the stir of annoyance in her voice and smiled to himself. A reminder of the way she'd once been.

'No,' he said. 'I can't. I'm the one who gave the order to keep it quiet.'

'I'll hear. You just said so.'

'I'm sure you will.' He winked. 'Just not from me. Hurry up, the tram's coming.'

The city felt every bit as busy as it had been before the fighting began. People bustled along the Headrow. Not as many vehicles, and the only horses drawing carts were worn-out nags; the rest had been commandeered by the army. But there were far more women around, in suits or all manner of uniform; most of the young men he saw on the streets wore khaki or the blue and white jackets of the wounded.

As he crossed Victoria Square, Harper glanced up at the clock tower on top of the town hall. One of the spotters was still up there, staring out over Leeds, although the darkness was fading. They'd been lucky, the city had had no Zeppelin attacks. Yet, he thought. Yet.

The squad was already at work in Parker's office. Ash had found a secretary to type up reports of all their interviews. Harper leafed through them, alert for any inconsistencies, the smallest thing that might jump out at him.

But there was nothing at all.

'Well?' he asked. 'Anyone have a hunch? Any feelings?'

Dixon cleared his throat. 'My guess is it was someone who took the chance and strolled in. I was talking to some of the workers. There wasn't any security worth a damn, if you'll pardon my French, sir. Someone could have come off the street, no questions asked.'

'And if that's the case—'

'We don't stand a cat in hell's chance of catching him.' Will Fenton's voice was flat.

'Have you gone through everyone who was there when it happened?'

'Yes, sir. There was one who didn't show up for his shift, but we checked on him at home. Down with the 'flu.'

Bob Larkin was leaning back in his chair, rubbing his chin and looking pensive.

'We're assuming we're looking for a man,' he began. 'All we have is what that fellow told you yesterday, and he was far from certain about anything. You said that yourself, sir.'

'True.' It had only been a glance, the man had said. But Harper had felt hopeful . . .

'There are plenty of lasses who work there, too,' Larkin continued. 'Maybe we should look at them as well.'

'We already did,' Walsh said. 'Went through the files. Women, too.'

'Take another look,' Harper ordered. 'At every one of them.'

A woman wanting to burn the place down? Christ.

THREE

A woman?

He sat at his desk, staring straight ahead. It was possible; his brain told him that. Most of the workers at Barnbow were women. But he couldn't believe it. When he'd heard Fisher, the witness, mention a man, that had made sense to him. It felt *right*. He couldn't explain it. And now he had to consider something completely different.

The suffragettes had used arson. But their targets had mostly been empty buildings. And they'd suspended their campaign for the duration of the war. Besides, this had nothing to do with votes for women. It was sabotage. If a blaze had started, it would have been destruction, pure and simple.

It was treason.

For an hour he kept busy with all the papers that Miss Sharp placed in front of him. He read the reports and signed his name with an appropriate flourish of his pen before putting them aside. When she appeared with a cup of tea, he realized he couldn't recall a single sentence from the pages. Only one thing filled his mind.

If there was any news, he'd hear from Ash. That was what he tried to tell himself. It was too early to expect an arrest. The investigation was just beginning. He knew all the phrases. He'd used them often enough himself. But none of it stopped him hoping.

At dinnertime he telephoned Chief Constable Parker, to bring him up to date. But there was so little to tell.

'Keep at it, Tom.'

'We will, sir.'

Twice he started to rise, ready to go upstairs and see what progress the squad had made. Both times he forced himself to sit down again; best to let them work without his interference. They were meant to be the best detectives in the city; that was why he'd put them together. He had to leave them to do their jobs without fussing around like a mother hen.

He managed to stay away until late afternoon. By then the pull had become too strong. Miss Sharp had left on time, blotter aligned on her desk, the cover pulled over her typewriter. The town hall was emptying; he could hear all the footsteps fading from the building.

Ash was the only one in the office, collating reports into a series of thick folders.

'Any leads?' Harper asked.

'A couple, sir, but I'm not expecting them to pan into anything worthwhile. It's like Dixon said this morning, anyone could walk into that warehouse.'

'Will we catch him, do you think?' Harper asked. 'Or her?'

He needed an answer and he desperately wanted Ash to say yes. But the man's face remained impassive.

'The honest truth, sir? I'm not sure. If it's someone who works there, then yes, I believe we will.' He frowned under the heavy moustache. 'If it's an outsider, we're going to need a mountain of luck. I wouldn't hold your breath.'

Harper attempted a smile. 'That's not what I wanted to hear.'

'No point in soft-soaping you. The men are doing everything they can.'

'I know.' He sighed. 'I know they are. Thank them for me. Is there anything else we should be doing?'

Ash exhaled slowly. 'If I knew that, we'd already be on it, sir. For what it's worth, I don't believe it's a woman.'

'No,' he agreed, 'it doesn't fit in my mind, either. Still, we'd better hope we have that bit of luck, shall we? If anything breaks—'

'I'll telephone you at home. How's Mrs Harper, sir?'

'Up and down,' he replied. 'The downs become lower and the ups are fewer. What about your Nancy?'

'Fighting fit. She's been talking about getting a job as a clippie.'

Harper smiled at the idea of Ash's wife as a conductress on the trams.

'You'd be able to get away without paying, there's always that.'

The Victoria was bustling; the dray had brought a delivery during the afternoon. Dan was pulling pints while Jaak moved through the crowd, collecting empty glasses. The air was heavy with the smell of beer and the fug of cigarette smoke. Men standing, talking, relaxing now their shifts were over. Some groups of women sat together at the tables with glasses of gin or port, something that would never have been seen before the war.

He slipped between them, nodding to a few familiar faces, then disappeared up the stairs and through the door to the living quarters.

Annabelle turned at the sound, smiling to see him. She was sitting at the table, working on a jigsaw puzzle with Mary.

'Just in time. Your dinner's in the oven. Pull up a pew and you can help us. We need a corner piece that's blue. You're a detective; you should be able to find it.'

He balanced the plate on his lap, eating as they worked together. He relished the plain, simple joys of his wife's laughter and a smile on his daughter's face.

By the time he'd made them all mugs of Ovaltine, the puzzle was complete, everything in place. Constable's painting *The Hay Wain*. Serene, a simpler, peaceful time. He stole a quick glance at Annabelle. She was smiling, happier than he'd seen her for months as she held the cup and sipped. All the strain had vanished from her face; she looked ten years younger. Mary's eyes were filled with joy instead of sorrow. And he hadn't thought once about a traitor and a saboteur. Who'd have imagined a jigsaw could work so much magic?

In the bedroom he helped Annabelle, standing behind her and unbuttoning the dress. For the first time, he realized how thin she'd become. Her collarbones jutted out; her shoulders were sharp.

Harper pulled her close. 'You know I love you, don't you?' he said.

'What's that for?' She pulled her head back to stare at him. 'Have you gone soft or summat?'

'Maybe I have.'

He rose in the dark, hurried through washing and dressing, and ran a razor over his stubble. The government had brought in summertime the year before, pushing the clock forward an hour to save energy. But it was no use during winter, he thought. Mary was already up, sitting at the table with her toast, tea mashed in the pot.

'That was a lovely evening, Da.'

'It was.'

A pause and the tone of her voice altered. 'I stopped in at Millgarth yesterday. They told me what had happened. Have you found him yet?'

'I can't tell you,' he replied. But he couldn't resist a little teasing. 'Who said it's a man?'

Her mouth opened wide.

Gently, Harper pushed her jaw up to close it and kissed her on the forehead. 'I need to go.'

The squad was busy, exchanging ideas and comparing notes. Harper talked to each of them in turn, discovering what they'd done, what they had planned for the day. Finally he stood in the empty secretary's office with Ash, the heavy wooden door closed behind them.

'What do you think?'

'I'm starting to believe we're chasing our own tails at the warehouse, sir. We've checked everyone who works there, and every visitor who logged in. There's nobody else left. We've gone seven ways from Sunday and there's nothing. The only clue is from the chap you talked to, and it's very thin, you have to admit that.'

So flimsy it might as well not have existed.

'And nowhere else to look . . .' A thought came to him. 'This is going to sound ridiculous, but what if it was a diversion, to keep us hunting there while the saboteur is planning something else?'

Ash chewed his lip. 'It's possible. What does he have in mind, though, sir? Where? And when? He's had time since then, and there's no shortage of possibilities in Leeds.'

That was the problem. Too many opportunities.

'I'll talk to the army, get them to make more searches.' He glanced back at the office where the detectives were working. 'Let them use their initiative today.'

After all, that was why he'd wanted them. Because they could follow their noses.

'Very good, sir.'

Usually it took longer to hit a brick wall. That was what had made him suspicious. Was the saboteur playing games with them? He didn't have enough evidence to guess.

'I can ask my men to search all around the places we're guarding,' Brigadier Fox said, but Harper could hear the note of doubt in his voice. 'What are we looking for, though?'

'Anything suspicious. Flammable things that aren't where they're meant to be.' How could he explain it? 'Something that doesn't *feel* right.'

Harper had a copper's instinct, honed over almost four decades. He knew at a glance if something was wrong. But he couldn't teach that to a bunch of soldiers who would probably rather be in the trenches.

'Do what you can, Brian,' he said. 'I'd rather your men were too cautious than let things go. My squad can take a closer look later. Let me know what they find.'

Two hours later the telephone rang. Harper had been sitting in his office, willing the time to pass. Wanting something to happen. Anything at all. He tore the receiver from the cradle.

'Deputy Chief Constable Harper.'

'Tom, it's Brian Fox.' He sounded triumphant. 'We've found him!'

'What?' He felt the pulse throb in his neck. 'Where?'

'The cattle market on Gelderd Road. They've been using it as another clothing depot for over a year now. He was siphoning petrol from one of the lorries into a can. Matches and a newspaper in his pocket.'

Harper let the surge of hope rush through his body.

'Keep him under guard until I get there. And well done, Brian.'

He told Miss Sharp to telephone for a car and rang Ash.

'The men are all out, sir. I'll come with you, if you like.'

'Like the old days,' Harper answered with a smile.

He sniffed as he entered the building. It still held the ripe, unmistakable warmth of cows. The place was a huge old shed, all the old metal barriers stacked against the walls. Like Swinegate, bundles of clothing stretched up towards the ceiling. The dry tickle from the fibres made him cough.

Fox was waiting outside one of the small offices, beaming and eager. Inside, a nervous young man perched on a chair, watched over by a Tommy with his rifle and bayonet at port.

'Caught red-handed,' the brigadier said. He pointed at a long rubber tube on the ground. 'Using this to try and siphon off the petrol.' From his pocket he produced the box of Swan Vestas and a copy of the *Daily Express*.

'You've caught him, but I'm afraid he's not your saboteur, sir,' Ash said. 'Are you, Sam?'

The man looked up, relief filling his face as he recognized the superintendent.

'I've been trying to tell them that for an age, Mr Ash. But they wouldn't listen. Talking about shooting me, they were.'

'Sam Johnston is a thief; he'll be trying to make a few bob on the black market,' Harper explained. 'Looks like it was petrol this time. He's been at this and that since long before the war. Sam will rob you blind, but he's no saboteur. He wouldn't know the meaning of the word.'

He saw the brigadier's face harden, then fall. He'd been cheated of his glory.

'Mind you,' Harper continued, 'if you hold him and do a little checking, I'll bet good money that he's either a deserter or evading conscription.'

'I'm in a reserved occupation,' Johnston said. 'Machinist.'

'You've never worked a day in your life,' Ash told him with disgust. 'Whatever papers you have are forged. You might want to have a think before you try that lark.'

Fox sighed. 'I was hoping we'd solved the problem. Are you sure . . .?'

'Positive,' Harper answered. 'Sam wouldn't have the nous.'

Johnston gazed at the floor, dejected. He realized that any run of luck had come to a crashing end.

'We'll hang on to him,' the brigadier said. 'Then I'll pack him off to Aldershot myself.'

'There was no way of knowing until we went out there, sir,' Ash said as they drove back towards Leeds. Another cold January day. The dark, sooty top of the town hall stood stark against a pale grey sky and chimneys belched out their smoke.

'True,' he agreed with a sigh. It felt like wasted time, but it wasn't; Johnston could have been their man.

Ash chuckled. 'At least Sam should be out of our hair for the duration. You can bet the army will keep a very close eye on him now.'

Small mercies. There were quite a few deserters and men who'd evaded conscription across the city. Harper tried to order a sweep every month, but he didn't have enough trained coppers to do a proper job; too many always slipped through the net. Their only big success had come in November: the police and the military had closed off Briggate and made every man who looked forty or under produce their registration card and exemption or rejection certificates.

'We'll see what the men have managed to turn up,' the super-intendent continued. 'The problem is we're not going to get much from our grasses about this.' He frowned and the moustache twitched above his lip. 'It's not something anyone's likely to talk about, is it?'

'I'll pass the word to the press about Sam Johnston's arrest. Make it sound like a general crackdown everywhere. That might make our saboteur think again.'

'We want him to stop, but we also want him to show himself so we can arrest him.' Ash raised his eyebrows. 'Horns of a dilemma, isn't it, sir?'

No leads. In the office he could see the frustration on the men's faces. Dixon doodled as they talked, drawing arrows on a piece of paper. Larkin listened closely to everything but added nothing. Fenton fidgeted and Walsh stared at the table.

They needed a push. A thread they could begin to tug.

'Keep at it,' he told them, but even to his poor ears they sounded like empty words.

He was walking down the stairs in the town hall, lost in thought as his footsteps rang and bounced off the high ceilings. Someone called out, 'Da.'

He looked all around for Mary, then finally up. She was leaning over a bannister, waving.

'Spotter duty for an hour,' she called. 'Got to go.'

Every night they had crews at the very top of the building, looking out for a possible airship attack. Harper had spent part of a shift up there once, a week after they began the watches. All he could remember was boredom and the cold. By the time his hour was over, he wondered if he'd ever be warm again. His hands shook, his legs were unsteady as he came back down. That was enough; he'd never agreed to do it again.

It was one of Annabelle's quiet nights. She and Johanna sat and knitted, making scarves for the troops. It was a way she could contribute, about the only one these days. Watching them work, the music hall rhyme came into his mind: *Sister Susie's sewing shirts for soldiers/ Such shirts for soldiers our sister Susie sews/ Some soldiers send epistles. Say they rather sleep on thistles/ Than the saucy sort of shirts that sister Susie sews.*

Once it was lodged in his head, it was hard to shake off.

'What are you smiling for?' she asked.

'Nothing,' Harper said. 'Happy to be home, that's all.' And he was. The pub ran smoothly. Dan handled all the paperwork. They'd increased his wages, and he was glad of the money and of Jaak's help. It was necessary; Annabelle couldn't concentrate on row after row of figures any longer. She grew muddled, then angry at herself, throwing the pen across the room in a fit of pique.

Harper read his way through the *Evening Post* then sat and considered the case. He kept willing the telephone to ring. Some new lead. Anything at all. But there was only silence.

FOUR

He opened his eyes. Five minutes to four on the clock and Annabelle was shaking his shoulder.

'Telephone,' she hissed.

The room was cold. By the time he lifted the receiver his arms were covered in goose pimples.

'Harper.' He heard his voice still thick with sleep.

'Duty sergeant, sir. We've had a shooting. One man dead.'

Suddenly he was wide awake, mind racing.

'Where?'

'East Leeds Military Hospital, sir. It was one of the soldiers guarding the entrance.'

For a second, he didn't know what to think. Christ Almighty.

'Send a car for me. Does Superintendent Ash know?'

'Yes sir. The driver will be with you in less than five minutes.'

'Good, good. Ring the chief constable and tell him what's happening, please.'

Annabelle gave a small grunt as he entered the bedroom, but she didn't wake again. Hurriedly he washed and dressed.

As he was about to leave, Mary emerged from her room. Her hair was loose, thick and dark over her shoulders.

'Sabotage?' she asked.

'Murder,' he told her. And he was gone.

A bitter January night with a keen wind scouring the ground along Beckett Street, past the soldiers' post at the entrance to the hospital. They were there to check everyone who came and went, to examine every vehicle.

Harper looked up at the building, thick, deep black against the night sky. A hospital for wounded soldiers. But to him it could never be anything but the old workhouse. Annabelle had been a Poor Law Guardian for nine years, visiting this place three or four times a week. Now it was filled with a different kind of pain. He'd been here a couple of years earlier, part of the official party accompanying the king when he visited the injured.

'Sir?' Ash's voice brought him back to the moment. He shivered. 'Give me the details.'

'One of the Tommies on duty nipped out on to Beckett Street to have a quick smoke. Single shot. Right through the heart. Instant. The guard working with him came running and raised the alarm. Brigadier Fox should be here any moment.'

He closed his eyes and took a breath. Poor man. 'Show me where it happened.'

Just outside the wall, a chalk outline marked on the flagstones. A dark patch where blood had soaked in. The body had been taken to the mortuary.

'What was his name?'

'Bertie Andrews,' Ash replied. 'Nineteen, a private. From Whitehaven, joined up last year.'

Harper stared across the road towards the cemetery. Its gates were locked.

'Did the shot come from in there?' he asked.

'Yes,' Ash replied. 'No point in searching until morning, we won't see a blessed thing. But no lights and a perfect shot . . .'

'A sharpshooter's bullet.'

No accident. Deliberate. And skilled. Murder, no doubt about it. The thoughts tumbled through his mind. A policeman's questions: had the killer been hunting Andrews in particular, or did he want to target any soldier? Why here? Why this way? Was it more sabotage?

He was talking to Ash, picking his way through all the things they needed to discover in the next two hours when Fox's staff car pulled up. The soldier was bundled in his heavy khaki greatcoat, bowing his head as he learned the details from a sergeant who appeared from nowhere.

Ash started questioning the other guard, a small, thin man with a stunned face who looked lost inside his uniform.

'What do you make of it, Tom?' The brigadier's voice was weary. 'Jesus God, what a bloody tragedy. Andrews was a good man, his sergeant said. He can't believe it. Nor can I.'

'We have to find the killer,' Harper answered. 'I don't know if it's anything to do with the sabotage, but it's definitely murder.'

Fox was staring at the cemetery.

'Bloody good shooting in the dark.' He shook his head. 'When we catch him . . .'

'He'll go to court.' Harper kept his voice soft, reasonable. He knew exactly what the man was thinking, and he needed to ease him away from it. They had to concentrate on finding the man behind the rifle.

'I need all the information the army can give me about sharp-shooters from Leeds who've been invalided out, and I need it as soon as you can get it to me. This morning if you can.'

'It'll take a few hours,' Fox told him. 'Probably more than that. At least it should only be a small group.'

'My men will find out if anyone had a grudge against Andrews. The post-mortem will take place first thing. As soon as it's light, we'll begin searching over there.' He nodded at the graveyard. 'We could make use of some of your troops.'

'Of course. If there's any other help we can give, just ask, Tom. I want him as badly as you do.' He turned, showing sad eyes. 'Maybe even more. Andrews was one of mine.'

They took over an empty room in the hospital. A soldier brought a large pot of tea and a handful of biscuits. Harper's belly rumbled.

'Who's best at going through records?'

'Larkin, sir.'

'Tell him to dig deep into Andrews. Everything he can discover. His history, talk to the NCOs and his comrades. Did he have any enemies, any grudges, all the usual.'

'Yes, sir.'

'I want Walsh and Fenton over in the cemetery at first light to see what they can find. The army's sending some men to help them. We might get lucky. We're certainly due. Maybe they can find a shell of his.'

'What about Dixon?'

'I've watched him work,' Harper said. 'He's good with people. Let's have him drifting around this place. He can chat to the patients and staff. Find out who's been discharged full of anger.'

'My guess would be a fair number of them,' Ash said.

'I've no doubt about that. But maybe if we put all our lines of inquiry together, they'll show a few names in common.'

He took out his watch. Almost seven. The early shifts had already been busy for an hour. Office workers would be up, getting ready for another day. He felt the clock ticking, the pressure on him. Solve this. Solve it *now*.

'What do you want me to do, sir?'

'The same thing you've always done – keep everyone in line. I need to go to the town hall.'

'My God, Tom,' Parker said. 'Do we have any leads at all?'

'Nothing yet, sir. The men are working on it and the army's looking, too.'

'Good—' On the other end of the line the chief constable's voice vanished into a series of barking coughs. Sounding that bad, it was going to be far more than a month before he was back to the fray. And right when the force needed him. 'Sorry. Damned illness. Make sure you push with everything. Use whatever you need. Nothing more from the clothing depot?'

'Looks more and more like a dead end, sir. Any more word on the Barnbow inquiry?'

'In the next few days, I've been told. But they're still inclining towards accident. Barring any changes, you can discount it as sabotage and focus on these other things.'

'Yes, sir.' Some good news, at least, if he could set that aside. No less awful for all the women who'd lost their lives, though. 'If anyone can solve this, it's you.' Parker was straining for breath, fighting to finish speaking. 'Keep me informed.'

At least someone had confidence in him. A damned sight more than he felt.

He dealt with the correspondence waiting on his desk, reading through it all, signing his name. The telephone rang again: Ash with the result of the post-mortem. A single shot, and Andrews had died immediately. The killer had used a .303 bullet. A sharpshooter; that seemed to confirm it.

Now they needed some clues. He sighed and returned to the papers in front of him. By the time he looked up, it was after eleven. All he'd eaten today was a couple of biscuits at the hospital. No wonder his belly felt empty.

The café at Leeds Market had bacon, and proper buns, not the tasteless grey muck they called war bread. He didn't ask where they'd got them; sometimes it was safer not to know. Instead, he sat back and relished the taste, slathering everything in HP sauce and washing it down with hot, dark tea.

The day hadn't warmed at all. He pushed his hands deep into his pockets as he trudged through Quarry Hill and Burmantofts up to the hospital.

Between them, Ash and Fox seemed to fill the office. A pair of big men in a cramped room, tracing lines across a map that lay on the table.

'My bods tell me the shot must have come from around here,' Fox said, jabbing his finger down. He turned and nodded at Harper.

'How far, though?' Ash asked. 'The middle of the night . . .'

'Couldn't be more than a hundred yards. And he'd have to be a miracle worker to manage that. More like thirty or fifty. Even then he'd be doing well.' He realized what he'd said; his face reddened with shame. 'I'm sorry, I mean . . .'

'How are your people doing on finding discharged marksmen, Brian?' Harper asked.

'We should have something for you later this afternoon.'

'Please, it's urgent. And there's something else. Where would he have come up with a rifle like that?'

'I . . .' the brigadier began, then pushed his lips together and shook his head. 'I'll have them take a full inventory today.'

'What have you managed to find?' Harper asked Ash.

'The sentries didn't see anything suspicious last night. Not a soul around on the street after the pubs closed. We think the shooter must have entered the cemetery the back way, from Stoney Rock Lane. It's out of sight of any houses and easy enough to clamber over the wall. They're still going through everything over there, but . . .' He shrugged, helpless.

Dammit.

'We're nowhere,' Harper said. 'That's what you mean.'

'Only for right now, sir.'

'We have a soldier shot dead outside a hospital and his killer's walking round smirking.'

Ash stared at him. 'Give us a chance, sir. We always get there.'

No, they didn't, he thought as he closed the door. Not always. He could cite chapter and verse of the times they'd failed. Too many of them. With this, though, the pressure to succeed was relentless. He could feel it crushing down on him.

'Deputy Chief Constable.'

The voice was imperious. It stopped him. He glanced at the woman coming down the staircase. She was only small, dressed in a clean, starched nurse's uniform, but she carried herself like an empress. And in this place, that was exactly who she was: Miss Kingston, the matron.

'The shot last night,' she said as she came closer to him. She was hard-faced, features like an axe. But there was compassion nestled away at the back of her eyes.

'You know what happened.'

She nodded. 'That poor young man. I used to pass him every day and say hello. The sound disturbed some of our patients. It was hard for my staff to calm them again. A number of them have shell shock. I'm sure you understand.'

What did she want him to do? He couldn't have prevented it.

'I'll have men patrolling the area,' he promised. 'It won't happen again.'

'Very good.' She smiled. 'I hope you find him quickly.'

'From your lips to God's ears.'

Dixon had spent his Thursday morning going around the hospital and talking to people had paid off. He read a list of ten names from his notebook, then snapped it shut with a flourish.

'All of them discharged now. Every one of them furious at the army, the nurses and doctors. You name it. Grudges up to here.'

'How badly wounded are they?'

'None of them will be going back to fight. Four have lost a leg or an arm. One's missing an eye.'

'How many are local?' Ash asked.

'Three, sir. I checked. And another two are staying on in Leeds a little while longer before they go home.'

'Talk to all those in town. Where the men have gone to their homes, have the local forces check on them. Make sure they're there.'

'Very good, sir,' Dixon said. 'I'm going to need someone to split the job.'

'Take Larkin,' Ash decided. He was about to add more when the door crashed open. Walsh, beaming. He placed his handkerchief on the desk, unfolded it and stood back, like a man displaying a treasure he'd just discovered.

'Shell casing.'

FIVE

'Fenton spotted it,' Walsh continued. 'Good eyes.'

Harper saw the man swell at the praise.

'Pure luck, sir. The light caught it.'

'Good job, though. You haven't touched it?'

'Hankie only,' Walsh assured him.

'Get that straight down to the fingerprint people and let's pray there's something on there.'

He stared at the casing as if he could will it to tell him everything.

As they watched Walsh and Fenton hurry off, Ash said, 'Even if there's a print it might not help much. Not unless we have him on record.'

'The army don't fingerprint recruits,' Fox said.

The cartridge was a start, Harper thought. The line they could twitch. 'But we're going to fingerprint everyone we interview about this.'

'Sir?' Ash's eyes opened wide.

'That way we'll have a record of them. If they try to object, use the Defence of the Realm Act.' Maybe it allowed the police to do that; maybe not. He didn't care; he'd argue the toss in court later if necessary. The only important thing now was to catch the killer.

Fox left to give fresh orders to his men.

Harper reached out to touch the side of the teapot and sighed. Cold.

'I should be back in the town hall.' He smiled. 'Miss Sharp will think I've gone AWOL.'

'One last thing before you dash off, sir.' Ash's voice was grave. 'Are you assuming that the same man is responsible for this and the paper and matches at the clothing depot?'

Harper stopped. He hadn't given it any proper thought yet. A sniper couldn't be a woman, surely . . .

'I suppose I am,' he added and stared at the superintendent as the implications sank through him. 'Christ, I hope he is. If not . . .'

'Exactly, sir.'

No need to say more. Harper sat inside the tram, staring out of the window and seeing nothing at all. More than one saboteur? It didn't bear thinking about. But now Ash had planted the seed, he had no choice but to consider it.

In his office, he telephoned the chief, letting him know what they'd discovered.

'It's progress,' Parker said.

'Not really, sir. Not enough.'

'Any is better than none, Tom. Maybe the fingerprints and this inventory at the barracks will give us something.'

He took a breath. 'Let's hope so.'

'I received word. The Barnbow inquiry has finished. They're definite – it was an accident. The report will be out next week. You can let that go now.'

Good news. One less worry. 'There's something Ash raised.'

As he finished, the chief began to cough, sounding as if he was hawking up his lungs. A long wait as he spluttered and finally caught his breath.

'Damned pneumonia.' Another pause. 'What does your gut tell you on this?'

'It's one man,' he answered without hesitation.

'I agree,' Parker said. 'We'll hope we're right. But let's err on the side of caution and entertain the possibility that we're hunting two different people. Just in case. I'll be glad to be proved wrong.'

'We ran out of leads on the clothing depot, sir.'

'Doesn't matter. Keep the investigation open. I want all your attention on this marksman, though. He's killed in cold blood. We need him out of the way as soon as possible.'

'Yes, sir.'

'Keep me informed, will you?'

'Of course.'

Miss Sharp was placing the cover on her typewriter, about to go for her dinner.

'Do you have any aspirin powder?' Harper asked. 'My head's killing me.'

She reached into her top drawer and drew out a box. 'You're working too hard.'

He attempted a smile. 'No choice. Not with saboteurs and dead soldiers.'

She looked as if she was about to chide him. Then she nodded and closed the drawer.

'We have a print, sir,' Walsh said. Even on the other end of a crackling telephone line, Harper could hear the triumph in his voice. 'Good and clear, too. It's a thumb, where he pushed the cartridge in. They never think about that.'

A surge of hope. He swallowed hard, scarcely daring to breathe as he listened. 'Have you sent it on to the records people?'

'Local *and* central, sir,' Walsh said. 'We ought to have answers tomorrow.'

Tomorrow, he thought. Roll on the morning.

'No, sir,' the man from records told him, 'we don't have those fingerprints on file at all.'

The voice buzzed and popped. Harper had to press the receiver tight against his good ear to make out the words.

Damn. He knew the odds were always against them, but he'd let himself hope . . . dangerous and stupid.

'What about London? What did Central Records say?'

'Same thing as us, sir. He's never been arrested.'

'I see. Thank you.'

Their only lead had turned to dust. For a second he wanted to pick up the telephone, throw it against the wall and hear it break. Very slowly, he exhaled, glancing up as Miss Sharp entered.

'Superintendent Ash is here.'

'Send him in.'

'I'll bring the pair of you a cup of tea. You both look like you can do with one.'

'No match in any of the records,' he told Ash as soon as he came through the door. 'No luck on that end. Where do your men stand?'

'Two possibilities from the interviews Dixon and Fenton conducted, sir,' Ash told him after he'd settled in the chair and pulled his waistcoat down over his stomach. 'One of them was very reluctant to be fingerprinted. They had to drag him down to the station.' His mouth turned down at the corner, the moustache drooping. 'No match to the cartridge.'

Of course. If it had been a break, he'd have already heard.

'What about the other one?'

'Prints don't match, but he couldn't account for his movements when the shooting happened, or when the saboteur was at the clothing depot.'

'They think he has something going?'

'No idea what, but yes, sir.' He paused as Miss Sharp appeared with two cups and saucers and a plate of custard creams.

'Broken biscuits,' she explained. 'They're the best I could find at the market, what with all the shortages.'

'Thank you,' Harper told her.

As the door closed, the superintendent began to speak again.

'His name's Graham Allen. Came back from France without a leg. They fitted him with a prosthetic, but he's very bitter.'

Who wouldn't be? Harper thought. Every second of every day the man would have the reminder and the pain. He'd relive whatever happened to him countless times.

'Any suggestions?'

'I've put a man on him,' Ash said. 'Just here and there and hope for the best, we don't really have enough to spare.' He took a couple of the biscuits. 'Dixon doesn't peg him as a saboteur, but he reckons there's something not quite kosher about him.'

'What about that list of sharpshooters the army promised us?'

'It eventually showed up about nine last night, sir. Four names. They don't match any that we have. The men are out talking to them right now.'

'For the moment, we're nowhere on the shooting, then,' Harper said. He scribbled a note on his blotter: *rifle inventory, barracks*.

'About all we can do is hope one of these pans out. Honestly, though, I have my doubts. The cartridge is our only clue. That means we have to keep hunting and asking questions.'

'I don't suppose anyone was looking out from the hospital when it happened?'

'One man,' Ash replied. 'I talked to him myself. He has trouble sleeping, so the staff let him wander a bit. He saw the muzzle flash and heard the shot. But it was too dark to make anything out.'

A tease, a hint. But nothing more.

'We can't let this be the clothing depot all over again, with everything petering away to fog. Someone killed a soldier on the bloody street in Leeds.' He could hear the anger making his voice rise, but he didn't want to stop it.

'We'll get this man, sir. I can promise you that.'

Fine, Harper thought when he was alone. They'd catch him. But how soon? The papers couldn't touch the story, that was one blessing. How long before he heard from the War Office, or the Home Office starting sniffing around and suggesting Scotland Yard should handle the case?

Time was one luxury they didn't have.

'We're missing one weapon.' Fox sounded embarrassed. 'A short magazine Lee Enfield. There's a scope missing, too.'

'Is that a sniper's equipment? Uses .303 bullets?'

The brigadier nodded. 'Exactly the kit we issue to sharpshooters. It's vanished since our last inventory a fortnight ago. I'm having them check the ammunition, but that's going to be harder.'

'At least now we know where the marksman got his gun.'

'Stolen.'

'Who'd be able to do that?' Harper asked. 'Who would be able to take a weapon? Unless you've had a break-in, it has to be someone at the barracks. Someone in uniform. Maybe they sold it. But think about this, Brian: if they didn't, the sharpshooter is one of your men.'

Fox straightened his back and started to bristle. 'I can't believe a soldier—'

'We have to consider it. After all, someone did it. Someone well-trained has that rifle and ammunition. And he's a murderer. Plain and simple. A saboteur. A bloody traitor.'

'I know,' Fox agreed sadly. 'I know.'

'We're going to find him and he's going to hang.' Harper stood and picked up his hat from the desk. 'The sooner, the better.'

They were getting nowhere. It was time to try something different. Anything at all, to see if it could bring results.

He didn't try to run up the stairs; those days had long passed. A steady pace, holding on to the bannister. A pause at the top to catch his breath, then down the corridor to the glass door marked *M. Harper, Secretarial School and Agency.*

Immediately, bright chatter and the constant quick clacking of typewriters engulfed him. Young women with their easy smiles and hair gathered up on their heads in buns, a blend of different perfumes filling the air.

He caught one or two of them glancing at him, heads moving down again as Mary came out of her office.

'Da.' Joy vied with worry in her eyes. 'What are you doing here? Has something . . .?'

'Nothing like that,' he told her. 'Honestly, everything's fine at home. Is there somewhere we can talk?'

The Kardomah on Briggate was quiet. They sat by the window, gazing down at the street. Trams passed, lorries, carts pulled by broken-down horses or men, and a welter of pedestrians on the pavements. He waited until the waitress brought their coffee before he spoke.

'You might be able to help me out. Professionally.'

Mary cocked her head, curious. 'How do you mean?'

'You know what happened at the depot and the hospital.'

'Even if you wouldn't tell me . . .'

He ignored the jibe.

'We've had a few leads, but they've petered out.' Harper spooned sugar into his cup, added milk and stirred, watching the colour lighten. 'When you're on patrol, you deal with girls and young women, don't you?'

Mary was listening intently, mouth pursed. 'You already know that. It's what we do, looking out for them and trying to keep them safe. What about it?'

'When you're doing the rounds over the next few nights, I'd like you to ask if they know of any men acting strangely, maybe boasting about doing this or that.'

'I suppose I can,' she agreed after a few seconds. 'But why not go through the proper channels, Da? You could have all of us out there asking.'

He shook his head. 'I'd like to try it this way first.'

It was his way of saying that it was a long shot. The idea smacked of scraping the barrel, and he'd rather not have that broadcast far and wide. Even Mary had her doubts; he could see it on her face. He'd start investigating at the barracks, but the more strings he had to his bow, the greater his chance of success.

'I'll try,' she agreed. 'You know we go out in pairs. I'm not sure when I'll have the opportunity.'

'If you can. That's all I'm asking.'

'Is the investigation going so badly that you need to do this?' she asked.

'It's not good,' he admitted. 'I think this is worth a shot. You know how it is; men boast to women. They want to impress, even if they're giving money to a prostitute.'

She nodded slowly. 'I can ask,' she said, 'but I don't know if it'll do much good.'

'It probably won't.' He gave a rueful smile and held up his right hand, index and middle fingers crossed. 'But let's see, shall we?'

'Pass the word,' he said to Billy Tanner. 'That's all I'm asking, for the landlords to keep their ears open.'

'I'm sure they can do that.' Tanner sat behind his desk, framed photographs of himself with all manner of local dignitaries spread across the walls. He was a vain man, hair glistening with pomade, a face that always looked freshly scrubbed. Clean hands and nails so perfect they must have been manicured. Every suit carefully cut to flatter and shoes polished like mirrors.

Tanner had run the Licensed Victuallers' Association, the group for public house landlords, since the beginning of the war. He'd fought for the pubs against beer shortages, rising prices, and changes to opening hours. It was always going to be a losing battle, but he'd done his best.

He took a cigarette from the wooden box on his desk, lit it and blew smoke towards the ceiling.

'And if they hear anything?'

'Send someone running for a copper. The thing is,' Harper added, 'you need to make them think it's an exercise, all caution. You can't let them know someone shot a soldier.'

Tanner snorted. 'Come on, Mr Harper. You think half of Leeds hasn't heard the news? You can't be that bloody daft.'

'I'm sure they have. But we're saying nothing, and the papers won't print it. So it didn't happen.'

Tanner clicked his tongue. 'Aye, fair enough. My people will be glad to do their bit.'

'Thank you.'

'How's your wife?'

'She's keeping well,' Harper said.

'We've not seen her at any of our dos for a few years now.' A shrug of regret. 'Never mind, eh? Tell her she's missed and give her my best.'

The Victoria ran smoothly; Dan and Jaak took care of the everyday things. Annabelle stayed around Sheepscar and avoided the other public houses. They weren't keeping her illness a secret, but there was no need for every Tom, Dick or Harry to know what was happening to her.

'I will.'

'I'm surprised to see you here,' Martin Collins said. 'Didn't expect someone like a deputy chief constable to show his face in a place like this.'

It was a through terrace house in Holbeck. Collins sat at the table in the kitchen tallying up columns of figures scribbled in pencil. He was grinning, relishing a copper coming to see him like a supplicant.

'What can I do for you?' he asked.

Harper hadn't minded being stopped at the door and patted down before the bodyguards let him in; he'd expected it. A simple precaution. He hadn't said a word when he had to wait for a quarter of an hour before Collins allowed him to enter. Hold your temper, he decided. He was the one who needed the favour.

'A question for you, Marty.' That seemed to take the man by surprise. 'What happened at the hospital up on Beckett Street the other night?'

'A soldier was killed.' He snorted. 'Everyone knows that, even if your lot won't admit it.'

Common knowledge. As he'd told Billy Tanner, it was an open secret they could never acknowledge. The same thing had happened with Barnbow. The death notices had appeared quietly in the paper, thirty-five women all the victim of accidents or something similar.

Private Andrews would have a similar memorial. Even his parents wouldn't learn the real reason.

'I want to find his murderer,' Harper said. He kept his gaze on Collins. Suddenly the man looked uncomfortable.

'It wasn't me.'

'I know that. But you can help.'

'Me? How?' He'd caught the man's interest.

'All those runners of yours—'

'I—' Collins began to object.

'Don't, Marty,' he said wearily. 'We both know you're the biggest bookie in Leeds these days. I don't give a monkey's about that. People are going to place their bets. Fine. Let them. I want to know if your people hear anyone drop a hint or a wink about a shooting or sabotage. You can be a bloody patriot for once.'

Collins fidgeted with the pencil between his fingers, staring down at it as he rubbed his thin moustache with his other hand. He was somewhere around forty-five, too old for the army, with his hair turning grey at the temples. He didn't hide his business, but he didn't flaunt it, either; he understood the unwritten rules between copper and bookie.

'All right. You put it that way, I'll do it. What if I hear something?'

'You telephone me.'

Three rolls of the dice. He wouldn't document a single one of them. They were his private gamble, and a damned sight more desperate than a shilling on an outsider in the three thirty. If one of them paid off, perfect. If they came to nothing, no one in authority would be any the wiser. But he was going to explore every single avenue to find the saboteur. The killer.

Carlton Barracks buzzed and jolted with the sounds of men marching and sergeants bellowing orders.

Brigadier Fox closed the door to his office; all the noise became a muted undercurrent of sound.

'Do you have any military policemen stationed here?' Harper asked.

He shook his head. 'No. The army doesn't have enough of them. Most are in France and Belgium. There might be a few in Aldershot, or up at Catterick Camp. We're too small.'

'Do you understand why I'm asking?'

A soldier had either stolen that weapon or arranged for it to happen. A copper, an outsider, didn't stand a cat in hell's chance of finding him inside the closed society of these walls. It needed someone in khaki.

'Of course.' Fox ran his hands down his cheeks. He looked as if he could sleep for a year.

'How about a former bobby?' Harper asked. 'Someone who was in the reserve or joined up?'

The brigadier brightened. 'Now there I can probably help you.' He picked up the telephone receiver and spoke a few quiet words. 'He'll be here in a moment. A corporal who used to be a policeman.'

'What's his name?'

'Carpenter.'

Five minutes passed, then a knock on the door and a large man hurried in, a ruddy face filled with worry. He stood at attention, offering a sharp salute to the brigadier.

'Sir.'

'At ease, Corporal.'

Fox outlined the situation while Harper studied the soldier. He had bulk, but it was muscle, not fat. He was alert, thinking and taking in everything that was said to him, his eyes shrewd and lively as he glanced around the office.

'Where were you a copper?' Harper asked.

'Chesterfield, sir. A sergeant. In uniform.'

He'd had some rank. Good. That meant he knew how to deal with people and assess situations.

'I'm Deputy Chief Constable Harper.' He saw Carpenter's back straighten a little. 'I have a very delicate job for you. Everything on the QT.'

'Yes, sir.' A tentative note. Caution and curiosity.

'I need you to find a thief and a saboteur.'

The man didn't blanch. His expression never changed.

'Very good, sir. What details can you give me?'

It was easily set up. Carpenter would report directly to Harper; less suspicious than regular visits to the CO. The brigadier wrote out a chit for the corporal to leave the barracks.

Now all he had to do was produce the goods.

* * *

'Penny for them?' Annabelle said as they ate supper. A bowl of thick vegetable soup and a couple of slices of the godawful, tasteless war bread that he left at the side of the plate. No wonder so many people preferred oat cakes these days.

'You'd end up with a ha'penny in change,' he told her.

Johanna narrowed her eyes. 'What does this mean? Penny for them. I do not know it. Penny for what?'

By the time they'd explained, the point was long forgotten. Probably just as well, Harper thought, as he watched the women clear away the dishes. He didn't have anything joyful to say.

His squad had a couple of leads, but they sounded like shreds of mist, gone as soon as they clutched at them. Not that his ideas were an improvement. They needed more. Something *solid*. The men were fingerprinting everyone they interviewed, but so far there had been no match to the cartridge.

Before he left the office, he'd spoken to the chief again. Told him about the copper at the barracks, but no mention of the other things he'd put in motion, of course; he hadn't even told Ash about those.

'You never did say what was on your mind,' Annabelle said as they snuggled in the cold bed.

One of her sharp days, he thought. The darkness hid his smile.

'Work.' A simple answer, and truthful.

'You mean the soldier who was shot.'

Yes, everybody knew. But it had still never officially happened.

SIX

Half past seven in the morning, winter and dark outside. A dank, gloomy day, with the drizzle edging towards rain. The room smelt of wet wool from the damp overcoats on the rack.

The meeting had already begun; they grew earlier every day. Faces turned to watch as Harper entered and stood in a back corner.

'The good news is that all the men you talked to were happy to be fingerprinted,' Ash told the squad. He chuckled. 'Funny what a mention of the war effort can achieve. Even the criminals are glad to oblige.' A pause, long enough to draw breath. 'The bad news is that none of them is our killer.'

'I might have something,' Dixon said. He tapped the ash off his cigarette. 'I was talking to someone I know in the Angel last night. He said he'd overheard a couple of men talking about guns and shooting.'

'Where? When? Shooting what?' Ash barked out the questions.

'Two nights before the soldier was murdered,' Dixon answered. 'Down in Burmantofts. He wasn't able to hear what they wanted to shoot. But,' he added slowly, 'they were in blue jackets with white facings.'

Silence as they all thought about what Dixon had said. Blue and white, the uniform of wounded, recovering soldiers. And Burmantofts was just down the road from East Leeds Hospital.

'Get a list of every patient in the wards who's allowed out.' Harper pushed himself away from the wall and strode to the front of the room. He counted off the tasks on his fingers. 'There must be some kind of register where they sign in and out. Check that. Talk to Brigadier Fox. Do we have any sharpshooters as patients? Grill anyone who's even vaguely likely. And make sure you get their fingerprints.' He paused for a moment. 'Then expand all that to other hospitals nearby. There's Gledhow Hall, Temple Newsam, Roundhay Hall . . . probably a few others. Take a look at every one of them.'

They should have done this earlier, he thought. His failing, no one else's. He was trying to think of too many things at once. Damnation.

'You can't come up with everything, sir,' Ash said once the meeting had ended.

'Maybe not,' he agreed. 'But that one was obvious.'

'It didn't occur to any of us, either.'

That was no consolation. He was the man in charge; it was his responsibility.

'The men want to catch him just as much as you do, sir,' Ash added.

'I know.' He'd seen their faces when he issued his orders. Eager to make a start. Hopeful that this might bring a result.

'You've got that copper at the barracks now, too.'

'Let's hope he's as competent as he seemed. He looked like he relished the idea.'

'It'll give him something to do instead of all that square bashing.'

A small cough. 'I took the liberty of ringing Chesterfield to ask about him. I have a pal down there.'

Of course. Ash had a web of friends and contacts all across the British Isles.

'What did he say?'

'Carpenter is clever and eager. He seems to do his job very well and the men under him liked him.'

'Go on,' Harper said. 'I sense a little hesitation.'

'He had a reputation for being a bit too physical at times, sir.'

No different from plenty of coppers. As long as he could keep his temper in check on this.

'Did we get anything from the marksmen list Fox gave us?'

'Nothing. I don't suppose you found anything yesterday, sir? I know you were gone for a while.'

All the gossip reached Ash. It had been that way as far back as he could recall; the man seemed to know every little thing that was happening all over the police force.

'No,' Harper told him. 'I haven't found a thing.'

It was the truth. He'd planted some seeds, that was all. Now he had to hope they'd flower. That morning, Mary shook her head when he gave her a questioning look. No chance for anything more when Annabelle was hovering around.

His wife had seemed bright as they ate breakfast. Her eyes were clear, her speech crisp and firm. But it could change in a second; he'd seen that for himself in the last few years. Thank God for Johanna. She, Jaak and Jef were the one good thing to come to them out of this damned war. The only one.

Half the families he knew in Leeds had lost someone or had someone wounded. The toll kept rising and there was no end in sight. The young men leaving every day for training were nothing more than cannon fodder. He'd never say that to a living soul, but it was in his mind. By the time all this was done, England would have lost an entire generation. His thoughts flickered to Mary, still caught in her grief over Len. Too many already mourned the ones they loved.

On the telephone, he gave the chief constable the latest news and heard his frustration at still being stuck at home. After that, Harper tried to lose himself in the daily paperwork. But every few minutes his eyes kept straying to the clock on the wall, willing the door to open or the phone to ring.

Yet when the bell sounded, it took him by surprise. He stared at it for a second before lifting the receiver.

'It's Brian Fox. I've tried your squad but nobody's answering.'

Harper smiled to himself. Good, that meant they were all out following leads.

'What can I do for you, Brian?'

'Your Inspector Walsh wanted to know if any of our marksmen are in hospital here. There's one, and he's ambulatory, allowed out.'

'Where is he?'

'Gledhow Hall.'

He took the name. The men were busy, he was ready for a break from the office; time to go and check on this one himself.

The building looked over a broad valley. In the summer it would be a glorious view, a green, beautiful place. Far enough from the city centre and all the industry to have clean air, grounds that seemed to run forever, yet still only three miles from Leeds. Town hung on the far horizon, shrouded in smoke.

He turned away from the window as the matron entered. Miss Cliff, the sign on the door read. She was a tall woman, somewhere in her middle forties, moving briskly with the air of someone who had no time for nonsense.

She placed a slim folder on the desk. 'James Openshaw,' she said. 'We call him Jimmy. The brigadier told me a policeman would be coming.'

Harper let the file sit on the desk. 'What can you tell me about him, Matron?' he asked, watching her face.

'Not Matron,' she corrected him. 'For some reason, my title here is Commandant. Don't ask me why. Jimmy arrived here three months ago with a bad case of shell shock. Poor man would probably be better in a place that specialized in treating cases of that, but . . .' She grimaced and let the sentence dangle. 'We're doing our best for him. He's making progress.' She paused for a second. 'Slow, but it's there.'

'He's allowed out?'

'He is,' she answered.

Harper sat back and rubbed his chin. 'What's your impression of him, Miss Cliff?'

She'd know every patient in the place. It was part of her job.

'Very quiet. Sits by himself a great deal, staring at the view. He tries to make himself small inside his greatcoat. He doesn't want much to do with the other patients, but I've seen that once or twice in similar cases.' She cocked her head. 'He seems harmless.'

'Does he often leave the grounds? Do you know?'

'Not to my knowledge. But I have my hands full here, Deputy Chief Constable.'

He smiled. 'I'm sure you do.'

'If you want to talk to him, I saw him a few minutes ago, sitting on a bench on the terrace. He smokes constantly, you'll see the dog ends around his feet.' Her mouth crinkled with distaste. 'Now, if you'll excuse me . . .'

She rose and he stood, extending his hand. 'Thank you. You've been very helpful.'

Harper skimmed the file. Nothing about the man's time in France. It was all about his stay here, the kind of treatment he was receiving. Long medical words he didn't understand. He set it aside and went to check the register. Patients signed when they were leaving the grounds and when they returned. He didn't see Openshaw's name.

Not that it meant much. Security was lax. Men guarded the main entrances, but there were too many ways in and out of the place. It was an easy stroll to Roundhay Road, slipping out unseen through the woods at the bottom of the valley. After that, less than a mile along the main streets and he'd be at East Leeds Hospital. Nobody would notice another recuperating soldier.

Finally he walked out to the terrace. A man sat by himself, staring off into the distance, but looking as if he was seeing nothing. A blue jacket with white facing, a corporal's stripes on the sleeve of his greatcoat.

His shoulders were hunched. Miss Cliff was right; Openshaw wanted to be inconspicuous, to disappear. Maybe he realized Harper was there; more likely it didn't even register in his mind.

'Jimmy? Jimmy Openshaw?'

He didn't look up, didn't even seem to hear. Instead, he took a packet of Woodbines from his coat and lit one, softly blowing out the smoke.

'It's beautiful out here,' Harper said. 'Almost silent.'

'It's never quiet.' The man's voice barely rose above a murmur; Harper had to strain to make out what he was saying. 'If you open your ears you can hear the birds and all the animals. I never knew that before.'

'My hearing isn't good enough.'

'Spend time out here and you learn.' He held the cigarette in a soldier's pinch, cupped inside his hand to hide the glow of the tip, grasping it with his thumb and his fingertips. Openshaw brought it up to his mouth. 'Stand out here just before it gets light and the birds are as loud as a brass band.'

'Very different from being at the front?'

Too late, he sensed the change in the man's mood. The wrong words. There was no movement, but everything had shifted, as if he'd lowered a shutter.

'I'm sorry. I shouldn't have said that.'

He waited for a reaction, anything at all, but Openshaw simply sat and gazed and smoked. Eventually Harper turned and walked away. On paper, the man remained a possibility. He'd been a marksman, he had the skill to make the shot that killed Private Andrews. But he couldn't bring himself to believe this man was capable of pulling a trigger now. Walking back to the car, he wondered how long it would take for Corporal Openshaw to find his way back to the world. If he ever managed it at all.

'Da.' The voice hissed in his ear.

Harper opened his eyes, wondering if he'd been dreaming. The bed was warm, Annabelle deep asleep beside him. He saw a shape move in the darkness and realized it was Mary, back from patrol duty in the wee hours of Monday morning.

Blinking, he rose, feeling the cold air, and shuffled to the parlour behind her, sitting at the table.

The room was all shadows, just the faint glow of the fire where he'd banked it for the night. He could make out a few planes of his daughter's face, nothing more; memory filled in the rest.

'What is it? Something important?'

'It might be.'

They were talking in whispers. She sat close to his good ear, leaning towards him.

'About the traitor?'

'I don't know.' She paused for a second. 'I was talking to a girl tonight, down by the open market. There was a group of them, all standing around together, quite a few, around about sixteen or so. She told me they'd been talking to some men who'd been passing; they'd left not five minutes before we arrived.' Harper said nothing, listening intently. 'She said one of the men had been drinking, and he started boasting to her. How he was part of a group helping deserters escape to America.'

Harper had heard rumours of things like that, tales, but nothing more definite. His throat was dry; he wished he had a glass of water.

'Did she ask his name?'

'Peter. That was all he told her.' She hesitated for a second. 'But he hinted at something else. That he knew about some people who were trying to disrupt the war effort.'

'Some people?' He pounced on the words.

'That's what he told her, Da. Word for word. She said he'd had a few, but he seemed quite serious. This girl has a cousin who's over at the front, she didn't want to hear it, but he kept pestering her until his friends dragged him away.'

'I need to talk to her,' he said.

Even in the night he could see her smile. 'She's willing to meet when she's on her dinner.'

'Where?' His mouth was dry, a sense of anticipation.

'She works in a place on Aire Street. I suggested we meet in City Square at noon and we can find a café.'

'We?'

'We,' she repeated. 'You need a woman there when you're questioning a girl, Da. Even in public. You know the rules.'

He did; they existed for a reason. And Mary had brought him the information. It was only fair she was there when he questioned the girl.

'What's her name?'

'Joanna Cummings.'

'Now we have to hope she turns up when she promises.'

'I think she will, Da.'

He placed his hand over hers. 'You did well.'

He drew Ash aside, watching the man's face as he told him about Joanna Cummings and Peter. Every phrase carefully weighted to make it sound as if he'd never prompted Mary to ask her questions.

'It's possible,' the superintendent said, but Harper could hear the doubt in his voice. 'I've heard rumours of people supposedly smuggling deserters away. But I've never come across any instance of it actually happening.'

'That's not the part that worries me. It's the idea of sabotaging the war effort. We need to find this man sharpish.'

'Maybe Miss Cummings will give you more of a clue later, sir.'

Perhaps, but he wasn't too hopeful. 'At least she can offer a description of this Peter, whoever he might be. After that, I want the word out to every bobby we have. If she can give enough detail, then between that and his Christian name, we ought to be able to track him down.'

'You know there are always some people don't want to be found.'

Harper shook his head. 'If he's shooting his mouth off like that, he can't be too bright.'

A little bit of digging and Peter would be wishing he'd never touched a drop that night.

Chief Constable Parker sounded brighter when they talked on the telephone. More alert, eager to return to work. 'I wish I could do more to catch him, Tom.'

'Every piece of paper you keep off my desk helps, sir. Believe me.'

A barking laugh that ended in a spluttering cough. The man's mind might be eager, but his body was nowhere near ready yet.

SEVEN

J oanna Cummings was bundled up tight against the cold. A thick coat, and heavy shawl draped over her hair. Mary was right, Harper thought; she looked very young, sixteen, seventeen at most. Nervous, too. Her gaze kept jumping around, glancing over her shoulder as if someone might be following her.

Once they were in the steamy warmth of the café she seemed a little easier.

'I only have forty minutes for my dinner,' she said. 'They'll dock my pay if I'm a minute late.'

'Don't you worry,' Mary assured her, 'we'll see you're on time.'

He was happy to sit back and let his daughter ask the questions. Easier if a woman did it. He'd explained to her what he needed. This way he could listen. He'd only need to speak if there was something she might have missed.

He stayed quiet for almost the entire meal, saying nothing until they were drinking their tea.

'How long were you talking to him?' Harper asked.

Her eyes moved to Mary. She gave a small nod.

'I don't know. Not too long. Five minutes. Maybe ten. I just wanted him to leave me alone. He kept coming close and he stank of booze. I don't like that.'

'No,' he agreed, 'it's not pleasant.'

He let Mary ask two final questions, then he paid the bill and they escorted the girl back to City Square.

'I'll go the rest of the way on my own.'

'Of course,' Harper said. 'Thank you. You've been very helpful, Miss Cummings.'

She blushed a little and hurried away, reaching into her handbag and bringing out a cigarette. Brazen, he thought, a woman smoking in public. But times were changing and leaving him far behind.

'What did you think, Da?' Mary asked.

'We need a long talk with this Peter,' he replied as they strolled back up Park Row. 'With everything she told us, we should be able to find him soon.' She'd given them a full, detailed description; Joanna Cummings had been observant. 'You did very well. Asked good questions.'

She beamed with pride and squeezed his arm.

'I really think so,' he continued. 'You'd be a natural for all this.'

Mary shook her head. 'Maybe if you had proper women coppers and I wasn't running my business.'

Harper stopped at the corner and turned to her. 'That's something I've wanted to ask you. What made you pick the volunteer patrol, anyway?' He'd initially accepted her choice as a reaction to Len's death. But there had to be more to it than that. 'It doesn't seem like the kind of thing to appeal to you. From what I've seen, they seem to spend most of their time breaking up couples enjoying a cuddle.'

'Oh, some of them love to do that.' She snorted. 'Dried-up old prunes. If I'm with one of them, I try to steer them away. For God's sake, let people have their fun. Who knows if the fella will come home again?'

He didn't know how to answer that. Silence seemed best.

'Do you remember that weekend I went to Scarborough after the start of the war?' she said after a while. They were standing on the Headrow, the town hall looming across the street. 'I said I needed some sea air.'

'I do.'

'Len had finished his training. We spent the time together.' She raised her head, eyes flashing and defiant. 'Same bed and everything, like we were wed.'

He reached out and brushed away the tear starting to roll down her cheek.

'You did right.' He saw her eyes widen and her mouth open in astonishment. 'I've known about it since it happened. You told your mam and she told me. You're our daughter. All we ever wanted was for you to be happy. We love you; we worry about you. And Len would have been a wonderful son-in-law. We're glad the two of you had some proper time together. It just wasn't enough.'

Her mouth tightened as she tried to smile. But it was a poor attempt as memories and sorrow rushed in. After a moment she gave a terse nod, turned and marched away.

Had he handled that well? Too late now. With a sigh he crossed the road to start his squad hunting for Peter.

'We'll give his name and description out at roll call today and tomorrow, sir,' Ash told him. 'Every copper in town will be looking for him.'

'Let's hope it doesn't take long.'

'I'd say we'll probably have him by this time tomorrow.'

Harper sat back and raised an eyebrow. Luck again. He hated having to rely on it. 'That's a big promise to make.'

'The description's much better than we usually find.'

True enough; it was almost enough to draw a good portrait of the man.

'One of the beat coppers will know him,' Ash added with certainty.

Before the war, he'd have agreed. Now, with so many specials, he couldn't be so certain.

'What about the men?'

'They're all off working their contacts. If we could break a ring smuggling out deserters as well as finding the saboteur . . .'

'Then we'd all be cock o' the walk,' Harper agreed. 'But I'll be a very happy man if we find whoever shot Private Andrews. We need him to hang.'

'We will, sir. I can feel it in my bones.'

Harper smiled to himself. In the bones, in the gut, in the water. A copper's hunch. If he had a penny for every one that had failed, he'd be a rich man. But they all still believed in them. He was as bad as the rest, and he'd been wrong just as often.

This time, though, they'd succeed. They'd find the killer. They had to.

Dark out, traffic moving along the Headrow. Harper reached for the telephone as it began to ring.

'Just to let you know, sir, nothing yet,' Ash said.

'Thank you.' Harper glanced at the clock. Just turned six. 'Anything at all, ring me at home.'

Mary was out on patrol again. The fire burned in the grate. Harper sat at the table playing pontoon with Annabelle and Johanna. A gentle, quiet night. He kept glancing at the telephone, willing it to ring as he lost hand after hand.

'I can't concentrate tonight,' he said finally.

'Tonight?' Annabelle clicked her tongue and turned to Johanna. 'He's always been rotten at cards. He just hates to admit it.'

'Guilty,' he admitted with a grin and held up his hands in surrender. 'But I'm off to bed. I'm a growing lad, I need my rest.'

'Did you think I'd forgotten about you and cards?' she asked as they settled under the blanket and she curled into him.

'I'm glad you haven't.' He ran his hand down her spine. 'I had dinner with Mary. She told me about the weekend she and Len spent in Scarborough before he went to France. I said I already knew.'

'You should have kept your mouth shut.' She raised herself on one elbow and stared down at him. 'Telling you like that, it was her gift to you.'

'I wanted her to know we were both happy for her.'

'Men.' He felt her shake her head, hair rippling against his chest. 'Useless, the lot of you. Of course she told me, I'm her mam. But saying it to her da, that's a different matter.'

Harper stayed quiet, mulling over what she'd said, the words Mary had used. He felt as if he'd hardly drifted off to sleep when the telephone bell brought him awake, shrill and loud.

'Fenton here, sir.' The man sounded crisp and alert. 'You wanted to know anything about that man, Peter.'

'Yes.' Harper's voice was heavy as sludge, slowly coming awake. 'Have you found him?'

'We've got him in custody, sir.' He could almost hear the man smile. 'Nabbed him at Central Station, trying to put a deserter on a train for Liverpool. The pair of them are in the cells.'

'That's excellent work.'

Part of him wanted to go down and start asking questions now. To get to work. By daybreak they might have the killer in handcuffs. He needed that.

But he also knew a few hours in a tiny little hole that stank of piss, down where the drunks yelled and cried, could make a man very eager to give answers.

'We'll let him stew until morning. See how happy he is to talk then.'

'Very good, sir. We took a statement from the deserter and handed him over to the army. Superintendent Ash said that was fine.'

'If we have the information, they're welcome to him. Go home, you've earned it.'

'Yes, sir. Thank you.'

Almost two, according to the grandfather clock; he'd been asleep longer than he imagined. But the telephone call had jolted him into wakefulness. His mind was working, filled with ideas and hope.

By five, he knew he had to go into town. The soles of his boots slapped along the pavement. Harper passed a few early workers on their way to the morning shift. He walked with purpose, a determined look on his face, never slowing as he climbed Eastgate and the Headrow until he could see the tower of the town hall.

None of the squad had arrived yet. Harper made his way down the stone steps to the bridewell, surprising the custody officer at his desk.

He studied the file. Peter Morton, twenty-one years old, machinist with Fairbairn Lawson. Just a single sheet with the bare bones of his arrest. In cell ten.

It was a small room, completely tiled in white. A bench for sitting and sleeping, with a mattress as thin as a wafer. The stench of old vomit clung to the walls, seeping into the throat and the clothes.

Morton's suit was creased, rumpled; he'd used the jacket for a pillow. The man had dirt on his hands, his hair was wild, a shadow of stubble on his face. He looked scared, Harper thought. And well he might.

'You're in trouble.'

A short nod of his head, patting his pockets for a cigarette. Morton's hands trembled as he lit it.

'Aiding a deserter. You know, the right judge might decide that's treason. Are you aware of the penalty for that?'

That made the man freeze, eyes wide in horror. 'But—' he began. Harper waited; no more words arrived.

'It's hanging at Armley Gaol,' he continued. 'Behind the walls. Everything done quietly, nothing in the papers. What traitors deserve.'

'I was only trying to help.'

'Help men who've decided not to do their duty? There are plenty in the trenches who would love to put down their weapons. But they don't. Of course, you might not last long enough to hang. Criminals are surprisingly patriotic. Once word spreads amongst the prisoners . . .'

He let the idea take root in Morton's mind. Make him completely terrified. Ready to spill everything.

'You don't believe in this war, do you?'

'No, I don't,' he answered. 'It's not just. It's ordinary people dying for the ambitions of royalty. Families and empires.'

Harper had heard it all before, often enough to be sick of the words. 'Is that why you became a saboteur, Mr Morton?'

EIGHT

'What?' He shook his head as his voice began to rise. 'No, not me. Nothing like that.'

'Torn paper and matches at the clothing depot, ready to start a fire. Killing a guard at the hospital on Beckett Street.' Harper cocked his head. 'We'll begin with those.'

'No. Honestly, I'd never do anything like that.' Morton was panicking. Flailing and drowning. 'I want to keep people alive. That's why I help the deserters.'

'I don't believe you.'

'It's the truth. I'm telling you the truth, I really am. I didn't have anything to do with those things. I wouldn't.' Morton was close to tears.

'We'll see. You'll be going in front of the magistrate this morning. From there, it's Armley Gaol on remand until your trial. We'll have plenty of time to find the evidence. But if you tell me everything now, I can make sure things are better for you.'

'I can't tell you what I haven't done.' He was pleading. 'Please. I didn't do that. I didn't.'

'Then why did you tell a girl you were trying to hamper the war effort?'

His head jerked up as if it had been pulled. 'What? I help the deserters get to America. That's it.'

'Who do you know who damages things and kills people?'

'Nobody. It's not like that. That's not peace.'

'We'll see.' He looked around the small cell. 'Enjoy your stay. You'll love Armley. It's loud there. Never a moment's silence, night or day.'

The metal door shut with an echo, then the loud turn of the key.

Harper climbed the stone steps, then out into the open space of the town hall. It felt broad and airy. Like freedom.

The squad was at work, writing reports and searching through files. Their heads turned as Harper entered.

'You did a good job last night.' He let them bask in the praise for a moment. 'Have we searched where he lives yet?'

'Yes, sir,' Ash replied. 'Came up with a list of deserters and where they're staying.' He grinned. 'Got bobbies out arresting them all right now. We've broken up that network.'

Good news, and God knew they needed some.

'You might want another word with him before he's taken to court. I think he'll be very happy to add to what we know.'

Ash nodded to Walsh and the man hurried down to the cells.

'An interesting name came up when he was questioned,' Dixon said. 'Graham Allen.'

Harper had heard it before, but he couldn't place it.

'He was discharged from East Leeds Hospital, sir. Lost his leg in France. A very angry man.'

Yes, it clicked into place. 'Is he part of this group?'

'He is, sir.' A quick smile of satisfaction. 'I knew he had something going. That tip you had was a good day's work, sir, uncovering something we didn't know existed.'

'Breaking this up is excellent,' Harper agreed. 'But I want to know if Morton or this Allen are connected to the sniper.'

'Nothing to indicate it, sir. Nothing at all.'

He nodded. 'That was my feeling when I talked to him. He was too petrified to lie.' Harper sighed. 'We need something useful.'

'At least we have this, sir. The papers will eat it up.'

'Milk it,' Chief Constable Parker ordered. His voice boomed down the telephone line. 'Give the press everything you can. Let them play it up as a great victory for police work.'

'All because one of the women on a Volunteer Patrol asked the right questions and passed on the information.'

'Then tell them that. Let's relish our moment of glory. God knows, we've earned it. It'll put some heart into people.'

'It still doesn't help us with the sniper, though.'

'Yes, it does. It all helps, Tom. Let's savour our victories where we can. Maybe we'll catch our man today.'

Maybe. Marching into town, he'd believed they might be close. But as soon as he heard Peter Morton, he realized the truth. It was good to have him off the streets; no denying that. But they were back where they'd started.

He slapped his palm down on the desk. A few seconds later, the door opened. Miss Sharp, looking concerned.

'Are you all right?'

'Frustrated,' he replied.

'You'll catch him.' A tight smile. 'Fancy a cuppa? At least we have some tea that made it past the German navy.'

'That sounds like an excellent idea.'

Back to square one. And if he felt like this, it must be even worse for his squad. They were the ones asking questions and wearing out shoe leather. He'd been in their place often enough, but never with quite so much riding on the result.

Apart from encouragement, he had nothing to offer. No directions, no orders. They'd have to use their initiative, their contacts, their experience. To show they were the best.

He picked up the Barnbow report from his desk. Exactly as Parker had said. A terrible, fatal accident. All those women who'd died. But not a trace of sabotage. It was something, but in the end cold comfort for so many families.

'I thought you'd want to know what happened,' Harper said to Mary after he'd told her about Morton. 'After all, you started it.'

She finished the slice of cake and pushed the plate away. The Kardomah was full, businessmen eating their dinners and talking shop.

'But he didn't have anything to do with the shooting?'

'No. But there was a . . . a group we didn't even know existed. We've closed that down. It'll be in the evening paper. You really have made a difference.'

That made the corners of her mouth curl upwards. The start of a smile.

'Not so much me. That was Joanna Cummings.'

'It was all because of you. You listened to her and passed it on. That's what good beat coppers do.'

'I must have inherited it from you, Da.'

He laughed. 'Not me, I hated being on the beat. Couldn't wait to become a detective. But keep asking questions. We need every bit of help.'

He'd barely been back in the office for ten minutes when the telephone rang.

'It's Billy Tanner here, Mr Harper.'

The head of the Licensed Victuallers. The words came through crisp and clear, the accent pure Leeds. Were all the seeds he'd planted suddenly starting to bloom, Harper wondered?

'Have you heard something?' No need for niceties; there was only one reason he'd ring.

'Maybe,' Tanner began. 'Course, it could be nothing at all.'

'Let's hope it's gold,' Harper said. He wanted the man to get to the point.

'Do you know Eddie Goss? He's the landlord of the Garden Gate, over in Hunslet.'

'No.'

'He rang me a little while ago. Last night he was collecting glasses and he heard a snippet of chat between a couple of his customers. Right shifty pair, according to him. They lowered their voices as soon as he came close, but he managed to pick out that they mentioned a dead man and one of them asked what comes next.'

Harper breathed slowly, feeling the thud of the pulse in his neck. 'Does he know who they are?'

'Not seen them before, but he did hear one of them say he worked at Hunslet Engine. Small lad, about twenty, blond hair cut very short. Missing one of his front teeth.'

Very helpful. A few words with the foreman at the locomotive works and they should have him. Maybe this time it would lead them to the sharpshooter.

'That's excellent.' He struggled to keep the hope out of his voice. 'Can you thank Mr Goss for me, Billy? And tell him one of my men will stop by.'

'Right enough. Glad to be of help. All helps us win, doesn't it?'

'It does.'

Upstairs, Walsh and Larkin were still in the office.

'You're going to Hunslet,' he told them with a smile, as he explained. 'Let's see if there's anything good in this.'

'What do you reckon, sir?' Ash asked once the men had gone.

'I want to believe it,' he answered after a moment. But all the other things he'd hoped were true had turned out to be mirages. 'We'll wait and see. It's something to pursue, at least. Any more leads?'

'Dixon and Fenton are running down a possibility. But I wouldn't put my pension on it.' Ash shrugged. 'We'll get there, sir.'

'Yes,' Harper said. But he saw the superintendent's eyes. They spoke the words, but neither of them was convinced.

Hunslet Engine. Where Mary's fiancé had worked until he'd volunteered back in 1914. He was a newly qualified engineer when he joined the army. He could have claimed a reserved occupation and stayed safe in Leeds, married. Maybe even a child or two by now. But young men needed to prove themselves with a war, even when they had every reason not to go. Two years later his body was consumed by the mud and the worms on the Somme.

Oh yes. Harper would find the bastard who was behind this.

'Do you know who I am?'

The young man shook his head, glancing around at the faces that watched him. He looked terrified, sitting with his hands tucked under his thighs like a scolded child.

He was small, a bantam, pigeon-chested. Little more to his hair than a blond colouring on his scalp. Right front tooth missing. Exactly as Goss had said.

'I'm the deputy chief constable of Leeds.' Harper stared at the lad. 'And right now you need to convince me that you're innocent.'

'Of what? I haven't done owt.' High-pitched. Fearful. He tried to stand. Ash placed a heavy hand on his shoulder.

'You're David Blenkinsop?' That was the name the foreman at Hunslet Engine had given as soon as he heard the description.

'You know I am.'

'Who were you drinking with at the Garden Gate last night?'

'What?' The young man blinked in surprise.

'It's a simple question.' Harper placed his hands on the desk and leaned forward until his face was inches from Blenkinsop's. 'Were you in the Garden Gate last night?'

'Yes.'

'You talked about a dead man and asked what comes next.'

For a second he looked confused. Then understanding came. His expression changed.

'It's a friend of ours who died. You know, over there. We were talking about whether we should join up.' He saw Harper's face. 'That was it.'

'I want the name of the friend you were with and where he works. And the one who died.'

'Yes. It's—'

Before he could give his answer, Harper had stalked out of the room. The squad would take care of the rest. Blenkinsop wasn't their man. He didn't have any guile; everything was written on his face.

Another dead end.

'Talk to the friend,' he told Ash when the superintendent entered the office.

'We will, sir. How did you hear about this one?'

'A tip.' It was easier to leave it at that than explain. 'A waste of time, but how were we to know?'

'One of these days it'll be the right one.'

'Maybe.' Harper sighed. 'The question is, how much time do we have?'

He'd just come out of the town hall into the cold evening air when the shout came. Fenton, pelting hell for leather and waving his arms.

'Sir! Sir! The super needs you.'

He followed, rushing as fast as he could up the flights of stairs as Fenton disappeared ahead. Harper was panting by the time he reached the office.

Ash looked grave. 'Another shooting, sir.'

He could feel the blood drain from his face. 'How bad?' It came out as a croak.

'Three, sir. One dead, two wounded.'

Christ Almighty. He knew it had to be awful, but this was worse than anything he'd imagined. Harper closed his eyes and breathed slowly as he pressed his palms against the desk to steady himself, to feel something solid while the world was disintegrating. 'Where?'

'Kirkstall Forge. One guard and a worker wounded,' Ash said.

'One dead, you said.'

'A woman, sir. She worked on the line.'

He exhaled. 'Let's get over there. I want two cars round here right now. I'll ring the chief and the brigadier and tell them.' He turned to Ash. 'I don't want people climbing all over the place before we can search for any evidence. Rustle us up some uniforms to guard the area.'

The forge reeked of hot metal. Sparks flew all around them. Work continued, the clanging of metal and the beating of hammers. Constant noise. They made axles for army lorries and artillery limbers. The things that would help beat the Germans.

Even with the office door closed, noise pounded through the building. Larkin and Dixon were outside with their torches, supervising the constables as they searched. Next door, Walsh and Fenton were talking to the two people who'd been outside when the shooting happened.

The works manager, a tired man named Jenkinson who appeared on the verge of tears, told them about the dead woman.

'Her name was Margaret Glover. We all called her Maggie. She worked on the day shift but she volunteered to put in some overtime today.' His voice failed for a moment. 'Everybody liked her. I know, people say that, but it's true.' He looked at the faces watching him. 'She was only twenty. Loved being here, said it was so much better than when she was a maid.'

'It sounds like you knew her well,' Brigadier Fox said, and the man nodded.

'We all did. Like a family here.' His eyes widened in panic. 'Oh God, I'll have to tell her parents—'

'We'll take care of that, sir,' Ash said gently. 'If you give me her address when we're done, I'll see to it.'

'What about the woman who was wounded?' Harper asked.

'Alice Pepper,' Jenkinson said. 'She was with Maggie. They were carrying a part over to shipping. It needed the pair of them.'

'The first bullet hit her in the leg,' Ash said. 'That's according to one of the witnesses. She fell down and the second shot caught Maggie Glover. It was over before anyone could help. Then there was a third that found the guard as he tried to raise his rifle.'

'Chest wound,' Fox said. 'Nasty, but he'll live. I'll go and talk to him once he's out of the operating theatre.'

Jesus, Harper thought. What a mess. Whoever had done it had picked their target well. Two soldiers on the gates, checking everyone who came and went, but only one in the yard. It made sense – who'd expect an attack there? The sharpshooter must have hidden in the bushes by the canal. He'd never be spotted.

'Our marksman again, sir,' Ash said.

'Oh yes.' He turned to Fox. 'Brian. You're the expert. What do you think?'

'I'm hardly an authority, but I'll have a better idea in the morning when I can see the landscape properly. He's good, though. The night shot at the hospital and now three shots when the light was fading and three hits. Thank God two of them will survive.'

'And there's one who hasn't,' Harper reminded him. He liked the brigadier, but the bloody military always thought in numbers, not human beings.

'Yes.' The man reddened. 'Of course.'

There was little more that Harper could do but sit in the office, drink endless cups of tea and think. Outside, the noise continued, but he was barely aware of it.

Fox's list had produced nothing last time. He'd have the men go over all the names once again, but he doubted they'd suddenly strike lucky. They needed somewhere else to look. And for the life of him, he didn't know where to begin.

Another telephone call to the chief, passing on the few fragments they'd learned.

'How do we catch him?' Parker asked.

'I don't know, sir. I really don't.' He heard his own voice and realized how fragile it sounded. On the edge of breaking.

'Go home,' the chief constable said. 'Sleep and come back fresh in the morning.'

'I—'

'That's an order, Tom. Do you have a car out there?'

'No, sir.'

'I'll ring for one. Get yourself some rest and we'll talk again tomorrow.'

Maybe it was for the best. Left to himself, he'd stay here all night to brood and worry.

The pub was dark, smelling of smoke and spilled beer. Everything tidied away after closing. Upstairs, a single light burned in the parlour and the fire glowed, already banked for the night. Johanna sat on the settee, knitting needles clacking, while Jaak was at the table with a deck of cards, playing patience.

Before Harper could speak, Johanna said, 'Annabelle had a bad day. Twice she didn't know me. She said I was trying to hurt her and kidnap her from here.'

He sighed. He couldn't apologize; she didn't know what she was doing.

'Did she calm down?'

'Yes. But it wore her out, so I put her to bed early. A hot water bottle so she'd be warm.'

'Thank you.'

If this bloody war ever ended, how would they manage without the Belgian family?

NINE

Seven in the morning. Still dark outside, but Kirkstall Forge was busy with banging and bumping and scraping of metal. Harper noticed workers watching him from the corner of their eyes as he passed on the way to the office.

Ash was already there, working steadily with his sense of calm and order.

'How are the two who were wounded?'

'Both recovering, sir,' the superintendent told him. 'The woman's injury was minor, thank God, but the soldier's likely to be invalided out.'

Poor man; it wouldn't have been the future he imagined for himself.

'Any developments? Do we have any leads?'

'Nothing yet, sir. Larkin and Dixon are over in the woods on the other side of the canal. They've got a few specials to help and one of the brigadier's sharpshooters to advise them. As soon as it's full light, they'll tear the place apart and see what they can find.'

But the best they could hope for was a .303 shell. A boot print if they were very lucky.

'What about Walsh and Fenton?'

'Out on the main road, asking questions. There are some streets full of houses going back off there. The marksman had to get here somehow and then get away again. Maybe someone there saw him.'

'It's hard to disguise a rifle,' Harper continued with a smile.

'Exactly, sir. Someone might have been nosy, especially after the shots.'

'Fingers crossed for two or three, all happy to gossip.' He nodded towards the forge. 'Anything more from the people here?'

'You've already spoken to the ones who saw it,' Jenkinson the manager said. 'All the others were inside. They didn't hear anything until the screaming and shouting began.'

With this cacophony, shots would pass unnoticed. He'd be surprised if they could hear anything at all by the time a shift was over.

'What about Miss Glover's family?'

Ash stared down at the floor. 'I saw them last night. I told them there'd been an accident here.'

He loathed this. They couldn't even give her parents the truth they deserved. National security forbade it. They'd probably go to their graves never knowing, and they were owed more than that. Maggie Glover was as much a war casualty as someone who lost his life in the trenches.

Harper read the workers' statements. Bubbling under the horror and shock was the fear that the murderer might strike here again. However much he willed it, Harper couldn't reassure them. Whoever was behind this was clever. He picked his spots carefully.

It had to be a trained man; killing from a distance was special-ized work, it needed patience and a very sharp eye. And he had the right weapon for it.

He pulled open his notebook and began to write.

Talk to all the discharged marksmen once more.

Ask the army to go through their records for all the marksmen who have any connection to Leeds.

Talk to Carpenter.

A few more minutes, thinking and pacing, not finding anything more to add to the list.

'I'm just dead weight here,' he told Ash. 'You're perfectly capable of handling everything.'

'I'll ring as soon as we have some news, sir.'

The brigadier answered the telephone with his rank.

'Brian, it's Tom Harper.'

'Have you found something?' He was eager, desperate for something to break.

'Not yet, I'm afraid. Can you arrange for Corporal Carpenter to come and see me as soon as possible?'

'Of course. I'll have my adjutant give him the message.'

'Are we agreed that the killer yesterday is the same one who killed Private Andrews?'

'Yes,' Fox answered after a moment. 'Definitely.'

'We've looked at all those discharged or in hospital here,' Harper told him. 'We'll go over them once more, but . . .'

'What do you need?'

'I need a list of every army marksman who might have some connection to Leeds.'

'For the love of God, that's a tall order, Tom. I don't even know if it's possible.'

'Private Bertie Andrews.' He paused. 'Maggie Glover. How many more do you want?'

The brigadier gave a loud sigh. 'All right. I'll start the War Office working. No guarantees. I don't even know how they'd put together that information.'

'As long as they find it, I don't really care.'

It was the army; they had records of every bloody thing. Some clerks just needed to pull their fingers out and sort through it all.

He had his head buried in a report on manpower when he heard Miss Sharp's familiar rapid tap on the door.

'A Corporal Carpenter to see you.' The glimmer in her eye showed she approved of the soldier.

'Send him in.'

He wanted to stand, only sitting reluctantly after Harper insisted, perching and tense on the edge of the chair.

'The marksman struck again.'

'Yes, sir. I heard. Nothing official, but rumours . . .'

No need to explain. It was the same everywhere. Word spread quickly.

'I—' Harper paused as Miss Sharp returned with two cups of tea and a plate of biscuits. 'I need to know what progress you've made.'

'Very little, sir,' Carpenter admitted. 'I'm working on my own, fitting it around all my other duties, and I'm trying to be careful. Only a few questions here and there, nothing to make anyone suspicious.'

'Of course.'

'I have to be honest, sir, something like this isn't my bailiwick.' Carpenter shifted on the seat. 'I've always been in uniform, on the beat then supervising constables. I left things like this to men like you in plain clothes.'

'You're who I have,' Harper said.

'I know that, sir. I'm not trying to back off or anything. I'm doing the best I can, but I'm feeling my way, so I might not have a result as fast as you'd like. I promise you this, though: if there's something to find, I'll dig it up.'

Harper believed him. He'd known men like this before. They were tenacious and honest; you could rely on them.

'I'm sure you will. Tell me, do you plan on going back to the force when this is all over?'

'Definitely, sir.' Carpenter smiled. 'It's what I know. I had ten years on the job before the war began.'

'Maybe you can go back as an inspector.'

The man looked horrified. 'Oh no, sir. That wouldn't suit me at all. Where I was, that's perfect, thank you, sir.'

At least he knew what made him content, Harper thought after the man had gone. Now he had to hope that the man's methodical ways turned up a name. But he couldn't bank on Carpenter alone. He needed to pursue every single possibility. He wanted that murderer in the dock.

*   *   *

Waiting and hoping. He'd never been a patient man. All through his career, Harper had preferred to be out there, stirring things up. This time, though, he'd already done everything he could. Some ideas had paid off, even if it had happened in ways he hadn't anticipated, like Mary's tip that had broken up the deserter ring.

It was good, but not the satisfaction he needed.

If they didn't find this sharpshooter, he'd kill again. And again. It didn't matter how much they tightened security, there were still too many opportunities.

'What do you suggest, Tom?' the chief constable asked when Harper telephoned. 'We can't keep everyone safe. I wish to God we could. And we daren't warn them, either.'

'What else can we do? I've been racking my brain and I can't come up with anything.'

'You're doing everything you can,' Parker told him. 'You've assembled some good men. You're using the army. Let them work. I know how much you want this man. Just accept that it might not be today.'

He already knew that. One more day lost. And now he'd worry about how many more this sniper might murder before they caught him. It was already too late for Bertie Andrews and Maggie Glover. A pair of names he'd never be able to forget.

'Sir,' Ash said, 'we might have something.'

'Go on.' Harper sat up straight, alert. The clock on the wall read just after half past six. He'd heard Miss Sharp tidy her desk then the click of her shoes on the floor as she left, but he kept working. A chance to burrow through the mountain of papers and keep the case from preying on his mind.

'You know we've been questioning people whose houses look down on Kirkstall Road. Walsh found someone who remembered seeing a man cycle away late in the afternoon, not long before dark.'

'Do we have a description?'

'All the woman can say for certain is that the man had very fair hair. Bare-headed. She was adamant on that, wouldn't be shifted. A young man on a bicycle. He had something long and wrapped in sacking on his back. She thought it was probably a fishing rod.'

Harper could feel the thud of his pulse. It felt like a sighting, a proper sighting. But he dared not let himself become too excited. How often had that happened before and he'd been wrong?

'Which way was he going?' Harper asked.

'Towards town.'

'Did she notice anything else?' He fired off a barrage of questions. 'How was he dressed? His manner? Hadn't she heard the shots? They must have been loud.'

'Walsh sat down with her. You know he's good, sir – women have always responded well to him. But she was just glancing out of the window for a minute when she saw the man. Sheer luck, that's all. And she wasn't looking at him, he was just there.'

'Yes, of course. What about the shots?'

'She never even noticed. It's always noisy near the forge, it doesn't register with people out there any more.'

No, of course; it would have just been another sound.

'Did anyone else see him?'

'We're still looking.'

'Get the men—' he began, but Ash was ahead of him.

'They're already going through the army records and singling out those with fair hair, sir. Not that we're going to ignore the rest. We all know what witnesses are like.'

Oh yes. They knew that all too well. But it was a place to start. More than anything, it gave them a spark of hope.

TEN

It was almost nine when he stepped off the tram in Sheepscar. The air was filled with the noise and stink of industry.

Home.

The Victoria was still open, the bar busy, filled with the buzz of conversation. In the corner, someone was playing the piano and trying to start a sing-song. Harper squeezed through the crowd, then up the stairs. The sound was quieter here, muffled.

For a second he thought the parlour was empty. Then he saw Annabelle on the settee, bent over and staring at the ground. She turned as she heard him, staring, face twisted with fear.

'Who are you?' she screeched. 'Don't you come near me. Don't you dare.' A moment and she was calling for Johanna. The woman bustled through from the kitchen, putting her arms round

Annabelle's shoulders and whispering softly in her ear to soothe her.

He didn't move. This behaviour had started the year before. She didn't know him, she believed he was going to harm her. This was only the fifth time it had happened. It passed quickly enough, but it always terrified him. Twice she'd been the same with Mary. The one she turned to, the one she usually trusted, was Johanna. That cut him more than anything. He knew it was the disease talking, that Annabelle loved him. But still it hurt.

Johanna's eyes urged him through to the kitchen. Out of sight and out of mind, banished in his own home. He took his supper from the oven, a dry, hard chop. Still some tea in the pot. He ate, trying to push his frustration away. It didn't work. The food was tasteless, like chewing a piece of leather. He slid it into the bin. A waste, but he couldn't swallow. The tea was just wet and warm.

He felt sorry for himself. A frustrating day and then this . . . it overwhelmed him. He stood, staring down at the lino, trying to convince himself it was nothing. Annabelle wasn't really scared of him. She didn't hate him. He knew it, he knew every word of this song, he could sing it note-perfect. But sometimes believing was so hard.

He must have drifted with his thoughts. Harper opened his eyes and Johanna touched his sleeve. A bashful smile.

'It's passed now. She'll be fine.'

Annabelle looked tired. Her skin had a grey tinge as she looked up with sad eyes.

'I didn't hear you come in.' Her voice was shaky.

'You were busy,' he said as he reached for her hand.

A frown passed across her face. 'I don't remember what I was doing, Tom.'

'You and me,' Johanna told her.

'Yes.' She nodded, uncertain. 'That must have been it. I'm very tired.'

'Come on,' he said as he helped her up from the settee. 'Why don't we go to bed? It's been a long day.'

A thankful glance over his shoulder to Johanna. He'd be lost without her.

Annabelle drifted off quickly, curling close against him as he put his arm around her shoulders. He felt her warm skin and muscle and bone. And just a few minutes earlier she'd thought . . . who knew what was in her head?

In the early morning she slept on as he woke and dressed. Mary was already moving around the kitchen; she poured him a cup of tea when he appeared.

'How's my mam? Johanna told me when I came home.'

'It passed. She'll be fine now.'

She stared at him. Neither of them dared to say more about it. Not yet.

'I could still do with you keeping your ears open,' Harper told her, 'the next time you're out on the beat.'

'I will.'

They rode the tram together. He read the morning paper, she made notes for the day ahead.

'Da,' Mary said as they stood on Vicar Lane. Still too early to be crowded, just a few elderly businessmen wrapped in heavy coats and mufflers against the winter cold.

'What?' He looked at her. A sideways glance and he saw her when she was five, precocious and already full of ambition.

'Are you going to catch him?'

'Yes,' he told her. He wasn't sure how, but simply being with her had given him heart.

'Fair hair?' the brigadier asked. 'Do you have any idea how many—'

'If you can just pass that to Corporal Carpenter, Brian. It might speed things along.'

'Of course,' Fox muttered. 'I've been chivvying the War Office for that information you need, too.'

As soon as you began to deal with a bureaucratic machine, things turned to sludge. That was Harper's experience. Maybe a request from a barracks would make them move faster; somehow he doubted it. Clerks moved like tortoises; it was their natural speed.

His squad had moved from the Forge back to the town hall, everything set out in the office on the top floor.

'What progress?'

'Not enough, sir,' Ash said. 'Truth is, we're all over the place. One of the specials found two cartridges in the woods across from the Forge yesterday afternoon. They look to be the same as the one from East Leeds Hospital. That's been the only real success. No idea what happened to the third cartridge.'

Confirmation, not that they really needed it.

'Where are we with this fair-haired man on the bike?'

'There was another woman who thought she might have seen him. Plenty who weren't at home.'

'Where are the men?'

'Following up on any scrap they can find,' the superintendent told him. He sighed and tapped the point of a pencil against his blotter. 'They've been going through the records, picking out the young men with fair hair. But that's no guarantee we'll nab him.'

'He needs to scout out his locations,' Harper said slowly. 'That must take time. He'll have to walk around and examine an area. Make sure of his shooting angles. It could mean more than a single visit somewhere.'

'Catching him doing that would depend on one of our lot spotting him, sir.' Under his moustache, Ash pressed his lips together. 'Or maybe someone local with a beady eye who tells us. Whichever way, it sounds an awful lot like luck to me.'

He was right. But still worth putting out the word to everyone on the beat: be even more attentive than usual. Challenge people if you're not sure what they're doing. The same message for all the army guards around town.

A very long shot. They needed something much more likely than that, and he'd run out of ideas.

'Keep them at it. And if you think of anything . . .'

'Don't worry. I'll let you know, sir.'

For another hour he sank into the papers and reports, drowning in a sea of ink. As soon as the telephone rang, he grabbed for the receiver.

'Tom.' Chief Constable Parker's voice was thin and scratchy on the other end of the line. 'The doctor's been out to see me again. My wife insisted; I had a little episode in the night.'

'Are you all right?' Christ, the last thing they needed was something else happening to the chief.

'He wants me back in hospital for a few days.' Parker stopped to catch his breath. 'It's just a precaution.'

It sounded to be more than that. 'Just make sure you look after yourself, sir. You'll be at the infirmary?'

'Yes. Same as the last time. But no visitors. Those are the orders. The bloody quack wants me to rest, as if shuffling around the house all day wasn't a quiet life.'

'I'll keep checking with the hospital, sir.'

'It'll only be for a few days. Nothing major.'

He didn't believe that for a minute. With all the wounded soldiers coming back, hospital beds were like gold. They wouldn't be taking him back in unless they were very worried. He knew it; Parker did, too.

'Let them work their magic, sir. You'll be back at home before you know it.'

'I'll be glad when I'm on the job again. There's more peace at the town hall than there is around my wife.'

If the chief returned at all, it wouldn't be for months. Not now, after this setback. That meant everything was firmly on his shoulders once more.

'All the post you've been sending to the chief constable at home,' he said to Miss Sharp. 'Start putting it on my desk again, will you?'

Worry flashed in her eyes. 'Why? What's happened?'

'He's going back into hospital. I don't know any more than that. And that's not to become public knowledge, please.'

'Of course.'

Harper needed some fresh air, a chance to think. A harsh breeze stung him as he came out on the Headrow. He strode out, up to the peak of the hill at Albion Street, then down the long slope of Eastgate, until he was no more than a stone's throw from Millgarth police station. He'd spent most of his years as a copper there, starting as a recruit and climbing to superintendent, running the division. The place was in his blood.

Without thinking, he walked over to the market and climbed the iron stairs to the small café. Condensation ran down the windows and he drew his hand across it to gaze down on all the people shopping. Always busy and alive.

Ash already knew about the chief. Of course he did, Harper thought.

'With a little luck, he'll be on the mend and back in his own bed again soon. Meanwhile we'll catch this saboteur and make him happy, sir.'

'I hope you're right,' Harper said. 'It feels like there's every chance he'll strike again before we find him.'

The superintendent nodded. 'The men understand how much is riding on this, sir. They all know people over there.'

The detectives were out, only the stale smell of tobacco lingering in the air.

'Any word from them?'

'Nothing yet.'

Was that good? Bad? He didn't know. Trust them, he told himself. Trust them.

The afternoon dragged past. More papers, the meeting with the heads of each division. There were only two real topics: the chief's health and the sniper. Every copper, every special in the city was searching for the sharpshooter. But one man in a place the size of Leeds . . . a population of well over a quarter of a million people. That was impossible.

He'd invited the brigadier. Each of the superintendents could name the places in their manors where a sharpshooter might be likely to strike. Between them all, perhaps they could come up with a plan.

Perhaps. A lovely word that meant so little.

Fox remained after the others had gone. He still looked crisp and groomed in his tailored uniform, the walking stick he used leaning against the desk. He gave the appearance of a man on top of everything. Only his eyes showed the truth. They were fearful, overwhelmed. He drew a hand through his hair.

'What they're asking is impossible, Tom. I'd need another division just to patrol the places they've mentioned. Even then I couldn't guarantee a blasted thing.'

'I never imagined you'd be able to cover it all,' Harper told him. 'I wanted you to hear what they're up against.'

'What do we do?'

'Whatever we can. Keep pushing, for a start. And keep hoping. Give Corporal Carpenter all the help he needs.'

Another visit upstairs. Still only Ash there, going through folders, looking at one then hunting through a pile for another and opening that as Harper watched.

'Something interesting?'

'Possibly, sir.' He gave a slow, dark smile. 'How do you fancy a little outing?'

ELEVEN

The car was noisy, and the driver kept apologizing as he shifted awkwardly through the gears. They followed the York Road, and beyond the Bank and Cross Green, where the streets were crammed with houses, the city quickly turned to countryside. Five more minutes and it was difficult to believe they were anywhere near Leeds.

Harper had kept silent this far. Now it was time for Ash to explain.

'Well? Where are we going?'

'There's a discrepancy between two of the files from the army,' he began. 'They discharged a man named George Johnson. A sharp-shooter. According to one of the files he had a head wound that left him seeing double much of the time.'

'That would stop him shooting. What was in the other file?'

The superintendent rubbed his moustache before he answered. 'That's where it becomes interesting, sir. No mention of a wound at all. But his behaviour became very strange. Erratic, they said. He was a danger to the men in his unit. Hospital didn't help. Not even seeing one of those trick cyclist doctors they have now. They ended up invaliding him out.'

'Are you sure it's the same man? Johnson's a common name.'

'Same address, sir. Seems he was supposed to have follow-up treatment here but he didn't show up.'

'What happened?'

'Nothing at all. It looks like he fell through the cracks.'

With his background, Johnson could be a prime candidate. They definitely needed to talk to him.

'Where does he live?'

'Seacroft. His mother moved there from Sheffield when she remarried, but her new husband died.'

He'd been through the place. A small village past the fringes of Leeds, a few streets and pubs, a couple of big houses. Miles and miles of farmland. That was all he could remember of it. Harper glanced out of the window. Already dark, nothing to see out there. Endless night.

'If he's local, why haven't we visited him before?'

'Fenton and Dixon stopped by, but the mother said he was out. They haven't had time to go back.'

The car slowed, and the driver turned off the motor. The only sound was the soft tick of the cooling engine.

'From the map I saw, the house should be just down there to the right,' the driver told them. 'It's the only one around.'

Harper raised his eyebrows. 'Ready?'

'Yes, sir.' Ash smiled.

Not a road, no more than a lane, barely wide enough for a cart. Hard, rutted dirt under his boots. And all around him, the soft sounds of the countryside. Animals snuffling, calling. Even with his poor hearing he could make out a little of it. What had that man at Gledhow Hall said? It was never quiet.

Harper felt his pulse starting to climb, the beating of his heart inside his chest. Why? This was a simple call. Straightforward. There shouldn't be any danger in it. But something inside was telling him to be careful. Maybe because they were so far from the comfort of buildings and familiar city noises. He felt very exposed and vulnerable out here.

A low wooden fence and gate, and the path to a house. Two small slivers of light showed through the curtains.

Harper knocked on the door. Once, twice, then a third time. Without thinking, he moved to one side. Whatever this uneasy feeling was, he was going to obey it. It was just common sense: never make yourself a target. He waited. Faintly, he could make out the shuffle of feet inside.

Without warning, a gun boomed and the door exploded.

Harper threw himself to the ground and rolled away to hide in the night. 'Are you all right?' he hissed.

'Fine, sir,' Ash replied.

'Send the driver to the nearest police station. We need everyone they have.'

He listened as feet scrambled over the ground, then the motor turned over. A few seconds and Ash returned, kneeling close by him.

'We're not taking any risks,' Harper said. 'If he's our marksman, I don't intend to give him the chance to kill us.'

'How can we take him, sir?'

He didn't know. This Johnson was deadly. And the man was on a knife edge. He'd already shown that.

The ground was hard, the cold beginning to seep through his coat and into his flesh.

'We can't just lie here until some help comes,' Harper whispered. 'You go and cover the back in case he tries to escape.'

For a large man, Ash moved lightly, hurrying off through the darkness. Harper looked around. His eyes had adjusted to the night, enough to make out the faint outline of objects. Slowly, cautiously, he crawled to a broad tree and propped himself behind it. In spite of the chill he was sweating, his heart racing.

Two of them couldn't storm the house. Even with reinforcements, any assault against an armed man would mean sending coppers to their deaths. He needed an idea that would work.

He slapped the tree trunk. The wood was old, solid, a good shield. Harper cupped his hands.

'Mr Johnson. George Johnson.' His voice seemed to fill the sky. The man would hear every word. 'This is Deputy Chief Constable Harper with Leeds City Police. We're here to talk to you, nothing more than that. Put down your gun and open the door.'

No reaction. He hadn't expected one, but he had to try. Talk him out of the house first, if he could.

'Who did you think I was when you fired at me?' Maybe a question would start Johnson talking.

A long silence. Then: 'The army. Come to arrest me.'

The voice was muffled by the walls, but still loud enough. It made no sense.

'The army discharged you,' Harper called. 'They don't want to take you into custody.'

'I ran. They're going to take me and put me back in the trenches. I can't go back there.'

The words came out in a howl of pain and fear. Harper exhaled slowly. How the hell was he going to make Johnson believe he was in no danger?

'We want to help you. I don't want you to return to France.' He was thinking quickly, thoughts racing through his head. 'You live with your mother, don't you?'

'Yes.'

'May I talk to her?'

'I killed her.'

Murdered his mother? Harper didn't move, stunned by what he'd heard. Johnson had admitted it so casually, as if it was nothing.

Christ. He really had gone off the deep end. If it was true . . . but maybe it had all happened in his head. They needed to get in the house and find out.

'Put down the gun and come out. You can tell me about it.'

'No. You'll shoot me.'

'The police don't carry weapons, Mr Johnson. I'm sure you remember that.' Stay reasonable, he told himself. Not angry or exasperated.

Harper turned in a panic at the sharp crack of a twig.

'Just me, sir.' Ash kept his voice low. 'I heard it all. He's not going to be running anywhere.'

'No,' Harper agreed. 'How are we going to winkle him out without anybody else dying?'

'I've no idea, sir. Remember, he's a trained marksman.'

He hadn't forgotten. Johnson had some deadly skills and madness had claimed him. That was a volatile combination. He couldn't see any chance of this ending safely.

'I think—' The words were swallowed as a shot exploded inside the house.

Harper didn't wait. He was on his feet, dashing across to the building. Ash was close behind. He kicked at the door. Once, then again, feeling the lock start to give. The third sent it crashing back against the wall.

The fire burned low, giving just enough light to see the two bodies on the floor. An older woman, curled on her side in a pool of blood. And at the far end of the room, sprawled in a doorway, a man. The shotgun had fallen from his hands. Half his skull was missing, brains and blood making wild patterns across the walls.

'She's dead,' Ash said, taking his fingers from the woman's neck. 'Quite a few hours, by the feel of it. The body's cold. Looks like he stabbed her.'

Johnson hadn't lied. He'd killed his mother and finished the job by putting a gun under his chin and pulling the trigger. Christ. What had been going through his mind?

Ash raised his head. 'Motor coming down the road, sir.'

'We might as well go outside,' Harper said. 'There's nothing we can do in here.'

The cold air was a welcome shock, a slap in the face. He breathed it in, filling his lungs. God. He'd seen some things on the force, but . . .

Four bobbies climbed out of the car, truncheons drawn, tentative, wary expressions on their face.

'In there,' Harper told them. 'I'll warn you, it's not pretty. I want an ambulance to take the bodies and someone to guard the place until the detectives get here in the morning. Understood?'

'Yes, sir.' A uniformed sergeant with more experience than the rest saluted. 'Don't you worry, I'll look after things.'

They barely talked on the drive back to town. What was there to say? He gave orders to have the squad out to the house as soon as it was light. Search all around for a marksman's rifle and ammunition. And anything else they could find, a journal, a diary. Something that might tell them more about whatever Johnson was thinking.

'Drop me at the Victoria on Roundhay Road,' he told the driver, then settled back and closed his eyes. But that gave no comfort. All he saw was a corpse with his head sprayed everywhere.

'We're here, sir.'

A nod to Ash and he ducked through the night into the warmth of the public house. Closed, empty, lights off, but so familiar. Home. Harper climbed the stairs and opened the door. Leave it all outside, he told himself. But he knew he never could. That was the thing about death: it followed you everywhere.

TWELVE

Harper sat behind the desk, watching his squad. Larkin was reading through his notebook, Dixon scribbled a few quick words then sat back to stare at them. Fenton looked down at the desk and chewed his lip. Walsh was glancing at a file, one of a small pile in front of him.

Ash leaned against the back wall, arms folded, his face showing nothing.

'Right,' Harper began, 'what do we know about George Johnson? How did it end up like that?'

It was a little after eleven in the morning. The men had been working since before first light. Poring over files, talking to people, two of them searching the house and garden where Johnson and his mother had lived.

Harper had been at the town hall earlier than any of them. A sleepless night. Each time he drifted off, the boom of a gun would pull him awake again and he'd see the shattered remains of the man's skull. Finally he slid out of bed, washed and dressed and walked into town from the Victoria.

Even at night, Leeds was alive; always the clatter of machines and industry and music to accompany life. Every shift running full pelt for the war effort. As soon as he reached the town hall, he telephoned the infirmary. The chief constable was comfortable. They refused to say more than that.

He read the newspapers each day. He'd seen the newsreels the few times he and Annabelle strolled down to the Newtown Picture Palace to watch a film. Everything carefully edited, of course, but they still showed enough of the horrors. Mary couldn't bear to watch, and he didn't blame her. Everything was still too raw in her heart.

What had Johnson experienced over there to make him murder his own flesh and blood then commit suicide?

'He'd been in hospital up in Scotland, sir,' Walsh began. 'There's a special place where they treat the bad cases of shell shock. According to the notes, they thought he'd be able to cope. He did have appointments to see a doctor down here, but it doesn't appear that he went, and they were too busy to follow up.'

'And the different diagnoses in his file?'

Walsh shrugged. 'Bureaucracy, sir. There was a wound, but it was minor. The problems seemed to be more in his mind.'

Silence filled the room. Harper took off his spectacles and rubbed his eyes. A subdued mood. No anger, just sorrow and hopelessness.

'When did he kill his mother?'

'We'll know more after Dr Lumb finishes his post-mortem,' Larkin said. 'He reckons about a day, but he wasn't willing to be more exact than that without an examination.'

Twenty-four hours sitting alone with the person you'd murdered. Impossible to imagine what he was thinking. All the demons running riot. No surprise that he'd fired as soon as he heard hammering on the door.

'Who searched the property?' he asked.

'Me and Dan, sir,' Fenton said, with a nod towards Dixon. 'There was the shotgun and a few shells. But no sign of a sniper rifle anywhere. Not in the house or anywhere in the garden. We tore the place apart. I'd stake my life it's not there and never has been.' He hesitated. 'A couple of other things, sir.'

'What?'

'That witness in Kirkstall mentioned someone with fair hair on a bike. There was no bicycle at Johnson's house. We talked to the people at the end of the lane; they've never seen him on one. And he had dark hair, sir, not fair.'

'Good work. Thank you.' He looked around at the faces staring back at him, all of them wanting to know what to do next. 'God only knows what we walked into, but it looks as if Johnson wasn't our suspect, the poor soul. Let's get hunting for that man with fair hair and a bike, shall we?'

Tragedy. Victims. The words always came too easily, Harper thought as he sat in his own office. But how else could anyone describe George Johnson and his mother?

He'd seen the dead often enough. It was part of the job. But this . . . this would stay with him, return in the nights to make him wonder if he could have done anything differently.

A tap on the door and Ash was there, a bulky presence as he sat and adjusted the knees of his trousers.

'Dr Lumb completed the post-mortems on Johnson and his mother. She'd been dead for over twenty hours before we arrived. There was nothing we could have done to stop that.'

Harper nodded. The man was trying to offer a little comfort. But instead he realized how much of life was beyond their control.

The bell on the telephone rang twice before he lifted the receiver.

'Deputy Chief Constable Harper.'

'It's Councillor Walton.' The chairman of the watch committee, the group that ran the police force. He had a brusque voice, a self-made businessman who was used to riding roughshod over objections. 'You'll not have heard, then?'

'Heard what?' He didn't understand.

'About Parker.'

The chief? A turn for the worse in hospital? What? 'I know he went back into hospital.'

A long pause. 'He died this morning. I'm sorry to be the one to tell you.'

He didn't know how to respond. He was stunned, unable to move. The man was bad enough to return to the infirmary, but he'd always been fit. A battler.

'I'd better . . . his wife . . .' Harper managed finally.

'All in good time,' Walton told him. 'I wanted to make sure you knew.'

'Yes. Thank you for telling me.' The words seemed to come out automatically, as if they didn't belong to him.

'There's something else. We discussed this possibility on the watch committee when Mr Parker first became ill.' His voice softened into the tone of someone trying to avoid responsibility. 'We needed to look at every eventuality.'

'Of course.' He was listening, but not really hearing. Parker was dead. Dead? 'Forgive me, sir, but was it sudden? When I checked first thing, they said he was comfortable.'

'I don't know the details,' Walton told him. 'The hospital telephoned me less than an hour ago.'

'I see.'

'I've talked to the others on the committee, and they confirmed what we agreed earlier. In due course we'll look for a new chief constable—'

'Yes, of course.'

'—but until one is appointed, you're our acting chief constable.'

'Me?' He'd thought about it of course, then dismissed the idea. He'd been doing the job for a while, but not in name. He'd still been Deputy Chief Constable Harper. He'd never believed they'd accept him for the top job, not even temporarily.

'I'm sorry it's under such terrible circumstances, Harper, but you're the right person for the job at present. I'll be sending you a letter so it's confirmed in writing.'

With that he was gone, just the faint hum on the line. He sat, the receiver in his hand, staring at the wall for a few seconds before he could move.

So much death. Everywhere you turned there was a list of names. And now Bob Parker was added to it. He took a deep breath, then stood.

'Miss Sharp,' he said as he stood in the doorway, 'I'm afraid I have some very sad news. The chief has died.'

He saw her face fall, and the start of tears in her eyes. The man had been well liked. A rocky beginning as he put his authority on everything, but after that he gained the respect and admiration of the entire force.

Only Ash was in the office upstairs. Parker's office. One look at Harper's face and he seemed to know.

'When did it happen, sir?'

'This morning. Councillor Walton just rang me.'

'That's terrible news.' He pushed his lips together. 'Does that mean you'll be the acting chief, sir?'

'Yes. That's what he said.'

It didn't seem real. Harper hadn't begun to think about that part yet. He was the lad who grew up in a back-to-back house on Noble Street, who started work rolling barrels in the brewery when he was nine. The young man who'd made his father proud the day he was sworn in to walk the beat. Now he was at the top of the tree. No one else to make the decisions, no one else to take responsibility. Just him.

'Sir?' Ash's voice brought him back to the present.

'What? I'm sorry, I . . .'

'Do we know anything about the funeral or a memorial service yet?'

He shook his head. 'The councillor didn't say. I'll tell Miss Sharp to ask.'

'Very good. And congratulations, sir. But I know you'd never have wanted it to happen this way.'

'I don't know that I want it to happen at all,' he replied with a shake of his head. He wondered when it might sink in. If it ever did. 'Tell the men when they return, will you?'

The day turned into a blur of faces as people in the town hall appeared with condolences and congratulations, one leading directly to the other. Wave after wave of them until he wanted it all to stop. He checked the chief's calendar; at least in wartime there were fewer functions. No need to wear a penguin suit and dicky bow until next month.

'You won't have any choice now,' Miss Sharp told him. 'You're going to have a car and driver. It comes with the job.'

He nodded. Some things he'd give in to and accept. But the city would have to do the same. He'd be the first chief constable to live in Sheepscar, not one of the green suburbs, and certainly the first to make his home above a pub. The thought cheered him.

He'd considered telephoning home to give Annabelle the news. But he didn't know what kind of a day this was for her; it was better to wait and see, and do it in person.

By six he was drained, unable to think clearly any longer. He climbed the stairs and walked into the chief constable's office. His office now, commandeered by his squad. Only Ash was there, broad and impassive behind the desk as he sifted through the files.

'You look as if you've been hit by a train, sir.'

'I feel like it.' He sighed, and for the first time that day, he smiled. 'It's been blow after blow. Johnson last night, then the chief.'

'For whatever it's worth, sir, we'll all miss him.'

'Yes, we will.' He had big shoes to fill, even if only temporarily. 'Have they found anything today?'

'A couple of blond men who fit the bill. Invalided out of the army, have bicycles. But it wasn't either of them.' He raised an eyebrow. 'Plenty of names on that list the army sent us. It'll take a while.'

'And we don't even know it was definitely him,' Harper said.

'Exactly, sir. I'm not going to put all our eggs in that basket. Walsh and Larkin are looking at other things. We'll get there eventually.'

'But he might strike again first.'

Ash nodded. 'He might. We don't understand how he thinks.'

'Is he a saboteur, do you think? Is he trying to damage the war effort?'

'Honestly, sir, I'm not sure his mind is working that way.' Ash frowned, hunting for the phrase he wanted. 'Something's gone wrong in his head, I'm sure of that. That's what makes him so unpredictable and so bloody dangerous.'

Harper raised his eyebrows. Ash rarely swore. The strain of this was showing on his face.

'Go home,' he ordered. 'See Nancy and get yourself a good night's sleep. And if there's anything . . .'

'I'll telephone, sir. Don't worry.'

The car was waiting, and the driver slid expertly in and out of traffic. He knew exactly where to go, turning into Manor Street and stopping in the spot where Annabelle used to park her Rex. She'd loved that car, only gave it up when she admitted she wasn't safe on the roads any longer.

'What time tomorrow, sir?'

'Six,' he said. 'What's your name?'

'Bingham, sir. Constable Bingham. I was the chief's driver. You know, before.'

'I'll try not to be too obtuse, Constable.' A pause, then he said, 'I'm sorry about Mr Parker. We'll both miss him.'

A small nod. 'That we will, sir. That we will.'

The bar was full, loud with the ring of voices and laughter. Dan and Jaak were hard at work, pulling on the beer pumps and filling glasses. Harper slipped through the crowd and up the stairs.

Annabelle, Mary and Johanna were all sitting at the table, talking nineteen to the dozen as they ate some scrag end with onions and potatoes.

'Your plate's in the oven, Tom.' His wife held up her knife and fork. 'We've only just sat down.'

He settled and watched them as they chattered away. Annabelle looked merry and alert, keeping up with the others. Her eyes were bright, her smile as sweet as ever. She caught him looking at her.

'What is it?' she asked. 'Have I grown a third eye and nobody said a word?'

He gave them the news about Parker, the little he knew.

'His poor wife,' she said. 'Is there anything we can do, Tom?'

'I don't think so.' He'd met the woman a few times, all official occasions, but he didn't know her at all.

'Who'll be the new chief, Da?' Mary asked. 'Have they decided yet?'

'Well,' he began, letting the word hang in the air, 'for now it's me. Acting chief, nothing more.'

A clatter as Annabelle dropped her cutlery. 'Chief constable?'

'It's not permanent.'

'That doesn't matter a jot, Tom Harper.' She shook her head in amazement. 'Who'd have thought it?'

'And it's only because Bob Parker died,' he reminded her.

'God rest his soul.' Without thinking, she crossed herself; that Irish Catholic upbringing she'd left behind was ingrained deeper than she could reach. 'Acting Chief Constable Tom Harper. And I thought I was getting a bargain when I married a detective inspector.'

Mary stood, her chair scraping over the floor. 'I have patrol duty tonight.' She pecked him on the cheek. 'Congratulations. Are you over the moon, Da?'

'No,' he told her honestly. 'I'd rather he was still with us and back at work. But I can't change things.'

'What does it mean?' Annabelle asked as she drew close to him in bed. The sheets felt harsh and cold against his body. 'Will it be any different. You've already been doing the job, haven't you?'

'I kept things ticking over, that's all,' he explained. 'Now I get the works. Meetings, all the formal dos. The lot.'

He felt her stiffen. 'I won't have to come, will I?' Her voice held an edge of panic.

'Don't worry, I'll make your excuses.' He stroked her back until the tension left her body.

'I'm proud of you. You know that, don't you, Tom? Even if it happened this way.'

'I know.'

'I love you. I always will. I know what I have makes it hard sometimes, but I do.'

'I know that, too.' He kissed her. 'And I love you, Mrs Chief Constable Harper.'

THIRTEEN

A new morning in more ways than one, Harper thought as the car moved quickly along the road. His first full day in this new position. But some things hadn't changed. They still needed to catch the sniper. That stood head and shoulders above everything else.

But there was a host of other, mundane things: everything that accompanied the job of being chief constable. Bigwigs to greet, meetings, correspondence. God knew what else. The grease that made the wheels of local government go round.

Miss Sharp was already in the office, sorting letters and folders into piles.

'There's a cuppa waiting on your desk,' she told him, 'although it's probably just warm by now. Superintendent Ash is upstairs if you want him.'

'Ask him to come down, will you? And see if you can find out when they're holding the chief's funeral, please?'

'A week on Tuesday,' she told him. 'Two o'clock at the Parish Church, then the burial at Lawnswood. You'll be expected to say a few words.'

He'd anticipated that. Still, it would give him the chance to bid a proper farewell to a boss who'd become a friend.

'Right.' He rubbed his hands together. 'Let's jump into things, shall we?'

'What's happening with those names from the army list?' Harper asked.

'Still working through them, sir,' Ash replied. 'So far, every possibility's ended up as nothing.'

'And meanwhile our man is out there, planning his next move.'

'All the bobbies on the beat have been warned to keep their eyes peeled. Same for the army guards everywhere.'

'Let's hope it pays off. You've had the chance to think about all this. What's your theory on it?'

The superintendent turned his head to stare out of the window as he gathered his thoughts. His hands were clasped together on his lap, and his eyes looked as though he was filled with sorrow.

'I reckon he's served at the front and he's come back with some problems that won't go away. I'm sure as I can be that he's doing all this alone. Nobody else knows.'

'That's going to make it all the harder to catch him.'

Ash nodded. 'I know, sir. We all do. I could be wrong in all this, but honestly, I don't think it's a deliberate attempt to damage the war effort here. He hasn't thought it through like that. It's not organized. My guess is he's someone who's taking his revenge for something we might never be able to understand. Someone living in a . . .' he paused, mouth tight, searching, '. . . I suppose we'd call it a distorted world.'

It made sense. More than some of the ideas he'd read. But it didn't bring them any closer to finding the man.

'Then how do we catch him?'

'We keep pushing. Follow every lead we can, sir.'

'Do you have enough men?'

'For now.'

'If you need more, just tell me.' God alone knew where he'd manage to find them, but he'd do it.

'Thank you, sir.' Ash stood. As he turned to go, he said, 'You're looking very dapper today.'

He'd had the suit made the previous year and barely worn it since. It came from Cohen and Sons, a tailor in the Leylands. He'd grown up with Moses Cohen, gone to school with him. Moishe had died of a heart attack; one of his sons ran the business now.

This morning had seemed right to put it on. Dark grey, a good, heavy worsted, it was a perfect fit. A chief constable's suit, he thought as he studied himself in the mirror at the Victoria. At least he could make a good impression for one day.

'The Home Secretary is on the line for you,' Miss Sharp said, with a hushed reverence in her voice.

Harper drew a breath and lifted the receiver. So this was what it meant to be the chief constable. The chance to talk to Sir George Cave in London.

'Good morning, Home Secretary. I trust you're well.'

It was a brief, formal call, an introduction. Condolences on Parker and a welcome to him. All done and dusted inside two minutes. But afterwards, his hand was clammy with sweat. Harper chuckled at himself. He'd stood close to a king, he'd talked to a prime minister, and now a phone conversation with a minister left him nervous as a child at school.

A tap on the door and Miss Sharp poked her head into the room. 'Inspector Walsh is outside. He says it's urgent.'

'Send him in.'

He looked as if he was wearing yesterday's clothes. A grubby ring around his collar, trousers rumpled. But the strain of the case showed most on his face. His skin was tinged grey and stretched taut over his bones. His usual easy manner had been replaced by sharp little gestures.

'Have you found something?' Harper asked.

'I don't know, sir.' He paced around the room, pushing his hands into his trouser pockets then taking them out again.

'Go on. We've worked together for twenty years now. It's not like you to be indecisive.'

Walsh stood and faced Harper. 'My neighbour came to see me

last night. He's a nice chap, honest as the day is long. He's heard about what happened.'

Everybody had, of course. But as long as it never appeared in print it remained a rumour, never a fact.

'What about it?'

'It's complicated, sir. And he's not sure it means anything. One of his sisters lives down south somewhere. Her son was a sharp-shooter in the army for a while, then moved to another unit because he was having problems.'

'What kind of problems?' Harper sat taller on his chair.

'My neighbour didn't know. But the lad was sent back to the line, down in the trenches. Then he had a Blighty wound and shell shock. Turns out he's been up in Leeds for a few weeks visiting someone else in the family. Evidently he acts strangely, goes off for hours by himself.' He paused. 'Likes to ride a bicycle.'

'Then go and question him.'

'My neighbour doesn't want it known that he told me all this.'

Harper shook his head. 'I'm sorry for him, but he doesn't get that choice. Not when two people have been murdered and there are two more still in hospital. Go and talk to this man. What's his name?'

'Albert Armstrong.'

'Do we have his file from the army?'

'It wasn't in the batch they sent,' Walsh answered. 'I've requested it.'

'If there's the slightest sniff of suspicion about him, drag him in.'

'Can I ask that another officer goes, sir? I met Armstrong myself once, before the war. His family would put two and two together.'

'They probably will, anyway. But ask Superintendent Ash. I'm sure he'll arrange it.'

'He's out, sir. They all are.'

'Give me the address. I'll go myself.'

'But you're the chief—'

He flared. 'I'm still a copper, *Inspector*. And we have a pair of killers out there. Don't you forget that.'

'No, sir. Of course not. I'm sorry.'

Grey, sullen skies. Buildings black from decades of soot. People dressed in muted shades of brown and blue. Sometimes Harper found it hard to recall if there had ever been any bright colours in

Leeds. While Bingham drove him up into Cross Green, he caught a flash of the river. As dark and bleak as iron.

The street looked down over the valley towards Hunslet. Smoke plumed from factory chimneys and gathered in low clouds.

'Stay ready in case I need some help,' he said.

The house was a well-kept through terrace. Door and window frames recently painted, windows clean and shining. A front garden the size of a postage stamp, dug over for winter. Harper stood by the low wall for a moment, praying to God this wouldn't be another George Johnson.

The woman answered the knock quickly, the sound of her shoes click-clacking down the hall. Small, prim, in her fifties, with dark, sympathetic eyes.

'May I help you?'

She tried to put a gloss on her words, but the accent was Leeds through and through. Her airs made him smile.

'I'm looking for Mr Armstrong.'

'I see.' She stared at his face assessing him and not pleased with what she saw. 'And who might you be?'

'I'm Chief Constable Harper.' That was enough to make her draw in her breath. 'Is he here?'

'No,' she said. 'He goes out every day on the bicycle and doesn't come back until evening.' She narrowed her eyes. 'Has he done something?'

'I don't know,' Harper told her. That was the truth. He had no idea yet if Armstrong was responsible for anything. 'We're following up on some files from the army. Have you had any problems with him, Mrs . . .? Any strange behaviour.'

'Mrs Emerson,' she told him. 'My husband's in the Clerk of Works office. Albert is his sister's youngest boy. He had a bad time over there and he needed a change of scene. He's no trouble, really, just quiet.'

'One of my officers will stop by tonight,' he said.

'He's done something, hasn't he?' the woman asked as he turned to leave. 'The chief constable himself doesn't come to talk to someone without a very good reason.'

'Nothing like that,' he assured her. 'Honestly. I was available, and I like to prove I'm still a policeman.' He raised his hat. 'Good day, Mrs Emerson.'

A wasted journey, Harper thought as he sat in the car. The woman didn't seem to notice much. Or perhaps there simply was nothing to see. He wanted this Armstrong to be their sniper, to have it all done. But he knew he needed to keep his mind open.

'Back to the town hall, sir?' Bingham asked.

'No,' he said after a second. 'Since we're in Cross Green, I have another stop first.'

He left a note for Ash about his visit to Armstrong, another report to add to the file, along with an order for someone to return that evening.

A summons to the Lord Mayor's office to discuss the order of service for Bob Parker's funeral. Five hushed minutes as they went through it. As soon as they'd finished, the politician in the mayor reared his head.

'Not planning any changes to the police while you're in charge, are you?'

'No, sir. I'm just here to keep the seat warm for a while.'

'Good.' A smile of relief crossed the man's face. Things would stay as they were. 'Let's keep it that way. We have enough on our plates with this damned war.'

Dismissal. But then, Harper was simply someone with a temporary promotion to fill the gap.

By seven he was exhausted. How had Parker managed it for so long? No wonder chief constables usually retired after a few years; he was ready to give it up now.

He was going to miss the man. The loss was beginning to sink in. They'd ended up working well together, a good team. He'd feel it deeply; he was beginning to realize just how much.

In the bar of the Victoria, the news of his promotion had obviously circulated; men shouted their congratulations and offered to stand him a drink. A wave of thanks and he vanished up the stairs, opening the door to the parlour with a sigh of relief.

Annabelle turned and gave him a loving smile. Her eyes were alert, her appearance was neat, the signs he always looked for whenever he came home. But today she was definitely here, working on another jigsaw puzzle with Mary and Johanna.

'A busy day, Chief Constable?' She began to giggle. 'I'm sorry, Tom. I'm proud as punch, but I can't still quite believe it.'

'That makes two of us.' He settled next to her, one hand rubbing the back of her neck. After a moment he stirred. 'I'll make us a cup of tea, shall I?

Harper emptied the old leaves into the bin and rinsed the pot. Suddenly he was aware of someone behind hm.

'You gave me the nod,' Mary said.

'Yes. I had to go up to Cross Green today—'

'Why? You're the—'

'It was important and there was no one else to do it,' he explained, pouring boiling water into the teapot to warm it. Before she could say more, he continued, 'I stopped to see Len's mother.'

'How is she?'

'Poorly. She looks a good ten years older.'

'Da . . .'

'I know.' Mary hadn't visited them. Mrs Robinson had told him that on the doorstep. She'd sounded confused by it, hurt rather than angry.

He made all the familiar movements, not saying any more. With tea hard to come by at the moment, just half a spoon per person, nothing for the pot. He felt her sigh.

'I can't,' Mary told him. 'If I even walked down their road it would just bring it all back. I can't do it. Do you understand?'

That was the problem. He saw his daughter's side. But he also saw a mother's grief.

'Maybe you could drop her a line. Meet somewhere for a chat.'

'Maybe,' she said. But from her tone he knew she was doubtful. To keep going she needed to cut away that whole part of her life.

'Tell your mother it's mashing,' he said.

A little after half past nine. They'd almost finished the jigsaw, only the final few inches in the centre remaining. Another evening that felt so comfortable and ordinary. Normal, except that things could change in a breath. Every moment was walking on eggshells.

The harsh bell of the telephone jarred him. For a moment, he didn't move.

Annabelle raised her eyebrows and looked at him. 'It's hardly going to be for anybody else,' she told him.

'Walsh, sir. I thought you'd like to know about Armstrong.' Even with the buzzes and clicks in the wire, he could make out the note of worry. 'Will Fenton stopped by about dusk, but he hadn't come back yet. Dixon was there half an hour ago. Still nothing. Mrs

Emerson said he's only been out late a couple of times. When Dan pressed her, one of them seems to be the same night as the shooting at the hospital. She's not certain, but . . .'

'Call Brigadier Fox. Tell him to have the guards at every facility on alert. A message out to all our lot on the beat to keep their eyes peeled. Did Dixon get a good description?'

'Yes, sir. The super's on his way in to take care of things.'

'I—' he began, then stopped. If he went down there he'd simply be in the way, everyone aware of him and looking over their shoulders as they worked. 'Keep me informed. Anything at all, I want to know.'

FOURTEEN

He was barely dozing. The telephone stirred him from the lightest of sleeps. Out of bed and into the parlour in seconds. 'Harper.' He was gripping the receiver so hard that his fingers hurt.

'No sign of Armstrong, sir.' Ash sounded weary, battered down by it all. 'He hasn't been home. I have a man watching the place. No bobby's spotted him anywhere, and the army hasn't seen hide nor hair round the places they're guarding.'

Where the hell was he? Harper wondered. Where had he gone?

'Is he our man?'

'I don't know,' Ash answered after a long silence. 'There's enough to suggest he might be. But with the shell shock . . . I wouldn't put all my money on it yet.'

'Keep on it. The bastard's somewhere.'

Short of catching Armstrong, he knew that would be the last he'd hear before morning. He could let himself rest for a few hours, at least.

But sleep refused to cooperate. He'd doze, then wake in a panic, imagining the phone was ringing. Every time there was only silence.

By five he was bone-weary and awake. He couldn't lie there any longer. Washed, dressed, shaved, he stood in the kitchen, spreading marmalade on his toast and waiting for the kettle to boil.

Armstrong had gone to ground somewhere. They needed to find

people who'd known him, discover where he might have gone, what he could be thinking.

Ash would already have his men working on that. And Harper knew he needed to think of other things. Manpower was threadbare, down to scraps. How was he going to cover everything? Tomorrow would see the monthly meeting of the watch committee. He'd appeared in front of them when he was deputy, but this would be his baptism of fire in the new job. At least they'd probably go easy on him. This time.

Six and he locked the door to the Victoria behind him. A foggy morning, the air rank with smoke and chemicals, the taste of soot on his tongue. He brought up his muffler to cover his mouth and nose and tugged up the collar of his overcoat. Months since it had been this bad; drivers would be crawling along the roads. He'd need men on point duty to direct the traffic. That meant they'd have to be diverted from other duties.

His mind filled with details and arrangements, not even hearing the car until it glided to a stop beside him. Right on time.

His footsteps echoed loudly as he climbed the stairs in the town hall. From somewhere above, at the top of the tower, he could just make out the voices of the spotters, still up and watching for Zeppelins, even though no airship would have a chance of finding Leeds in the fog.

At the door to the office, Harper stopped to stare at the wooden plaque on the wall. *B. Parker, Chief Constable* picked out in gold. Would there be one for him, he wondered, or didn't an acting rank deserve that?

The squad was already at work. Walsh smoked a cigarette as he read through the papers in front of him. Larkin scribbled notes. Dixon and Fenton were gone. Ash paced, hands clasped behind his back, a frustrated expression clouding his face.

'No sightings of him?' Harper asked.

'Nothing, sir,' Walsh replied. 'Not likely with this pea-souper, either. At least he can't go riding around and he won't be able to shoot.'

True enough. Small mercies. It offered them a little time to try and catch up with Armstrong.

'The army's been helpful,' Ash said. 'Names and addresses of people who know him. A couple of men who served with him and are on Blighties, wounded.'

'Anybody local?'

The superintendent shook his head. 'We've been in contact with forces all over the country. Another hour or two and we ought to start hearing back.'

Down in his own office, he asked the operator to connect him to Carlton Barracks. Then the long wait until they found the brigadier.

'Anything on Armstrong?' Harper asked.

'Nobody would be able to spot him in this. There's no point in them even looking, Tom, you know that. But I've told them to keep on top of the security. Plenty of patrols. It's all we can do.'

'Don't let up, Brian. If he's planning another attack, we might be able to find him before it happens.'

'My men know. Congratulations on the appointment, by the way.'

Harper snorted. 'I'm just a stopgap to take the blame when everything goes wrong.'

'Find this man and they might want to keep you.'

He didn't believe that. The watch committee would want an appointment from outside, someone fresh, experienced. That was always the way. Not a working-class lad whose politics were different from most of those in power. He couldn't believe they'd accept someone like him in charge of the police for more than a few months. Permanent? The idea gave him the first chuckle he'd enjoyed in weeks. Fox might understand the army, but he didn't have a clue about local government.

At dinnertime he strode down the steps of the town hall, patting the stone lion for luck as he passed. The fog was starting to thin a little, but people a few yards away vanished into the haze as they moved, insubstantial as ghosts.

Crossing the Headrow meant taking his life in his hands. The fog muffled and deadened every sound. With his bad hearing, all he could do was hope no lorry was close. At least the trams had bells that sounded as they rattled along.

A bowl of soup in a café, glancing at the *Post*. Harper wasn't particularly hungry; he simply needed to escape from the town hall for a few minutes. He'd learned to cope as deputy chief constable. Now he felt overwhelmed again. He'd get a grip on it, he knew that; but it would take time.

Still no sign of Armstrong. In this weather a man could stay hidden all too easily. There were other leads, faint strands, but none of them was more than a whisper.

Outside it was dark, the murk of fog and a winter Sunday night. Corporal Carpenter waited in Miss Sharp's empty office.

'I think I've discovered who took the rifle, sir,' Carpenter said once they were alone.

Harper's hand curled into a fist. 'How certain are you?'

'More than ninety per cent,' the corporal answered after a moment. He had an iron look in his eye. That was enough.

'Have you told Brigadier Fox?'

'Not yet, sir. You wanted me to report to you, and that's what I'm doing. You can take it up with him.'

'Who's your suspect?'

'A private who works in the quartermaster stores, sir.' He drew an envelope from the inside of his uniform and placed it on the desk. 'I wrote everything down, sir.'

'Very good.' He could read it later. 'Any leads on a sniper?'

Carpenter shook his head. 'The lads have been talking about it. It's not anyone from the barracks, I'd stake my life on that, sir.'

'No one's come up with a name of someone outside, perhaps?'

'No, sir.'

It was probably too much to hope. But the name of the man who'd sold the rifle; that was gold. They could follow things from there.

'One request if I might, sir,' Carpenter said. 'If you could keep me out of it when you question him. It'll make my life easier up there if they don't know I'm passing word to the police.' A brief flash of a smile. 'And I'd still be able to work for you if you need it.'

'Of course. And well done.'

Alone, he picked up the telephone receiver. 'Carlton Barracks, please,' he told the operator.

Four of them filled the room. Fox behind his desk, Harper sitting close by, Ash and Walsh against the walls. Then the sound of boots and a knock on the door.

The soldier wore a feral look as his eyes moved from one face to another. He knew he'd been rumbled, and now he was burrowing, hunting around for some way out.

'Private Pearson,' Fox said, 'we have information that you've been selling weapons.'

'Me, sir?' He tried to sound innocent, but his guilt shone bright as a flare.

'We know of a .303 rife and a sniper scope vanished from the stores. Very likely some ammunition, too.' The brigadier stared at him. 'What do you have to say?'

'Not me, sir. Honest.'

Harper took over. Carpenter had given him enough detail to trap Pearson. He led the man along, step by step, until his story was a tangled mess, then closed the snare around him. Let him damn himself.

'You're guilty,' Fox told him. 'You've just proved it.'

'But—'

'You might be able to help yourself.' Harper dangled the lifeline. 'Who bought the weapon?'

They eased the details from him. A meeting in a public house, talking over drinks, back there again a few nights later. The temptation of good money and the belief he'd got away with it. Until now.

'I'll ask again,' Harper said. 'Who bought the weapon?'

'He told me his name was Clarence,' the soldier said. He was nervous, voice uneasy, hands trembling in his lap.

'Clarence what?' Ash asked. Pearson had to turn his head to see him.

'I didn't ask. He didn't say.'

'What did he look like?' Walsh from the other side of the room, the questions quickly following each other, keeping the man off balance.

Pearson never stood a chance. A few minutes and they'd stripped him of every scrap. But Walsh and Ash knew how to do this. They'd interrogated experienced criminals. Pearson was an amateur, a chancer looking for a little cash.

After he'd been escorted away, the prospect of a court-martial in front of him, Fox said, 'That's one thing solved.'

'Not really,' Harper told him and saw the brigadier's face fall. 'We still need to find the man who bought it and follow things from there.'

'Carl Whittaker,' Ash said. 'Seems to me that he's used that name Clarence before—'

'He has,' Walsh agreed.

'—and the description sounds close enough. We'll bring him in later tonight.'

He felt a small glow of satisfaction as Bingham edged the car down the hill towards Sheepscar. Real, undeniable progress. For a brief moment he wished he could pick up the telephone and tell Parker. But those days had ended.

Annabelle was herself again, lively, bright, talkative. A few days of this and he could start to lull himself into the feeling that maybe everything would be well once more. Then some new thing would happen, the world would turn upside down again, and he'd be forced to remind himself that life would be like this from now on.

But there was no chance to enjoy the peace. An hour and the telephone rang. Harper could feel the dryness in his throat as he lifted the receiver. Fenton's voice, round and deep.

'We've got Whittaker in the office, sir.'

'That was fast.'

'Found him in the first place we tried. The super thought you might want to come down for the questioning.'

'Yes,' he said. A glance out of the window. The fog had thickened again, so thick he couldn't even see Manor Street. 'Better send a car.'

'On its way, sir. Whittaker looks like he's bursting to talk.'

If he wasn't yet, he would be very soon, Harper thought.

FIFTEEN

C arl Whittaker was an anonymous man. A bland face with no defined features, light brown hair. Not fat, not thin. The type of person the eye glided over, too easy to miss in a crowd. Perfect for a criminal; no one would remember him.

But here in the interview room he was sweating like the devil, reaching for a glass of water with quick, terrified movements as silent, menacing policemen surrounded him.

'What am I supposed to have done?' he asked finally. He had a faint, stupid smile, as if this might all be a joke.

'Inciting a soldier to steal British Army weapons,' Walsh began. 'A rifle and a telescopic sight.'

'Receiving and handling stolen property,' Larkin continued.

'Selling the rifle to someone,' Ash finished. 'That's a fair list for starters.'

'Not me.' Whittaker shook his head. 'I would never do something like that.'

'You're lying,' Harper said, and the man turned to stare at him.

'Maybe we should call him Clarence,' Ash suggested. 'He might answer to that. After all, it seems to be his business name.'

Relentless statements, questions, tying him up with words and pushing him through hoops. It took two hours to wring out the truth. He was beyond deception by then, ready for the cells, court tomorrow, then on remand to stand trial, with a hefty sentence looming.

'Right,' Ash said once he'd gone. 'Whittaker was paid to get hold of the rife and ammunition.' He frowned. 'The thing is, I don't recognize the name of the man who wanted it. Charlie Croft. Any of you know him?'

'I'll check the records, but it doesn't ring a bell,' Walsh said.

'Wait a minute.' Harper felt a faint stir of memory. He'd come across the name before. But he couldn't place where or when. Years ago, perhaps. 'I'm not sure,' he began, then it sprang into his mind. 'Tosh Walker.'

'Sir?' Ash asked.

'When Tosh was finally released from jail, he had nothing, do you remember? We'd taken it all away. Confiscated every one of his businesses and left him broke. Someone tried to help him. I'm as certain as I can be that it was Charlie Croft. It was a new name back then. After Tosh died he seemed to vanish again.'

Where had he been, and why was he surfacing again? It must have happened around the turn of the century, long before there were any beacons of war. Back when he was still in charge of A division.

'I want him down here for questioning in the morning,' Harper said. 'Get out there and find him.'

He watched them leave. Determined men. They were exhausted, but they had a purpose now. This would galvanize them.

'What do you think?' he asked Ash.

The man shook his head. 'No idea, sir. Tosh was a long time ago.'

'And I hope he'll be rotting in hell for eternity,' Harper said. 'Croft. I'm positive it was the same man. But it doesn't make sense. He's probably fifty or sixty now. He has to be a middleman. And that brings too many questions.' He pulled the watch from his waistcoat pocket. Quarter to three. Was it worth going home for a couple of hours of sleep? No. Easier to settle down in his office. There was one comfortable chair and he'd be here if anything happened. God, he thought, I'm too old for all this.

Harper ached. A pinched nerve in his neck from the angle of his head against the cushion. Knees that felt they might creak if he moved. His body was heavy, as if someone had filled his pockets with stones.

He opened the cover of the pocket watch and wound it, glancing at the time. Twenty past six. Harper ran a hand over his face, feeling the rough stubble.

When he stepped outside, huddled in his overcoat, the fog was little more than a memory, only a few shreds caught in the ginnels and at the back of buildings. Down at Midland station, the tea in the café was strong and hot, the porridge creamy, and they offered kippers on the menu. His body might still hurt, but at least his belly was full. Over at the Great Northern Hotel, the barber was in early. A full shave with hot towels, pomade on his hair, and he felt more human.

Miss Sharp stared at him as he entered the office. 'Well, I suppose you've made an effort,' she sighed. 'But you still look like something the cat dragged in. You could do with a fresh collar on that shirt and your suit looks like you slept in it.'

'I did.'

She raised an eyebrow and sighed. 'You're the chief constable now. There are other men to do that work.'

'And we have a saboteur and a murderer,' he reminded her. 'A sniper, killing people here in Leeds.'

'Yes. I'm sorry.' Her expression softened. 'Would you like me to send someone to buy you another collar when the shops open? Maybe another tie, too?'

She was trying to be helpful, to warn him and remind him of his status. And she was right. But it was hard not to bristle. He'd been doing his job. The one he'd signed on to do. As deputy chief, he'd been able to hide. Nobody cared, he could still be involved with real police work. But the chief constable was a public figure. People noticed what he did. Newspapers reported it.

'Yes. Thank you.'

'You were right about Charlie Croft, sir,' Ash said. Some small consolation: the superintendent looked no better than he did.

'Do we have him yet?'

'Still on the hunt. The men spent last night tracking down a current address for him. The last thing in his record was his involvement with Tosh.'

'Makes you wonder what he's been up to all this time. And why he's suddenly in the business of buying rifles for people.'

Ash glanced at the clock on the wall. 'With any luck they should be on their way back with him now.'

The early morning raid. It was an old tactic. Catch them when they were still asleep, handcuffs on before they could resist.

He returned for a glimpse of Croft. He hadn't been able to picture the man; seeing him didn't stir any memories.

He was fleshy, bald. The hair at the sides and back of his head was too long, grey and curling at the ends, and three chins nestled one on top of the other above his collar. A thin moustache that did his face no favours. Anger and resentment in his eyes.

Harper stood for a moment, watching as the man settled on his chair, legs spread with the palms of his hands resting on his knees. Defiance. Interesting. Croft definitely had something to hide.

Harper beckoned to Walsh, then led the way to the outer office.

'Do you have men searching his house?'

'Of course, sir.'

'I'll lay odds he has an office somewhere, too, some kind of hidey-hole.'

Inspector Walsh smiled. 'We're looking, sir. I'm just about to go back to the house and talk to his wife.'

Perfect. Walsh had a good way with women. A few minutes and he could charm them into telling him almost everything.

'I don't want him slipping out of this.'

'He won't, sir.'

Leave them to do their work, he thought. Not that it helped him concentrate on the papers that waited on his desk.

'You're meeting the leader of the council at eleven,' Miss Sharp
told him. 'Three o'clock there's the watch committee.'

'I hadn't forgotten about them.' How could he? His first real tests
in the new position.

'I know what you said, but I sent someone to buy you a fresh
collar and tie. Your wife would never forgive me if I sent you
somewhere important looking like a rag and bone man.'

Harper smiled. 'Thank you.' She was right. Women always
were.

He waited until the last minute, hoping for some word from Ash's
men. Nothing.

The leader of the council was a man who hid his nerves under
a bluff manner. He looked as if he was being very careful around
the acting chief constable.

Interesting, Harper thought. But after almost thirty years on the
force, he knew where all the political bodies were buried. And
some politicians had disposed of more than their share. Good; let
the man worry a little, that could be useful. But he still breathed
a deep sigh of relief once it was over and he could step back into
the world.

Larkin and Fenton were smiling as they sat smoking.

'You're looking very pleased with yourselves,' Harper said.

'We broke Croft, sir,' Bob Larkin answered.

'Took an age, but we tore him apart.' Will Fenton beamed.
Exhaustion filled his eyes, but he was happy.

'And?'

'He admits he bought and sold the rifle and the scope.'

'Who did he sell it to? Armstrong?'

'He says he doesn't know Armstrong and the description didn't
mean anything. Croft said it was man called Ronald. Claims he's
known him for years, but somehow he never managed to learn his
surname.'

'And this man just happened to ask if he could find him a .303
rifle?' At this rate, pigs might fly.

'More or less, sir.' He snorted. None of them believed a word.
'We haven't been able to shake him on that one. He's in the cells
now.'

'Where are the others?'

'Walsh went to see Croft's wife and Dixon's digging into his past.'

'The superintendent?'

The men glanced at each other for a moment. 'Not sure, sir. He left a few minutes ago.'

Ash had something going on, something he wasn't meant to know.

'I'd like to see him when he returns. I don't suppose Armstrong's shown up at home yet?'

'No sign of him, sir.'

Damnation. Vanishing like this made it appear more and more as if he was their man. But they still needed to connect him to that bloody stolen rifle. Croft was the key, him and the mysterious bloody Ronald, if he even existed.

He wasn't going to solve that now. He needed a change of scenery. He picked up the telephone and asked the operator to connect him to the Harper Secretarial Agency.

'How do you fancy a spot of dinner?' he asked Mary. 'My treat.'

As he emerged from the town hall, happy to feel the shock of cold air against his cheeks, he noticed a knot of people gathered around a car at the kerb. Dark blue coachwork glimmered in the pale light. Even from fifty yards away, Harper could make out the winged figure of the bonnet sculpture. A Rolls-Royce. The uniformed chauffeur stood by his vehicle, making sure the kids kept their grubby hands off the vehicle.

Someone had money, he thought, and started to cross the Headrow. A woman's voice cut through the noise of the traffic. 'Chief Constable!'

He turned. From the back seat of the Rolls, she waved. Not a face he could remember ever seeing, and he certainly didn't know anyone who owned a car like that.

She was wrapped in a thick, heavy coat, the fur so dark that it seemed to steal the light. In her forties, plenty of cosmetics trying to cover the wrinkles and signs of time. But they couldn't hide the pinching around her mouth.

He lifted his hat. 'You'll have to forgive me. I have no idea who you are.'

'Of course not. How silly of me.' Another practised smile. 'I'm Barbara James.'

Harper shook his head. He was still none the wiser.

'I imagine you know of my husband, Sir Richard James.'

That name was familiar. The man had made a fortune supplying soap to the army. Enough to afford a Rolls and expensive furs for his wife, it seemed. But he wasn't from Leeds. He had nothing to do with the city. What brought him here, and how did his wife recognize Harper?

'By reputation,' he replied.

'He's meeting some people on the council to talk about . . .' She waved the thought away. 'Business. And meanwhile I'm stuck out here.'

'How did you know my name?'

'Frederick. Our chauffeur. He told me. He used to be a policeman here.'

Harper glanced over the car's soft top. He couldn't forget that face. PC Tierney, dismissed for consorting with prostitutes while on duty and accepting bribes. No loss to the force. That must have been back around 1906. A different time.

'I'm surprised Mr Tierney isn't in uniform,' he said.

'Richard considers what he does to be war work, so after a fashion, any employee of his is serving.'

A safe, cushy billet. Tierney turned towards him and gave a mock salute.

'It's been a pleasure to meet you,' Harper told the woman, 'but I'm late for an important appointment.'

She pouted. 'I was hoping you could join Richard and myself for luncheon. Maybe show us around. I've never been here before.'

'I'm sorry, it's a very busy time. I'm sure one of the councillors would be happy to do that. Or Mr Tierney. He probably knows some very interesting places.'

A dip of the head, then he turned and strode away, lost in the crowds. Curious. He knew James by reputation. A very poor one with the troops; they claimed his soap fell apart as soon as it was wet. But the army still bought it, and he was making money. James knew the people at the very top of government and industry. Why would his wife want to cultivate someone as lowly as an acting chief constable?

'Maybe she collects people, Da. Some people are like that,' Mary said as she finished the last mouthful of stew at the Kardomah on Briggate.

Harper snorted. 'Come on. I'm hardly important enough. She hobnobs with ministers and royalty.'

She shrugged. 'You're here, and a chief constable has status.' Before he could object, she added: 'Even an acting one.'

'Perhaps.' He pushed the bowl of soup away. 'Heard anything else suspicious on the volunteer patrols?'

'It's all been very ordinary. That other time was pure luck.'

'I know,' Harper agreed. 'But you picked up on a remark. You asked questions and took it further. That's not luck. That's police work.'

'There hasn't been anything else to pursue,' she insisted.

It was probably too much to hope that he might have two dips from the same well, but it was still worth asking.

'Anyway, I heard you'd found the man who took the rifle from the barracks and was selling it on.'

Harper raised an eyebrow. That wasn't meant to be common knowledge.

'I ran into the sergeant who trained our group,' she explained. 'Is it true?'

'Yes. But we're still not much closer to finding the shooter.'

'It's awful,' she began, breathing slowly and looking down at the table. 'After all, you expect people to die over there when they're fighting. That's war.' She pressed her lips together. 'Most of the time I can even accept that it happened to Len. But shooting people over here . . . they're supposed to be safe in England.'

'I know. That's why we need to find this saboteur.'

Mary put down her knife and fork. 'You know, I was thinking about what you said. Stopping in to see Len's mother.'

He didn't say a word. For once he'd keep his big mouth shut. Let her say what she needed to without him chiming in.

'Maybe you're right and it's time I went over there,' Mary continued. 'I just couldn't before. I . . . needed to keep him all to myself.'

He reached out and placed his hand over hers. This was more important, more satisfying than any meal with a rich man and his wife.

'Any sign of Armstrong? What about this man Ronald?' Harper asked. 'Do we have any idea who he is yet?'

'We might have an inkling, sir,' Dixon answered. His desk was littered with old files, the musty smell of old paper rising. 'I've been going back over Charlie Croft and people he's supposed to have worked with. Came up with someone called Ronnie Pickering.'

'I know him,' Ash said. 'Ran him in a couple of times myself. Had him up for burglary and affray. He managed to duck out on both charges, as I remember.'

'He did,' Dixon said, 'and one or two more besides over the years. We'll have a current address for him this afternoon.'

It was all they could do. Piece by painstaking piece, they were making progress. Pickering sounded as if he might be the right Ronald. But the only really worthwhile thing would be arresting the marksman. The saboteur.

'Let me know when you have him down here. Go through his house with a nit comb. And if he has any kind of shed or warehouse, do the same there.'

They already knew what to do, but he had to say it. All frustration; it was there on each of their faces, too.

'A chauffeur came and left a note for you,' Miss Sharp said as he entered her office. Her eyes glittered with the idea of something hidden. 'I put it on your desk.'

He smiled and said nothing. Let her imagination run riot for a few seconds.

A thick envelope, heavy cream stationery.

> Dear Chief Constable,
>   It was so unfortunate that you were previously engaged for luncheon. My husband and I shall be in Leeds until tomorrow morning. We both hope you'll be able to join us for dinner tonight, along with your wife. We have rooms at the Metropole. Perhaps seven o'clock would be convenient.
>   Most sincerely,
>   Barbara James

He opened the door. 'Can you take a letter, please?'

A little before three, Harper checked the knot on his new tie and left the office. A thumbs-up from Miss Sharp. He presented himself at the committee room, where Councillor Walton was sitting behind a table with the two other members of the watch committee. Tucked away in the corner, almost out of sight, was a woman to take down every word in shorthand.

'Welcome, Acting Chief Constable. Have a seat. You know Councillors Smith and Wright.'

An hour. Plenty of questions about the sniper, the incident at the clothing depot, even the explosion at Barnbow. Could he cope with this new responsibility? By the time he emerged, Harper felt as if he'd gone ten rounds with the middleweight champion. And the day wasn't over yet.

SIXTEEN

Half past four, dark outside, but no lamps lit along the streets. The city prepared for night in wartime, the rumble of motors and the constant clang of the trams as they passed.

A shout rising through the town hall drew him out of his office. Walsh and Fenton were pulling a man up the steps. He was yelling, screaming, dragging his feet.

'Need a hand?' Harper asked.

'I think we'll be fine, sir,' Walsh answered as the man lashed out with his foot, kicking against a heavy marble newel post. 'We found Mr Pickering. He's very pleased to be assisting us.'

'I can tell.'

It was impossible to see the man's face as he flailed around. No matter; he'd make sure he took a good look later.

'The uniforms are giving his house the once-over.'

'Where does he live?'

'Mushroom Street, sir,' Fenton replied. 'Just off Skinner Lane.'

He knew the area well, at the bottom end of Sheepscar. Old houses, the wood in the window frames soft and rotten, buildings that should have been torn down years ago. But he knew they'd probably still be standing long after he was put in the ground. The constables would need a disinfectant bath after they'd finished that job.

'It's a good job most of your suspects aren't like that,' Miss Sharp said.

'Why do you think we carry truncheons?' he told her with a wink and returned to his desk. He had plenty to fill his time into the evening. But he knew he'd be drawn upstairs soon enough, eager to hear what Ronald Pickering had to say for himself.

Fenton was in his shirtsleeves, the cuffs neatly folded back to show thick, hairy forearms. Pickering sat in a hard-backed chair, wrists cuffed behind him, head slumped forward.

No need for an explanation. Harper knew exactly what was happening. Pickering lifted his head. He looked to be in his late forties, a shock of dark hair shot through with grey.

'Is this the man you remember?' he asked Ash.

'The very same, sir. A bit older and fraying round the edges, mind. But give him the right encouragement and he's very voluble.'

Harper stared at the man again. His trousers were shiny at the knees, shirt collar worn and dirty, shoes unpolished and down at the heel. 'Has he said anything encouraging?'

'Not yet,' Ash replied pointedly. 'But he's getting there.'

He could take the hint. Some things it was much better for a chief constable not to see. And to find the killer he'd gladly turn a blind eye. 'Telephone me at home as soon as you know something.'

After a run of good days, the bad was inevitable. As soon as he walked into the parlour, Harper could sense it. The air almost crackled, and Annabelle had a glint in her eye.

Johanna gave him a tight, weary smile that said so much with no words at all.

'I was just talking about Mrs Daley. You remember her, don't you? Used to live on the other side of the street, two doors down.'

He had no idea what she meant. Their home had been above the Victoria ever since they were married. Nobody called Daley, not even in any of the houses on the other side of the Roundhay Road.

'Yes,' he answered. 'Of course. What about her?'

'We saw her at the shops today, didn't we?' She turned to Johanna. 'Hadn't run into her in donkeys' years. Ended up having a chinwag for a long time.'

'That's good,' he said. Johanna gave a slight shake of her head: it never happened. 'How is she?'

'She's fine. All her kiddies are grown now, off and married. Would you believe her Eric's gone to live in South Africa? She was asking after everybody on Leather Street. I told her it was all different now. The Rileys and the Learys have moved away.' Annabelle glanced up, beaming. 'She looked well.'

'I'm sure she did.'

Leather Street. She was thinking of the Bank, where she'd grown up. There had been no Mrs Daley at the shops. She lived somewhere back in his wife's history, a figure from when she was very young. Annabelle had woven a whole story around it, drawing ideas from . . . he couldn't even begin to guess. At least she seemed happy for the moment; she was smiling. But there was a brittle edge to it that could crumble at any time.

The trick would be to keep her like this until bedtime. In the morning, God willing, she'd be back to herself. None of this would have happened and she wouldn't remember a thing.

The coals slumped in the grate, and for a moment they all turned towards the hearth to watch the dancing flames. Then Annabelle was talking again.

'I told me mam I'd seen Mrs Daley and she was full of questions. You know, what she was doing now, what about her husband, all of that.' She hesitated for a second and her eyes widened. 'Do you know, I'd never asked her. That's not very good, is it?'

Her mother had died before Annabelle was nine years old.

He encouraged her to talk, listening and making a few neutral comments. Johanna disappeared into the kitchen and came back with a pot of tea.

After half an hour, Annabelle was beginning to wind down. Her speech slowed and her thoughts were drifting.

'You look like you're ready to sleep,' Johanna said.

'Yes,' she agreed. 'Maybe I am.'

'Come on, we'll get you ready.'

'I'll be in later,' Harper said as he kissed her.

'It was seeing Mrs Daley that brought it all back,' she told him. 'I'm sure it did.'

For once, he was glad the phone hadn't rung. The smallest inter-ruption could have shifted her mood. He wanted that sniper, but far more, he needed his wife to be content.

Harper sat by the fire, letting its warmth seep through him. He must have begun to doze; the sharp ringing of the telephone bell made him blink his eyes and gaze around.

'Pickering decided to help us, sir,' Ash said with grim satisfaction. 'Very public-spirited once we explained things to him.'

'You got a name? Was it Armstrong?' He needed that link. The confirmation.

'Not him, I'm afraid, sir,' Ash told him. 'Someone called John Best. The men are looking for him now.'

'As soon as you bring him in, I want the whole squad to go home,' Harper ordered. 'That means you, too. A good night's sleep for everyone and we'll come to it fresh in the morning.'

'Good idea, sir.'

Johanna was sitting at the table, reading one of her son's schoolbooks as she tried to improve her English.

'Was she like that all day?' Harper asked.

A nod. 'But it's harmless, no? Was there a Mrs Daley? She talked about her so much.'

'I don't know. She's never mentioned her before.'

'She's sleeping now. There's something else. We didn't go to the shops today. Annabelle hasn't even been outside.'

'I see.' He exhaled slowly. 'I can't thank you enough, all of you. I don't know how we'd cope without you.'

'You give us somewhere safe to live,' Johanna said. 'Work. Not home but . . . home. Do you understand?'

'Yes. I think I do.'

'And now the telephone rings late in the evening. You police are always busy.'

'Sometimes,' he agreed. 'It's part of the job. Especially now.'

'I know it's not my place, but you look . . . weary, is that the word?'

'It is,' he told her with a small laugh. 'Exactly right.'

'Maybe you should not work so hard. I'm sorry, it's not my business.'

'No, you're right. I just don't have the choice.'

The men looked rested. Eyes alert, in fresh clothes, their suits hung overnight.

Harper had been in the office since just after six, trying to conquer the mountain of papers waiting for him. At seven he climbed the stairs, moving past the early clerks, and down the corridor to the squad's office.

A new plaque by the door: *Acting Chief Constable T. Harper.*

He stopped for a moment, staring at it. His fingertips traced the letters. It was right there, so it had to be true. Another second, then he turned the handle.

'Good morning, gentlemen. Do we have John Best?'

'He's down in the cells, sir,' Larkin told him with a grin. 'You should have seen the surprise on his face when he opened the door and saw us.'

'Did he have the rifle?'

'Not in his house, sir. Some uniforms will be searching outside as soon as it's light.'

'Does he have any connection to Albert Armstrong? Has he turned up yet?'

'Still missing, sir,' Ash answered. 'His relatives are growing frantic; they think he might have tried to kill himself. We're searching for him. But we haven't come up with anything to tie him to Best.'

Damnation.

'See what the man has to say about that. Wring him dry.'

Harper left them to do their job. He didn't even need to see Best's face.

It was a morning of meetings, one after another after another, until he felt exhausted by straining to hear voices from the other end of the table. Nothing resolved, of course; when did a meeting ever achieve anything worthwhile? It was simply a chance for some men to feel important and pad out their day.

By the time he returned to his office, he'd had enough. He wanted to escape. Once he'd believed that rank brought freedom. Now he knew that once you passed inspector, the world grew more and more restricted.

'Superintendent Ash asked to see you as soon as you came back,' Miss Sharp said.

They had something. That had to be it. It put a spring in his step as he hurried up the stairs.

'What does Best have to say for himself?'

Ash pressed his lips together. 'Denies everything, sir. Claims he only ever met Pickering twice and he's never bought anything from him.'

'Is he lying?'

The superintendent nodded. 'I'm sure of it. The men are out, trying to find some evidence. But he's sticking to it and for the moment we can't disprove it.'

'No rifle?'

'Nothing at all. That's the problem. We haven't come up with anything that looks stolen, so we don't have any kind of lever to use with him. This is what he owns.' He pushed a list across. Not too much on it.

'Question Ronnie Pickering again?'

'He was up before the magistrate this morning; he's over at Armley Gaol on remand now.'

That would make it harder, interviewing someone over there. And with a Crown Court appearance ahead, they'd have to hold back and leave no bruises and bumps showing in court.

'Save it as a last resort, if you're sure Best is lying.'

'I'm certain of it, sir.' If Ash was convinced, Harper believed him.

'Where is he?'

'Down in the bridewell.'

It couldn't hurt to take a look. Maybe even a word or two.

John Best was thin as a branch, with the kind of face that had probably looked hollow and haunted since childhood. There were men just like him all over Leeds, most likely all across the North, Harper thought. Grown up poor and hungry in the shadow of industry. Probably rejected by the army as unfit. Scraping a living from this and that. A single glance was enough to tell his story.

'Who are you?' Best asked. Sullen, still defiant, ready for a scrap he knew he'd lose.

'Seems like Ronnie Pickering doesn't like you.' Harper didn't bother to introduce himself.

Best shrugged. His eyes were filled with cunning. He'd been behind bars before. Right now he knew he was winning, that they had nothing they could use to charge him. But Ash was right; he was guilty, no doubt about that. It practically shone out of him. Prove it, his face said.

Five pointless minutes. Best was cautious, he wasn't about to admit anything at all. If he kept his mouth shut, he could be home and dry.

As he banged for the warder to open the cell door, Harper said: 'The constable said you have a decent bike.'

It was a shot in the dark. No reason he wouldn't own a bicycle.

But he didn't seem the type for more exercise than was necessary.

Best looked suspicious. 'That better still be there when I get out—'

'What make is it? A good one?'

'It's all right.' He seemed to close in on himself, to become defensive. 'A Raleigh, it gets me around.'

'Better than spending money on the trams all the time.'

'Like I said. Nothing special.'

Another quick stop to see Ash. 'The bike that Best owns. See if it has a serial number on the frame. If it does, check if it's been stolen.'

A slow smile spread across the superintendent's face. 'I'd never thought about that.'

And if it was nicked? That didn't mean much. But it was one tiny wedge they might be able to use to start cracking open his defences.

With a sigh he sat behind his desk. Back to the ordinary work of being a chief constable.

Late afternoon, a winter dusk when night seemed to fall quickly. One minute he looked up and there was still a hint of light in the grey skies. The next time he glanced out of the window, it was full dark.

Harper grimaced and lowered his head. Budgets, figures always made his head spin.

Suddenly he was aware of voices in Miss Sharp's office. The door crashed open and Fenton was standing there, wild-eyed and frantic. 'We've got another shooting, sir.'

'What? Where?' He was already on his feet, dropping his pen on the blotter.

'The barracks up on Woodhouse Lane.'

Harper pulled his overcoat and hat from the rack, hurrying out and down the stairs. 'Anyone dead or hurt?'

'We don't know, sir. Two shots fired at the sentries on the gate. That's all the information we have.'

Two minutes in the car. Hardly any distance at all from the city centre, not even as far as the university and well before the expanse of Woodhouse Moor. The barracks still looked like the grand private building it had once been.

The last time he'd been out here was three years ago, before the war. Striking council workers had planted a bomb that didn't go off.

Brigadier Fox was already there, walking around awkwardly with the help of his stick; Carlton Barracks was close. He moved among the men, listening and asking questions.

Several soldiers stood alert, holding their rifles, on edge and ready to take aim at the slightest provocation.

Everything felt tense, as if it could explode into action at any second.

Walsh and Larkin were talking to a group of soldiers. Ash and Dixon had the civilians who might have witnessed it. A uniformed inspector was supervising the constables searching for the cartridges.

Buildings stood all along Woodhouse Lane and in the streets on either side. As easy to disappear among them as in a wood. Who'd notice one man, walking, cycling, however he'd made his escape? The best they could hope was a description to confirm it was Armstrong.

Harper spent time with the uniforms, encouraging and sympathizing. By the time he returned, Ash was surveying the scene.

'He picks his targets well.' A grim compliment, but it was true.

'He does, sir. We're just lucky no one was hurt. Missed with both shots.'

'This time.'

'From what I can gather, he was probably put off by a lorry backfiring just up the road. He probably thought someone was taking a pop at him and it put him off his aim.'

Thank God for that, he thought. 'Did anyone see him?'

'We haven't come across anyone who had a decent look at his face. The best we've managed is a young man wearing a cap with something strapped to his back, riding away on a bicycle. About the only thing that's certain is it's not Best. He's still in a cell at the town hall.'

'A cap this time? Not fair hair and bare-headed?'

'No, sir. Don't know if it means anything at all.'

'Have you come up with anything?' he asked Fox when the brigadier joined him.

'One of my men saw the muzzle flash. That's only because it was almost dark.' He banged his stick against the ground in frustration. 'Two shots and gone again. The soldiers would have been cautious about firing, anyway.'

Woodhouse Lane was a busy road, traffic and pedestrians always passing. If they'd returned fire, they could have hit a civilian.

'We're nowhere, aren't we?' Fox asked.

'Maybe not quite that bad,' Harper said.

'We don't have him—'

'We're learning more about him. And maybe someone had a good, clear sighting of him.'

'Hardly anything concrete, though, is it, Tom?'

'No,' he agreed with a sigh. The brigadier was right. They were just words puffed up to sound good.

'Is it this man Armstrong?' Fox asked.

'It seems like it,' Harper answered. The pieces all seemed to fit, yet something held him back. He couldn't bring himself to say with utter certainty that Albert Armstrong was their man. He had no idea why, only a feeling inside, a hesitation. Was he right? Time would tell. 'My men are seeing what they can find out.'

'He'll do it again,' Fox said.

'I hope we can catch him before then.' He stared at the brigadier. 'You know we're doing everything we can.'

The man nodded. 'So are we. Is there anything more Corporal Carpenter can do for you?'

'Just keep his ears open. Maybe ask a few questions. Gentle ones, things that come up in conversation. Maybe someone will have a thought about who's behind all this.'

'I'll let him know.'

'Everything's worth trying at this stage, Brian.'

Fox glanced over his shoulder at the barracks. 'Yes, I suppose it is.'

He walked back to the town hall, Ash by his side.

'We found the cartridges quick enough, sir. They're still canvassing for witnesses.'

'Anything definite?'

'Not yet.'

'He manages to fade away and blend in,' Harper said. 'How? He goes from making his shots to disappearing in seconds.'

'Very ordinary-looking, perhaps,' Ash suggested. 'People don't notice.'

'Yes. I don't think it's deliberate. I . . . I'm not sure what I think.'

'That's the problem, isn't it, sir? We don't understand him.'

It was like trying to grasp fog. They carried on in silence, locked in their own thoughts, down Great George Street and up the steps of the town hall.

'You've had reporters on the telephone,' Miss Sharp said.

'I'm sure I have. Tell them all there's nothing to print. Defence of the Realm Act.'

'Very good.' She hesitated for a second. 'Was it bad?'

He sighed. 'Nobody hurt. We were lucky this time.'

'Any more clues?'

He shook his head and vanished into his office. Back to paper and writing and words. But his squad had everything covered. Harper knew he should be working, but he sat back and tried to sort through his thoughts. Why did he have doubts about Armstrong's guilt? What was holding him back? There had to be something.

Another half-hour and he still didn't have an answer. There was nothing he could pinpoint. At best it was a feeling, with no evidence at all.

Finally he gave up, rang for his car and shrugged into his overcoat. Any word and they'd know where to find him.

SEVENTEEN

A nervous, uniformed special constable was waiting outside his office when Harper arrived in the morning. As soon as he saw the new chief constable, he straightened his back and saluted.

'Good morning,' Harper said. 'You look like a man bearing news for me.'

'Superintendent Ash wanted you to know that Albert Armstrong showed up at home, sir. His aunt discovered him this morning. We're bringing him in.'

'Thank you.'

He tried to swallow, but his throat was tight. A few more minutes and they'd know the truth.

One hour, then a second. He pretended to work, but however many times he read a page, nothing sank into his brain. He was waiting for the telephone to ring.

In the end it wasn't a call, but Dixon entering his office, the cuff of his left sleeve empty where the hand had gone at the start of the war.

'Well?' Harper asked. No need to ask why he'd come.

'You won't credit it, but Armstrong's not our man, sir.' He spoke the words as if he couldn't quite believe them himself.

Harper let out a low breath. That explained the reticence he'd felt. But if it wasn't Armstrong, then who was the sniper? 'What did he have to say for himself?'

'He rode up to Masham to stay with a comrade he served with in France. Another one who'd been invalided out. Didn't even know there had been any shootings here.'

'Have we corroborated it?'

'Yes, sir. The local bobby paid a call. All above board.'

'Why did he go without telling anyone?'

'He claims the idea came over him while he was out and he decided to do it.' Dixon pursed his lips. 'He seems like an odd duck that way, sir. Half the time he isn't really here at all. Set off for the Dales on a whim on that bike.'

A shell-shocked man. Who could tell what he was thinking?

'What made him come back?'

A shrug. 'He felt ready, he said.'

'We had reports of a man near the Kirkstall shooting with a long package on his back.'

Dixon shook his head. 'Armstrong says he hasn't handled a rifle since France. They scare him. And he doesn't own a fishing rod. His aunt confirmed that.'

'Are we one hundred per cent certain?' Harper asked.

'I am. But you'd need to ask the super, sir. It's his decision.'

'If he's satisfied, you can let Armstrong go.'

'Very good, sir. And we're about ready to release Best.'

Back to square bloody one yet again. Every time they'd had someone in their sights, they'd been wrong. But this time . . . this time. It felt as if they'd been chasing Armstrong forever. And it had come to nothing. Crumbled in their hands.

* * *

'Fenton and Larkin are going back over every scrap of paper that we have,' Ash said. 'Walsh is up at the barracks and Dixon is having a last crack at Best. Not as our sniper, but he's hiding something.'

'I want him questioned again. Be relentless.' He felt the frustration boil up inside. 'At this point I don't bloody care how you do it. We need some proper answers.'

'We will, sir. I can promise you that. And as soon as Walsh has finished, he's going to Armley to have another long chat with Pickering.'

'Tell me what I can do to help,' Harper said.

'I'm not sure there's anything,' Ash replied. 'The answers are out there. We just have to shake them loose.'

'You're certain Best is lying?'

'Positive, sir.'

'Who's he protecting? And from what?'

'I don't know,' Ash answered after a long moment, then shook his head. 'Truth is the deeper we go in this, the less I'm sure of anything, sir.'

'We've followed the damned trail. The rifle was stolen from Carlton Barracks. We know Pickering had it. That gives us two possibilities: either he's lying about selling it to Best, or Best isn't telling us the truth. We need to press them both until we get some answers.'

'I agree, sir. And there are uniforms asking questions all around Woodhouse Barracks, trying to come up with a witness.'

'Nothing yet?'

'A few bits of this and that. But we've seen what this sniper is like. He fades away as soon as he's done.'

'He's not a bloody magician, we can be sure of that. He's not vanishing into thin air.'

'No, but he's definitely clever, sir. Cunning. He goes for places we'd never anticipate.'

'We were lucky nobody was hurt yesterday,' Harper said. 'He'll be back again. Probably very soon, since he missed his targets.'

'Everyone's keeping a close watch, sir.'

But when you didn't know what you were looking for, how could you keep a close watch?

'He has a sharp sense about him. He knows the right places to try. And a bicycle means he can go all over Leeds.'

'We can't stop every cyclist, sir.'

'No.' Too many ordinary people used them as transport to work, for pleasure. There were thousands across the city. 'But I want them checking everyone cycling with a long package. Anything that might be a rifle.'

'I'll pass the word.'

'And squeeze Best and Pickering until the pips squeak. I want to be able to hear them from here. We need some truth.'

It made the superintendent smile. 'I'll pass on your orders, sir.'

The morning was spent going from pillar to post, different rooms in the town hall to meet with one group or another. A small respite for his dinner. But as he came outside and stood by one of the stone lions, he saw the blue Rolls-Royce parked on the Headrow and turned around. He didn't want to see Mrs James or Lady James or whoever she was. Weren't they supposed to have left this morning?

At least the Victoria Hotel across Great George Street served a decent roast beef sandwich. He could keep his head down, read the paper, and no one would bother him. But it always felt like a vague betrayal to go into another Victoria.

Five minutes after he'd returned to his office, Miss Sharp tapped on the door, entered and came close to the desk.

'Councillor Walton's outside,' she said quietly. Then leaned close enough to whisper in his good ear, 'He looks like he's on the warpath.'

'Better send him in.'

He knew it would happen sooner or later, and that Walton would be the one to do it. After all, he was the head of the watch committee. It was his job to fire a salvo at the police when they were failing.

'Acting Chief Constable.' A handshake, and he settled in the visitor's chair. The harsh, forthright voice from the fleshy mouth. 'You know why I'm here. We might as well dive right in, eh?'

'Yes,' Harper agreed.

'What happened yesterday, and why hasn't anyone been charged yet? I hear you've been questioning some likely suspects.'

'We were fortunate yesterday. I'm not going to deny that. It was pure luck that nobody was hurt. But I don't believe anyone could have predicted where the sniper would strike. Quite honestly, if you have any ideas, Councillor, I'd love to hear them.'

A snort that could have been acknowledgement or dismissal. 'What about these suspects?'

'That's all they are at present. One seemed likely, but he has a proper, full alibi. He wasn't even in Leeds. A shell-shock victim.'

'A lollygagger.'

Harper ignored the remark. No need to wade into that swamp.

'Two others we're questioning again, and we'll have answers from them. But right now, we're stuck.'

'Do you think that's good enough?' Walton asked. 'It's been over a fortnight since that incident at the clothing depot and you still don't have anything.'

'No,' Harper told him, and saw the astonishment on the councillor's face. 'The only thing we do know is that Barnbow isn't part of this; the inquiry established that. But you're right. We do need this to be over. You know there's been nothing in the papers, but word still spreads quickly enough. People hear, and it's hurting morale in Leeds. They're scared. I don't blame them. We don't even have the killer's name. He's a murderer, but he's also a saboteur.'

'Fine words, Chief Constable, but what are you going to *do*?' A vague smile of satisfaction on his lips, as if he'd just moved his opponent into check.

'Find him and arrest him. We haven't managed it yet, but we will. I'm sure about that. That's what the police do. As I'm sure you know.'

'How?'

'Good coppering.' He dredged up a phrase Parker had used to him. 'Not everything is solved in a day.'

'It's been a good deal longer than that. We have two people dead, another pair wounded.'

'I'm fully aware of that,' Harper agreed. He stared at the other man. 'I know it all too well. Don't you think I wish I could change it? You can be absolutely certain I'm doing everything I can to make sure there are no more casualties. So is Brigadier Fox. But I'm not going to give you guarantees there won't be other bodies. I can't.'

Walton stayed silent for a long time. He pursed his lips together. 'Fine. We'll give you a little while longer yet. But I expect progress, and I want it bloody fast. Leeds needs that. And if it doesn't happen, you can bet your boots I'll be on the phone to Whitehall, asking them to send men from Scotland Yard to solve this. I'm putting you on notice, Acting Chief Constable.'

And he was gone. No second handshake, just the door closing quietly behind him.

Well, he'd tried, Harper thought. The squad was already doing everything possible. Going upstairs and haranguing them wouldn't help a damned bit. Now he had to hope they could come through before Walton picked up the receiver and asked to be connected to London.

He'd been staring at the wall for a few minutes when Miss Sharp appeared. That made him stir. She had a cup and saucer in one hand, an envelope in the other.

'I thought you might need this,' she told him. 'And that man who was here yesterday came and left this for you. The chauffeur.'

Another letter from Mrs James, or her husband. He opened it as he drank. A brisk, masculine hand.

> Chief Constable,
> It was unfortunate not to have the opportunity to meet you on this trip. I've heard about some of the things you've done as a policeman and I was curious to meet the man behind all that, especially someone who's managed to rise so high.
> However, as my business in Leeds appears likely to continue, my wife and I will be returning, so I hope we can meet then, and we can have the pleasure of dinner with you and your good lady.
> Sincerely
> Richard James

It was friendly enough, without any stiff formality; the man hadn't even added the title to his name. But whatever Sir Richard James wanted, he didn't intend to be a part of it. The man had something going on in Leeds, but Harper refused to be party to any war profiteer filling his pockets. He crumpled the letter and threw it into the bin.

Back to the important matters.

Harper scrambled for the telephone as soon as it rang.

'We've gone over Best every which way,' Ash said. 'He still insists he doesn't know anything about a rifle. Never bought one or sold one. Says he wouldn't even know how to shoot one properly.'

'So what's he hiding?'

'All the other little fiddles he's been doing. Turns out he cheated Ronnie Pickering out of fifty pounds last year.'

A very handsome sum. 'Giving us his name was Pickering's revenge?'

'Looks like it, sir. At least we still get Best for his bits and pieces. That's something.'

'We'd better get some proper answers from Pickering today.'

'We will, sir. I can guarantee you that.' That small cough and slight hesitation. 'A little bird told me that Councillor Walton visited you.'

He smiled. 'Your little bird was right.'

The man knew everything that happened.

'He wasn't too pleased?'

'You could put it like that. We have a few days' grace, then he's going to call in Scotland Yard.'

'Don't you worry, sir. We'll spike his guns.'

'Will we?' Harper asked. For all he'd said to Walton, he didn't feel confident.

'Yes, sir.'

Harper hoped he was right. 'Tell me, what do you know about Richard James? *Sir* Richard James.'

'Apart from the fact that he's had that blue Rolls-Royce parked outside a lot lately, you mean, sir?'

'Yes.'

'Not much, sir. Want me to have a nosy around?'

'It wouldn't hurt. When you have the chance.'

Scratch John Best. Scratch Albert Armstrong. All he had was a growing space where there should be a list of suspects. He needed names.

Brigadier Fox sat down across from him in the office. The officer looked thoughtful.

'What is it, Brian?'

'You're looking for a sniper.'

'You already know that,' Harper said.

'Do you know how they operate?'

'I'd guess that they hide and camouflage themselves where they can see the enemy, then fire when they have a good shot.'

Fox nodded. 'I thought that might be it.'

'Why? Am I wrong?'

'In part. The sniper works with another man. A spotter. They're a team.'

'What?' It beggared belief. 'Why didn't you tell me?'

'Because everything pointed to one man. It struck me, though, what if he was operating in the military way, with someone else.'

'For Christ's sake, we need to go back over everyone now.' He could feel the fury rising. All the time wasted since the first killing at East Leeds Hospital . . . all for the sake of one piece of information.

'I'm sorry, Tom. Honestly, I never thought. I was like you, I imagined one man, a loner.'

'Come with me.' Not a request. An order. Fox followed as if he was a private.

'That puts a different face on things, sir.' Ash frowned after Fox had explained. 'There will be quite a few we need to look at again.'

'Get them on it,' Harper ordered. 'Draft in some other CID and uniforms to help. We need to know as soon as possible.'

'I'm sorry,' the brigadier said as they made their way back down the stairs. With his limp, they were always awkward for him; he winced as he moved. 'I should have thought.'

'It's a cock-up, all right.' Harper sighed. At least the first part of his anger had passed. Blowing up at Brian Fox wouldn't help at all. 'But we can't change it. Maybe it won't make any difference.' Or maybe it would change every bloody thing.

'If I'd thought properly . . .'

'Never mind.'

'As soon as I realized, I . . .'

But Harper waved the words away. He didn't want to hear them. Fox was a very good soldier. He ran the three barracks in Leeds efficiently. He'd made a mistake. But they all had; they'd assumed snipers operated alone, and none of them had thought to find out how it really worked. Maybe it really wouldn't make any difference. If it did, maybe Walton would be right to bring in the Yard.

As the clock on the wall softly chimed seven, Harper put on his overcoat and hat, then made his way out into the darkness. The car was waiting, and purred along the Headrow, the New Briggate and North Street.

He wanted to banish all the thoughts swimming through his mind, just to let them go for the night. But he couldn't. Rosters, meetings, promotions, the possible sacking of a uniformed inspector for dereliction of duty: they swirled around. And above them all, this case. Shootings that had never officially happened to people who died from accidents. All a fiction, all a lie, because the truth could scare and scar.

EIGHTEEN

'Pickering, sir.' Harper pressed the receiver to his ear. The connection broke then returned; he'd missed a few of the words Walsh had said.

'You faded,' he said. Hearing was difficult enough; Annabelle was crying. It had come out of nowhere, and he'd been comforting her until the telephone rang. Now Johanna had her arms wrapped around his wife, whispering in her ear.

'We finally winkled the truth out of Pickering. It took a while.'

'What happened to the rifle?'

'It's a long story, sir. It ended up with a man called Gibson.'

Gibson, Gibson . . . it didn't ring any bells. He was sure they'd never come across him before.

'Who is he?'

'We're still digging into that, sir. Bob Larkin swears he saw the name somewhere, but he can't quite place it. Between that and this sniper spotter thing, we're tearing every file in the office apart.'

'Let me know as soon as you find something.'

Back to Annabelle. She was growing more and more frantic. Her mood had turned on a sixpence, from calm and easy to this. Nothing had set her off; the wind had simply shifted in her head.

Johanna eased away as he returned. Harper pulled Annabelle close, her head against his chest. The tears kept coming as he stroked her hair and softly told her that everything was fine now.

It took time, but eventually she calmed. The sobs turned to gentle hiccoughs, the tears stopped, and her breathing became quiet snuffles. He kept her close, where she could feel safe.

Finally she said, 'I'm jiggered, Tom.'

He smiled. She was back. 'Me too, it's been a long day. Let's get off to bed, shall we?'

He hadn't expected to sleep, but when he opened his eyes the clock read a little before five. Annabelle gave a snort and turned over as he slid out of bed. Wash, shave, breakfast, and he was waiting on the corner for the car by six.

A cold morning, with the kind of chill dampness in the air that cut through to the bones. He'd hated days like this when he walked the beat; no matter what you did, you could never feel warm.

But back then he only had to worry about a small area. These days the whole city was his manor. Every inch of it, everyone who lived here.

'Could you give me a lift into town?'

The voice interrupted his thoughts. Mary, wearing her black coat with the ratty fur collar again, a black felt hat jammed over her hair.

'I think I can manage that. Early start?'

'Plenty to do. We've been asked to put in a bid for part of the secretarial work at the Department of Works.'

'Don't they have enough clerks?'

'That's what I asked. Some po-faced chap just asked if I was interested in the job or not.'

The car arrived. As they moved along Sheepscar Street, he asked, 'Patrol last night?'

'Yes. Jaak told me about Mam. Was everything all right in the end?'

'She's been worse.'

'And she won't be getting any better.'

'I know,' he told her. 'Believe me, I know. I don't suppose you've heard any more whispers when you've been out there?'

'Nothing to do with a sniper or sabotage,' she answered.

'Oh?'

'Bits and bobs, that's all,' Mary said. She glanced out of the window for a second. 'Do you remember what I said about maybe going to see Len's parents?'

'Of course.'

'I popped over the night before last.' She gave a hesitant smile. 'I didn't know how they'd feel, with me not visiting them after the news.'

'What did they do?'

'We had a talk. His mam and me, we had a little cry together. It helped a little bit. It'll never be the same as . . . but . . .' Her words faded to nothing.

'I understand.'

'If you hadn't gone round there, I don't think I would, Da.'

'Going to see them again?'

'For my supper on Sunday. They invited you and Mam, too, but I explained you couldn't go.'

'It's for the best.'

Bingham stopped the car on Albion Place outside her office, moving away as she stood by the door, pulling out her key. Maybe she really did need an early start, he thought. Or more likely she'd simply wanted a quiet place to tell him about seeing the Robinsons. Something to say to Annabelle on one of her good days.

'Right, what have you been able to find out about this man Gibson?'

None of the squad looked as if they'd been home. They were unshaven, suits rumpled, and surrounded by a flock of empty white china cups.

'According to Pickering—' Dixon began.

'Was he telling the truth this time?' Harper asked.

'Yes, sir.' He glanced at Fenton, who massaged his knuckles. 'No doubt about that. He says he met Gibson at the General Elliott public house.'

They all knew it. Small, poky, sitting across from the market at the corner of Kirkgate and Vicar Lane, it was the kind of place men went when they were looking for stolen goods. Sometimes taken to order.

'Pickering arranged for the rifle and sold it on, made five pounds for his trouble.'

'And he never thought to ask why anyone might want a rifle, a telescopic sight and bullets?' Harper said.

'Claims it was none of his business, sir,' Fenton added.

'Gibson knows his way around Leeds if he's going in a place like that.' He looked around the faces of his men. 'Who is he?'

'All we've got is Pickering's description, sir,' Ash said. 'Tall, fair hair cut very short. Walks with a limp.'

'Invalided out of the army?' Harper asked.

'We don't know yet,' Ash replied. 'We've gone through our

records of men who've been arrested. There are a few Gibsons who might fit, but it's a common enough name. I've put in a request to the War Office for anything they can find.' He frowned. 'You know what it's like trying to deal with them. Like wading through treacle. I had a word with a chap I know. That might gee it up a bit. I'm hoping we'll hear something today.'

'I want this Gibson in custody. Let's not rely on the army for information or we'll be sitting here till Doomsday.'

He wasn't going to let himself hope too much, Harper thought as he went downstairs to his office. He'd made that mistake far too often. But inside, every nerve in his body tingled.

Miss Sharp interrupted his meeting. He was sitting with the division heads, listening to their problems, when she tapped on the door, entered and placed a note in front of him. He put on his spectacles: *Supt Ash says they have an identification for Gibson.*

'Gentlemen,' Harper said, 'I need to end this. My apologies.'

Even as they gathered their papers, he was hurrying out of the room and up the stairs. With every step he could feel the urgency and purpose. Outside the squad's room, he paused and ran his hand over the plaque with his name, then entered.

The squad had all gone, only Ash left.

'Well?'

The superintendent picked up a sheet of paper. 'Gordon Gibson, age twenty-two. Grew up in Colchester. Joined up the day war was declared. Did his time in the trenches, then someone saw he had very good eyesight. He ended up as a spotter for a couple of snipers.'

Harper drew in his breath. 'Who? Anyone we know?'

'One of them was a man called James Openshaw.'

Oh yes. He recalled that name. The man he'd met at the hospital, Gledhow Hall. The chain-smoker who kept his distance from the world. Shell-shocked, gazing at the world through distant eyes.

'Who was the other one?'

'He's dead, sir,' Ash replied. 'The three of them were out on a mission, all hidden away, when a stray shell exploded right by them. The other sniper was killed. Blown into pieces, evidently. Gibson and Openshaw were buried under parts of him and a ton of mud for hours. It took that long to find them and dig them out.' He put down the paper and pinched the bridge of his nose. 'A Blighty for them both. Gibson was discharged a month ago. Anger still burning inside him, the doctors said.'

A month. Plenty of time for everything that had happened here.

He couldn't begin to imagine what they'd experienced. Under the mud with the brains and blood and limbs of a comrade, it must have felt like suffocating in hell. No wonder Openshaw was so damaged.

'You said Gibson is from Colchester.'

'He spent a week with his parents after he got out of hospital, then said he needed to be away from there. He felt constricted.'

'I don't suppose we're lucky enough to have an address for him up here?'

Ash shook his head. 'Not a clue. Walsh has gone out to Gledhow Hall to see what he can discover. I talked to Colchester police; Gibson didn't have any kind of record before he went in the army.'

Harper cocked his head. 'And after he came home?'

'A couple of instances of brawling and drunkeness. With everything he'd been through, they never charged him. But they were able to give me a good description, and one of them has been to see his parents to try and come up with a photograph. That will be here tomorrow.'

Harper stared down at the desk and thought. 'We need everyone searching for him,' he said. '*Everyone*. Ask in the lodging houses, the hotels, anywhere someone might stay. Talk to women who are renting rooms in their homes, the lot.'

'Yes, sir.'

'It'll be difficult to get anything from Openshaw. One wrong word and he completely shuts down.'

'You know Walsh is good, sir.'

He was good with women. Maybe he'd have some luck in teasing answers from Openshaw. Anything was worth a try.

'Why not? From what I've seen of him, though, it's hard to imagine Openshaw as a sniper.'

'Stranger things have happened, sir.'

They had, all too often. 'You've made some good progress. I want to know as things happen.'

His pulse had quickened. Things were really moving. In his office, Harper picked up the telephone receiver.

'Gledhow Hall, please.' He waited, and finally a thin voice came on the line. 'Commandant Cliff, please. It's Acting Chief Constable Harper.'

Maybe he'd never become used to the title, but it made people move.

'We already have one of your men here, Mr Harper.' Commandant Cliff's voice was cool, concerned.

'I know. He'll do all he can not to disrupt things. Tell me, please, is Openshaw still allowed to leave the grounds?'

'Yes,' she said. 'There's been no reason why not.'

'I'd like you to revoke that.' There were too many ways in and out of the place. Once the man stepped out of the building, keeping him close would be impossible. 'In fact, not allow him outside at all.'

'I see,' she said. 'Might I ask why?'

'All I can tell you is it's a matter of national importance. Possibly life or death, and believe me, I'm not using those words lightly.'

She was quiet for so long he wondered if the connection had been cut. 'It's his doctor who makes that decision,' she told him. 'It's not in my power. But I can ask him.'

'What's his name?' Harper said. 'I'm happy to talk to him myself.'

'Dr Bishop.'

'Is he there?'

'He left a few minutes ago for his practice in Park Square. Chief Constable—'

'Thank you. I'll talk to him at his office.'

A glance out of the window. Another dry, bitter day. Bishop's office was no more than a two-minute walk from the town hall. Some fresh air might clear his head.

'Do you have proof, is this a suspicion, or merely a precaution?' Bishop asked when Harper finished speaking.

'At the moment it's a precaution, verging on a strong suspicion.' He spread his hands. 'That's the best way I can describe it.'

'Do you definitely need Corporal Openshaw restricted to the hospital building?'

'You know the grounds there, Doctor. As soon as he steps out of the door, it's child's play for him to walk away.'

The man nodded. 'The problem is that if we take away that privilege, we might jeopardize his recovery.'

'If you don't, and he is the sniper, not removing it might cause more death. Wouldn't that go against the Hippocratic oath you take?'

'I won't reveal anything about the patient's treatment, but I can tell you I've seen nothing to indicate he might harm other people. I doubt he'd be capable of being a sniper again. I can't see him even picking up a rifle.'

'That was my impression, too,' Harper agreed. 'But now we have facts that lean the other way. And until we have proof to the contrary, this is what I need.'

'I have my doubts about what you're saying,' Bishop said. 'And believe me, I've seen a great deal to astonish me since this war began. Still, I'll issue the order' – he raised a hand before Harper could speak – 'but only for the next three days. You'll have to settle for that compromise.'

'That should give us enough time.' He hoped to God it would.

'I trust it will, Chief Constable, and it shouldn't cause any lasting damage to my patient.'

Openshaw was caged at the hospital. Now they had some leeway. A little time to track down Gibson and the weapon.

'Nothing from Openshaw, sir,' Walsh said. 'As soon as I tried to talk about anything with him, I could feel the wall going up.'

'He was exactly the same with me,' Harper agreed. 'What was your impression of him? Can you see him as the sniper?'

'Honestly, no,' the inspector replied. 'He seems like he's in another world most of the time.'

At least he wasn't the only one to think that. If Openshaw really was fooling them all, he was doing a bloody good job of it.

'What about visitors?'

Walsh smiled. 'There we've got him. Gibson has been to see him eight times. The first was a few days before the shooting on Beckett Street. The staff all know him now, he's the only visitor Openshaw has, and about the only person who can talk to him.'

'Was the first visit before the incident at the clothing depot?' That seemed to have happened an age ago. But he hadn't forgotten about it, even if it didn't fit with everything else that had happened since.

'The day before, sir.'

No, it was impossible to tell.

'But,' Walsh added, 'Gibson was a visitor on the days of each of the shootings. They only have to sign in, not out again. However, Openshaw did sign himself off the grounds all three of those days.'

'Times?'

He shook his head. 'Not required, sir. Only that they're back before nine at night.'

'Do you think Openshaw is capable of deciding to take shots by himself?'

Walsh chewed on his lower lip. 'No, I don't. I talked to the nurses. They have to remind him to go to meals or to bed. About the only things he can manage for himself are getting up and going outside to smoke.'

'If these two really are behind the murders, that means Gibson is running everything.'

'It looks that way, sir.'

'I want someone in plain clothes up at Gledhow Hall. We'll nab him when he visits again.'

'It's already been arranged. Will Fenton's on his way.'

As the inspector was leaving, Harper called him back. 'A thought just struck me: why isn't Gibson doing the shooting himself? Why does he need Openshaw?'

'According to the army records, Gibson has very sharp eyes, but he can't hit a barn door with a banjo. He failed to qualify three times as a marksman, barely passed as a rifleman.'

Harper chewed his bottom lip for a moment. 'Instead, he's doing all the work, finding the targets and the place to hide, then wheeling Openshaw out to do the killing. And so far we don't have a single shred of evidence on either of them. Very neat.'

'At least Gibson doesn't even have a clue we're on to him, sir. That's something to help us. It gives us an advantage.'

'If he has any sense, he'll be wary. And as soon as he goes up to Gledhow Hall and discovers Openshaw can't leave, he'll realize.'

Thursday afternoon. Couples still walked arm in arm around town, looking in shop windows. Yet while the wages were good, women earning more than they ever had, there wasn't as much to buy. The restaurants and cafés were crammed, everyone pretending the food was what it had once been.

Habit took him to the café at the market, looking down on the stalls and the clock. Things changed – new faces, a different building – but the market itself was timeless. People calling out their wares, people looking for the best bargain. It was easy to imagine business had always been done that way, down through the centuries. A far cry from County Arcade, just the other side of Vicar Lane. Maybe it was more than habit that kept bringing him back here; maybe it was where he felt most comfortable. Part of the old Leeds.

He took the long route back to the town hall. Up Kirkgate, its face changing and brightening as it neared Briggate. Along Commercial Street and Bond Street, all the way to Marshall and Snelgrove, then turning on Park Row. A chance to hope that the men had been busy on the trail of Gordon Gibson.

'We've learned more about him,' Ash said as he sat on the other side of the desk. 'I talked to someone in army records who has a bit of a spark about him. I told you that Gibson was in the trenches before he became a spotter.'

'Yes, I remember.'

'Turns out his two best pals were caught by a shell in no man's land. Just disappeared into the mud, nothing to find. They'd gone over the top in the first wave of an assault. Gibson was in the second wave.'

'That's awful,' Harper said, 'but it must have happened to plenty of others.'

'Gibson threatened to kill the platoon subaltern if he didn't search for the men. He didn't, and no action was taken against him. But between that and what happened to him when he was with Openshaw, he's brimming with anger.'

'He was treated after he was shipped home, though.'

'There was some improvement. But he was looked at by one of those head doctors who said Gibson is very good at hiding things and manipulating people. Recommended the discharge, said he could be a danger back at the front.'

'And instead he's a bloody danger here.' Harper sighed. 'Do we know where the hell he's been staying?'

'We're working on it, sir. And Fenton will be ready as soon as he shows his face at Gledhow Hall.'

'We have three days. That's how long the doctor was willing to confine Openshaw.'

'It'll crack open in that time, sir.'

Harper gave a hopeful smile. 'From your lips to God's ears.'

NINETEEN

'If it's not too nippy on Saturday afternoon, maybe we could go out somewhere,' Annabelle said.

They were sitting in front of the fire, finishing a supper of water biscuits and cheese. Mary was curled in a chair with a book in her lap. She glanced up as her mother spoke.

'I might be able to manage a few hours. What do you fancy?' Harper asked.

'There's always the tram up to Roundhay Park. It feels like an age since we've been there.'

They'd gone the June before. As they'd started to stroll, all the people and the unfamiliar faces had suddenly scared her; in the end they'd turned around and quickly come home again. In winter, though, the park should be quiet.

'I'd like that,' he said. 'Like I said, it depends on work. We have a very important case. If something breaks, I'll need to be there.'

'Couldn't the chief handle it?' she asked. 'You need a day off.'

He gave her a gentle smile. 'I am the chief now, remember? Acting, since Bob Parker died.'

'He . . .' Confusion filled her face for a second, then cleared. 'Yes, of course. I forgot for a second, I don't know how. Poor Mr Parker, I'm so sorry for his wife.' She turned and beamed at him. 'My husband the chief constable, eh? Who'd have thought that?'

'If Da can't go, I'll come with you,' Mary offered.

'Thank you, love,' Annabelle told her with a nod. 'Maybe all three of us, a real little family outing. What do you think, Tom?'

'It sounds like a wonderful idea.'

The times when the world turned upside down were terrible. But these small moments tore deepest into his heart.

Saturday morning and she'd forgotten all about any jaunt. It was no day for it anyway, with a cold drizzle and a thin wind. At half past seven in the morning, Harper stood by the window looking down at the street. Puddles glistened in the dim, early light.

He was growing soft in his old age – no desire to stand outside in this weather and end up soaked. But no day off for him at the moment, either.

'I'll try not to be late,' he promised as he kissed Annabelle.

Dixon was in the office, busy sorting papers with his one hand, a cigarette dangling from his lips as he worked.

'Gibson?'

'Nothing yet, sir, and he hasn't been to Gledhow Hall.'

Where are you? Harper wondered. Busy finding your next target? What are you thinking? What do you really want? How many dead will satisfy that hunger of yours?

'Let's see what happens this morning.'

He worked listlessly. Outside, the rain became steady, a constant tap-tap-tap on the glass. The canteen in the basement was closed for repairs.

Finally, a little after five, he climbed the stairs to the office the squad was using. Ash had his head down, busy. Larkin smoked, staring into the empty distance, and Walsh was writing up a report. A damp overcoat hung on the rack, filling the room with the smell of wet wool.

'We know where Gibson was a week ago,' Ash said. 'A boarding house in Burmantofts. The owner remembered him.'

Burmantofts. Just across from East Leeds Hospital, not far from Gledhow Hall. But a week ago; that was another age.

'What was he calling himself?' Harper could feel the pulse thudding in his neck. They were growing closer to him, on his heels.

'Gibson.' Ash shrugged. 'Probably thought he had no reason to hide the name. He had a bicycle, carried what he owned in a knapsack. And,' the superintendent added, 'he had something long and thin. He told the owner it was his fishing rod.'

'Why did he leave?'

'He said his business here was done. Cool as you please. But we know for a fact he's been with Openshaw since then.'

'He won't still be in Burmantofts in case the man from the lodging house sees him and starts asking questions.' Harper was trying to piece his ideas together as he spoke. 'But he won't want to be too far from Gledhow Hall, either.'

'Where?' Ash scratched his chin.

'Talk to the stations. They'll know who's renting rooms. With all the war workers, it could be plenty of people. We need coppers going to each one and asking in person about Gibson.'

'Good idea, sir.' He smiled. 'I'm going to post another man with Fenton up at the hospital. We're not going to let him get away.'

Still raining the next morning. Only his squad was working on the Sabbath. They knew what to do without any prompting. If they found some results, he'd know quickly enough. The quiet gave him time to catch up on all the paperwork, more of it than ever, it seemed.

By one o'clock, he had gone through it all. A walk upstairs. They had gone off working.

Nothing more he could do at the town hall. Still wet outside; from the look of the clouds, it was set in for the day. He telephoned for the car.

The bar at the Victoria was busy as men enjoyed their day off. Two tables of women talking and laughing. He slipped through, waving to Dan and Jaak, then up the stairs.

Jef had his exercise books spread across the table, doing his homework. The parlour was filled with the tempting smell of roasting meat. In the kitchen, Mary moved around by the range, wearing a pinafore. On the settee, Johanna and Annabelle were playing whist and giggling like young girls.

'What are you doing here, Tom?' Annabelle asked with a frown. 'It's the middle of the day. You're not poorly, are you?'

'It's Sunday,' he reminded her.

'Oh yes. Of course.' She smiled. 'Silly of me.'

He saw Johanna give a very small shake of her head. Let it go.

Harper was shooed out of the kitchen before he could even set foot inside.

'Tell Jef it's time to put his books away and lay the table,' Mary said, and for a moment he could hear the echoes of her mother's voice from years before.

The ringing of the telephone jarred him awake. He didn't even realize he'd been dozing in the chair after the full meal. He hurried across the room, blinking at the clock. Almost four and already dusk outside.

'Chief Constable Harper.' His voice was still thick with sleep.

Ash. 'You wanted me to keep you up to date, sir.'

'Do you have Gibson?' That was the only important question.

'Not yet. But we know he's been lodging with a couple off Roseville Road.'

Not five minutes' walk from the Victoria. Harper might have seen him and never known.

'Walsh is over there right now if you fancy stretching your legs and talking to the people who own the place.'

The rain had finally ended; the winter cold would wake him up.

'I'd enjoy that. Maybe he'll show up while I'm there.'

The inspector was standing on the corner of Gledhow Place, outside a little shop that was closed for Sunday. He was smoking a cigarette, hat pulled down, huddled in his overcoat.

'Been here long?' Harper asked.

'An hour, sir.' He tried to smile. 'Mind you, it feels more like five. I'm perished. This damp cold goes right through me.'

'Let's see if we can find a little hospitality indoors, shall we?'

The house was a back-to-back, like almost all of them in the area. The Booths rented out the spare bedroom. Their daughter was away, a nurse in a military hospital down south, and the extra money came in useful.

'We put a note in the window down at the newsagent,' Mrs Booth said. 'Mr Gibson came and he seemed pleasant enough, didn't he?' She turned to her husband.

'Sound fellow,' the man agreed.

'Could we take a look in his room?' Harper asked. 'We won't disturb anything.'

She produced a key. 'It's on the left at the top of the stairs.' The woman seemed astonished that a chief constable would come to her house.

He let Walsh handle the search. His skills were still honed; he'd spot the smallest thing that was wrong. And the Booths might have some useful information.

'Does Gibson have something long and thin? He might say it's a fishing rod.'

'That's what he told us it was,' Mr Booth replied. 'Takes it everywhere with him. I told the lad he'd not be catching much round here with the state of the beck.' He smiled at his joke.

'He's probably going farther afield.' No need to tell him the truth and terrify the man. 'And he has a bike?'

'Leaves it outside. People respect things round here, it's safe enough.'

'What time did he leave today?'

The couple looked at each other.

'About eight, I suppose,' she said. 'Later because it's Sunday. I did him a good breakfast, then he went on his way.'

'Did he say when he'd be back?'

She shook her head. 'He has a key, so it doesn't matter. What's he done?'

'Probably nothing. We're just keeping an eye on people who aren't from round here. All part of being careful because of the war. Don't tell him we've been asking, please.'

The pair of them nodded eagerly. Walsh came back down the stairs

'Anything to tell us more about him?' Harper asked as they strolled back down the street.

'A few clothes. Nothing personal unless he has it well hidden.'

'As soon as he returns, he'll know.' He inclined his head back towards the house. 'They might not say a word, but it'll be written all over their faces.'

'We'd better nab him sharpish, then, sir. He's the one, isn't he?'

'Yes,' Harper replied after a long moment. 'This time I'm definitely going to say it's him.'

His heart was thudding. He could smell Gibson; he could almost see him riding along with the long package strapped to his back. The man was close. He could come around the corner at any moment.

But he was going to be alert and very careful. The slightest suspicion and he'd run. That would leave them with absolutely nothing. Openshaw? He was being used. He might not even be aware of what he was doing.

'Who's going to take over from you?'

'Bob Larkin,' Walsh answered. 'He's supposed to be here at six, and I hope he's on time for once. My mother-in-law's coming over tonight and there'll be the devil to pay if I'm late.'

Mary and Annabelle were sitting at the table, playing Pank-a-Squith. As far as he could see, his daughter was winning. The game was as close as Mary came these days to being a proper suffragette; all their political activities were suspended for the duration of the war. Annabelle had been a suffragist speaker, giving talks all over Leeds, but since her illness, there was no more of that. She never even mentioned votes for women now, as her world grew smaller. Seeing that spark flicker and die in her had been one of the hardest things for him to accept, a part of her that had vanished.

'Superintendent Ash telephoned a quarter of an hour ago, Da. He said it was important.'

He felt dread pressing down on him. If it had been good news, Ash would have passed it on. This had to be bad.

'Well?' he asked as soon as they were connected.

'Gibson, sir. He's scarpered.'

Exactly what he'd feared. 'How did it happen?'

'He stopped at Gledhow Hall to visit Openshaw. Hadn't even got off his bike when Fenton showed himself and told him to stop. Gibson turned round and pedalled away for all he was worth. Not a cat in hell's chance of catching him.'

He'd be too clever to return to his lodgings.

'Did he have the rifle?'

'Strapped to his back, sir.'

'Tell the squad to stand down for tonight. They can go home and sleep. I want a message to all the stations to have every bobby stopping all men on bicycles with large packages. That's our best bet for now. And we want to know about anyone looking for a room.'

'Understood, sir.'

When he returned to the parlour, Mary had gone.

TWENTY

He hadn't expected to sleep, but it was almost six when he woke; he had to hurry to meet the car waiting on Roundhay Road. No telephone calls during the night, no news. Gibson was still out there and he had that bloody sniper rifle with him.

He walked outside to a damp morning with a bitter drizzle.

'Better watch out later, sir,' Bingham said as he pulled up by the town hall. 'This stuff's going to freeze. It'll be treacherous, you mark my words.'

At least that would make it dangerous to ride a bicycle, Harper thought as he clattered up the stairs. Maybe Gibson would break his neck.

Larkin was in the squad room, smoking a cigarette and looking on the verge of exhaustion. But this case was pushing them all. It was bad enough to try to police during wartime, but this . . .

Was Gibson really a saboteur and a traitor, someone who hated the country? Or was this some twisted revenge for everything he'd suffered? Maybe the distinction didn't matter; the effect was the same. People were dead, as surely as if they'd gone over the top into no man's land.

Openshaw? If they were right, he was the marksman, he'd done the killing. Did that make him a traitor, too? If the police ever had the evidence, he'd probably be prosecuted as one. But Harper couldn't force himself to believe it. The man was too damaged to make any real decisions on his own. Gibson was using him. He was a tool, nothing more. Openshaw pointed the rifle, Gibson used him.

But before any court case, they needed Gibson in a cell.

'Any more leads during the night?'

'A couple of possible sightings, sir. By the time our men arrived, nothing at all. If he'd even been there.'

'Whereabouts were they?'

'One in Kirkstall, another in Horsforth, and a final one near Roundhay Park.'

Harper thought for a moment. Horsforth seemed unlikely, too far away from anything else. Still, they'd had the shooting at Kirkstall Forge . . . Roundhay Park was a different matter, though. It offered endless places to hide, and was no more than a hop, skip and jump from Gledhow Hall and Openshaw.

'I want every spare man beating the bushes in Kirkstall and at the park,' he ordered.

Larkin raised his eyebrows. 'Yes, sir. I'll get them on it.'

'Where are the others?'

'Not in yet. The super told them to have a good night's sleep and report at nine.'

'What about you?'

A grin. 'I drew the short straw. Night duty.'

'Go home once the others arrive. You've earned the day off.'

Larkin's smile broadened. 'Yes, sir. Thank you.'

He felt as if he'd been mired in ordinary work all day, arranging meetings and signing letters, when Miss Sharp tapped on the door.

'Corporal Carpenter from the barracks,' she said, with that eager little glint in her eye.

'Sir.' The soldier stood to attention, forage cap under his arm, puttees precisely rolled on his calves, boots bulled and glowing.

'At ease,' Harper told him. The man shifted stance, arms behind his body, legs slightly apart. 'What can I do for you?'

'I know you nabbed the man who took the rifle, sir, but I thought I'd keep my ear to the ground, anyway.'

'Have you heard something interesting?'

'Yes, sir. Nothing related to your case, but I thought you should know, anyway. It seems there's a bit of a racket going on with food supplies disappearing then coming to light in shops. Under the counter, if you know what I mean.'

'I know exactly what you mean.' There was a thriving black market. Soon enough, food would be rationed; that was the rumour. But plenty of items were already in short supply, ships bringing food torpedoed by the German U-boats. 'Do you have any names of people handling the stuff outside the base?'

'Right here, sir.' He took a folded piece of paper from the breast pocket of his uniform.

'Very good. And what about the ones at the barracks?'

Another slip of paper with three names written in a neat copper-plate hand. 'I think that's all of them, sir. They must be making a pretty penny.'

'Excellent work, Corporal,' he said. The man grinned with pride. 'I'll make sure the brigadier receives this, and that he knows the source.'

'Thank you, sir.'

'If you come up with anything else, let me know.'

Once he was alone, Harper telephoned Fox.

'That ex-copper of yours has come good again.' He gave the details and heard the brigadier sigh.

'It's suppose it's too much to hope for an army of honest men. This lot will think I'm the proverbial ton of bricks when I fall on them. Thanks, Tom. Any luck with this chap you're after?'

'Close,' he answered. 'But that never wins any prizes, does it?'

'I wish it did. I'll keep Carpenter's name out of it, but I'll see there's a commendation in his record for uncovering the food thefts.'

Another ten minutes and everything was in motion. Shopkeepers and soldiers would be arrested. Carpenter was proving to be a goldmine. A pity he didn't want a move to CID once he went back to civilian life; he'd be a natural for the job. But then, being in uniform didn't bring the frustrations of plain clothes.

Another pair of possible Gibson sightings too. But none of them was him, of course; that would be too easy.

At twelve, Harper put on his overcoat and tied his scarf around his neck. Gloves, then hat, and he was ready for the cold. There was a mix of sleet and ice that left the pavements dark and slick. People trod slowly and carefully, watching the ground in front of them.

He saw a motor car slip and slide up the small hill of the Headrow while he waited to cross to East Parade. Would Gibson know how to bivouac and keep himself dry? Maybe he'd found an empty house where he could hide, out of the weather. He'd set the constables searching this afternoon.

A ten-minute wait while Dr Bishop finished with one of his private patients.

'Is this about Corporal Openshaw, Chief Constable?' He had a flicker of irritation in his voice.

'It is. I need his restriction to the building extended.'

'I examined him this morning. He's fretful and anxious at not being able to go outside.'

'I'm sorry about that.' He paused, not wanting to use the words, but needing something powerful. 'It's a matter of national security. I have to insist. Either that or transfer him to a quieter facility. Somewhere rural.'

Bishop shook his head. 'Moving him would probably send him into a spin.'

'I appreciate that. Your cooperation was helpful before. I hope I can count on it again.'

Bishop sighed and Harper knew he'd won. 'How long will you need him kept indoors?'

'Until we catch this other man. Soon, I hope.'

'Very well.' His voice was filled with reluctance. 'I'll send them the order.'

'I'm grateful.'

'I have to tell you: I'm not convinced Jimmy Openshaw has done anything wrong, Chief Constable.'

'I'm not sure he's aware of it himself. But we have two people dead and one in hospital here from a sniper's bullets. Believe me, it's very real.' He gave a small bow. 'Good day to you, Doctor.'

Gibson could have cut his losses and left Leeds. His only connection to the city was Openshaw, and he'd probably realized it was impossible to reach the sniper now. He had the bicycle; it would be easy enough to go. And it would be the sensible thing to do.

Then why did he believe that Gibson was still here? It niggled and wormed its way under his skin.

'You need to send the division heads the details for this month's deserter sweep,' Miss Sharp reminded him.

'I know.' The routine of wartime England. The early, eager flow of volunteers had long since become a thin trickle. The government had brought in conscription to replace all the young men dying and wounded on the front. People at home had seen the bitter reality of war, and all those early thoughts of patriotism and glory had vanished.

Men deserted, more than the government cared to admit, and the police had to catch them and send them back. Cat and mouse. Part of being a copper.

He scribbled a copy of last month's orders and left it on her desk as he went to see Ash.

'No nearer to finding him?'

The superintendent shook his head. 'A lot of it's going to be luck, sir.'

'I'm sure he's still around. I can feel it here.' Harper pressed a hand against his belly. 'I just can't understand *why*. Gibson knows we're on the hunt, and Openshaw's confined at the hospital. We've taken away his killing machine.'

'Maybe he knows something we don't,' Ash said. 'Or he's desperate.'

Either of those was possible. 'What does he want?'

'To destroy. I'm not sure it matters what or who.'

That made sense. 'What about that incident at the clothing depot?' Harper asked. 'The one that started all this. Do you fancy him for that?'

Ash shook his head. 'It's not his style. It could be we were reading more into it than existed. We haven't seen a repeat, not even anything like it.'

He saw Ash glance out of the window. The rain had stopped, but the roads and pavements were slick and icy.

'Not going to be pleasant for him if he doesn't have a roof over his head tonight,' he said.

'I doubt he'll turn himself in, if that's what you're hoping,' Harper told him.

'He's not going to have much in the way of food, or anywhere to keep himself warm and dry. If he doesn't have a room tonight, he'll be desperate for one tomorrow, and a hot meal and a drink.'

'Make sure everyone knows to tell us if someone comes looking for somewhere to sleep.'

'Exactly, sir. We keep ramming it home with them. In weather like this it can only be a matter of time before we find him.'

If that turned out to be true, it would be the first time he'd ever been grateful for winter. At least with Openshaw confined to the hospital at Gledhow Hall there would be no more sniper deaths. Harper felt that the net was closing. But he wasn't going to rest easy until Gibson was caught. There was still too much that could go wrong; he knew that from bitter experience.

As he finished for the day, sorting papers into piles on the desk and closing the top of the inkwell, he looked up to see Mary standing in the doorway.

'Your secretary's gone,' she began.

'Past her clocking-off time,' he said with a smile. 'What brings me the pleasure of your company?'

'Any chance of a lift home? It's nasty out there. Even the trams are slipping and sliding on the tracks.'

'No patrol tonight?'

'I'm off. I pity the ones who have duty. Not that I expect they'll have much to do.'

'Go on,' he said. 'We can squeeze you in the car. That's not the real reason, is it?'

'No,' she admitted. 'I went over to Len's parents for my supper last night.'

She'd vanished quietly after the board game and came home when Harper and Annabelle were already in bed. 'Did it go well?'

'It was awkward at first.' Mary tucked her arm in his as they went down the stairs and out into the night. The pavements were like glass and she held on tight.

'I hope it improved.'

'It did.' Satisfaction and relief filled her voice. 'After a while we were all able to talk about Len. Not in any strange way. Laughing, happy. It seemed . . . natural, I suppose you'd say. They told me things about him when he was young, things I'd never known. And I could tell them what he was like with me. All the plans we had.' She smiled, content. 'You know, they really treated me like I was their daughter-in-law.'

'In a way, you are,' he said, and she nodded.

'Yes. I felt like part of the family. I think it helped us all.'

'Going over again?'

'In a while. We haven't set a day. But when I was coming back, it set me thinking about other things.'

'Oh?' Harper asked.

'Like me mam. We need to have a plan for the future. The war's not going to last forever. Johanna and her family will be going back to Belgium. What will we do then?'

She was quite right. He knew he hadn't considered it. Maybe it was the war and work; that was his excuse, anyway. But he knew the truth: he hadn't *wanted* to think about what would happen, the way Annabelle would decline.

'Do you have any suggestions?'

'Just a few thoughts.' She shook her head. 'About the only thing that's certain is that it won't get any better. Has the doctor told you what to expect?'

'I haven't asked.' The only thing he knew with certainty was that Annabelle wouldn't live many more years. That awful knowledge was enough. He didn't want to know a damned thing more. It was too painful.

'You should, Da.' Her eyes were pleading. 'Please. We need to come up with a plan. I know you have plenty on your plate right now, but this is important, too.'

'Yes,' he said. She was right, of course she was right. He needed to grow up and take his head out of the sand. Mary had done it. So could he. Ignoring the future wouldn't make it go away.

TWENTY-ONE

No warmer the next morning as Harper put on his dress uniform, the first time he'd worn it in years. Tight around the waist, but it still fitted. He'd sooner have kept it in the wardrobe than wear it for Bob Parker's funeral.

Annabelle slept on. The evening before, she'd begun insisting that he was her father, talking about the times when she was a child, the Saturday nights when all the neighbours would come together for dances at the end of a week. He'd listened, saying little, hearing all these things she'd never mentioned to him, memories she probably hadn't realized she still possessed. Now they were more alive in her mind than something that had happened that afternoon.

'We're still searching everywhere, sir,' Ash told him. Like Harper, he was in uniform for the service. They both had a strip of ribbons across their chests for the medals they'd received over the years.

'If we don't have any luck this morning, I'll send more crews into the parks to look. In case he's camping.'

Harper worked through dinner, making a tiny dent in the mountains of paper that were part of being chief constable.

He'd just put down his pen, massaging some life back into stiff fingers, when the telephone rang.

'Harper.'

'Dixon here, sir. I thought you'd like to know: we have a lead on Gibson.'

He sat up straight, one hand gripping the arm of his chair. 'Go on. Where?'

'Bottom of Beeston Hill, sir, not far from the Leeds City ground.'

Harper's mind sparked. These days the football pitch was used by the army for drilling. Men standing and marching. But completely the other end of town to Gledhow Hall.

'Are you sure it's him?'

'It certainly looks like it, sir.'

'Then flood the area. I want every spare copper down there going house to house. As wide an area as you can manage.'

'Very good, sir.'

Was Gibson simply running, or had he found himself another target? And if he couldn't use Openshaw to kill for him, who did he have lined up for the job?

There was no time to discover more. Miss Sharp came through to tell him that the car was waiting. She straightened his tie, stepped back and assessed him.

'You'll do him proud.'

'I hope so,' Harper said. 'He deserves it.'

A grand and glorious service. Hymns and eulogies. The Lord Mayor in his finery, councillors, the heads of all the police divisions in Leeds, chief constables from the surrounding forces. Businessmen. And tucked away on the front pew, Parker's widow, his children and grandchildren.

Harper stood at the lectern and spoke a few words when his turn arrived, then gratefully sat down again, glad to be away from the spotlight.

Finally it was over. The hearse left for the cemetery, the family in two cars behind it. It would be a small, private burial, leaving the rest of the congregation to mill around in the desperate cold outside the Parish Church at the bottom of Kirkgate.

He was chafing to return to the town hall, to discover if Gibson had been found yet. That was more important than any of this. But Harper knew he was trapped by his rank. He had to stay and make small talk. More congratulations and commiserations.

As he tried to ease away, a figure appeared in front of him.

'Chief Constable. I finally have the chance to meet you.'

A bulky, fleshy man with a salesman's ready smile and the sheen of money. A careful appearance, well-tailored clothes. His hand was extended.

'I'm sorry,' Harper replied, 'I don't—'

'Richard, you found him.' The woman seemed to appear from nowhere, her voice too bright and loud for the occasion. He knew *her*. Barbara James, the woman in the blue Rolls-Royce. The man had to be her husband, the one who'd made his fortune from selling poor soap to the army.

Something about James repelled him. He glowed with the same self-satisfaction Harper had seen in criminals who thought they owned the world. The only difference was this one had a title. *Sir* Richard.

'A pleasure to make your acquaintance. Unfortunately, I'm in the middle of a very important case. Perhaps we can talk another time.'

With that, he hurried across to his car.

'Get us out of here,' he told Bingham. As they pulled away, he caught a glimpse of the Rolls-Royce parked on High Court. The chauffeur, former PC Tierney, stood by it, smoking.

Why did Sir Richard James want to cultivate him? Whatever it was, it couldn't be good.

'Well?' Harper asked. 'Any progress?'

'Nothing definite yet, sir. No report of Gibson actually renting anywhere near Elland Road. We have three different people who claim to have seen him. We're following up on those.'

'That lead from this morning: what was it?'

'He approached a woman about a notice she'd put in the local newsagent with a room available. But she said there was something about him she didn't trust, so she told him it had already gone. Definitely him, though. He even used his own name.'

Gibson had used a card in a shop window to find his last room.

Not too long after four, a thin, withering drizzle began. Along with the cold, this was weather for neither man nor beast. Parker was six feet in the ground now, and Gibson would certainly be wanting somewhere warm and dry.

Maybe they had a chance, after all.

The car dropped him off on Manor Street. Harper hurried through the rain with his head down, almost crashing into a man who stumbled out of the front door of the Victoria. The man turned, a surly, vicious look on his face. But Jaak stood in the doorway, solid as stone, and the man thought better of it, wandering away hatless.

'A problem?'

'He cannot hold his drink. He wanted to fight.' Jaak shook his head and returned to the bar. They'd definitely been lucky with the Belgian refugee family they'd taken in.

Upstairs, Annabelle made a fresh fuss of him in his uniform, as if she hadn't seen it that morning. Mary was going over Jef's fractions homework with him.

He changed into comfortable clothes, trousers that didn't threaten to split him in two at the waist, and made himself a sandwich in the kitchen.

'She has been up and down all day.' Johanna appeared beside him. 'This morning I found her putting on her hat and coat. When I asked where she was going, she didn't know. Then she began talking about what she's been doing with a man named Harry.'

'He was her first husband,' Harper explained. 'Harry Atkinson. He left her this place when he died.'

She cocked her head. 'Do you know if she loved him?'

'Yes,' he told her with certainty. 'She did.'

A nod, as if everything made sense, and she drifted away. Week by week, the past was becoming more real to his wife than the present. At some point she'd never return. Mary was right. He needed to talk to the doctor and make a plan before things grew worse.

He sighed. As he chewed the last bite of food, the telephone began to ring.

'It's Superintendent Ash,' Mary said as she held out the receiver.

'Have you found him?' Harper asked.

'One of the uniforms did, sir. A special named Townend.' Ash's voice was solemn. 'Gibson was riding his bike. As best I've heard it, our man started chasing after him.'

'Go on.' He felt the heavy throb of the pulse in his neck.

'As he was pedalling, Townend kept blowing on his whistle to bring other bobbies. Gibson stopped, took out the rifle and shot him. Ten yards. Doesn't matter how bad a shot he is, he could hardly miss at that range.'

'How—?'

'His leg, sir. Through the fleshy part of the thigh. Missed the artery. He's at the infirmary now.'

Thank God for that.

'Townend was lucky in a way,' Ash continued. 'Fell behind a parked lorry, so he was out of the way. Fenton and Walsh are over there now, taking statements. Larkin and Dixon are leading the house-to-house questioning.'

'Any more sightings?'

'No, sir. We know he started heading back towards town. After he'd shot Townend, one of the witnesses said Gibson put the gun back in his knapsack, picked up his bike and cycled away as cool as you please. Not even hurrying.'

Cold, confident.

'Is there anything I can do out there?' Harper asked.

'Not really, sir. The men are on top of it. I'm not even going myself. More use here.'

'I'll go and see Townend tomorrow. One thing's certain, Gibson won't be showing his face in Beeston again—' He stopped. 'Do we still have anyone at Gledhow Hall?'

'Someone from the station at Chapel Allerton, sir.'

'I want him especially alert. Gibson might try there again. If anything comes up . . .'

'We'll let you know, sir.'

Harper picked up the newspaper. The Germans had begun unrestricted submarine warfare and were threatening to sink hospital ships. Bastards. Australia was looking to form a war government. There were rumblings of revolution in Russia; that could change the balance of the powers.

'Harry,' Annabelle said, staring at him, 'where did we go last Sunday? It's slipped my mind.'

'Was it the park?' Anything he said would be a guess.

'No, it was York. That's it.' Her face brightened. 'We took the train with Clarence and his wife and the Bensons and we ate that big meal for dinner and the cream tea later. It was lovely, wasn't it?'

She continued to talk to him as if he was her late husband. The things she mentioned had happened over thirty years before. But once she fixed on it, everything was clear, as sharp as crystal in her mind.

He encouraged her, simply for the pleasure of seeing her happy. But believing he was Harry Atkinson was new. Harper glanced at Mary. She raised her eyebrows, her silent way of emphasizing what she'd said to him before.

At five he was up, alert, washing and shaving in cold water, dressing in a starched shirt and collar, putting on his new suit with its four buttons and lapels on the waistcoat, all set off with a deep burgundy silk tie.

By six he was standing on Roundhay Road, ready when the car arrived then purred away towards town. Dry today, maybe it even felt a touch warmer; everyone out on the beat would welcome that.

But so would Gibson. Where are you? Harper thought. What are you planning?

'Town hall, sir,' Bingham said, shaking him out of his thoughts.

The only sounds in the building were the echoing voices of the spotters up in the clock tower. Harper hung up his coat and hat, then picked up the telephone and asked for the infirmary.

'You have a patient called Townend, admitted last night,' he began.

Ash sat behind his desk, his face so drawn and weary that the skin was tinged with grey. All the others were busy writing up interviews and statements from their notebooks. No sleep for any of them, by the look of it. The air was thick with sweat and stale smoke, the window cracked open to try and draw in some fresh air.

'Gibson,' Harper said.

'Vanished into thin air, sir. About the only thing we can say for certain is he's not in Beeston now.'

'He'll know we're hunting him. He shot a copper in the middle of the road, for Christ's sake.' He knew his voice was rising, but he couldn't stop it. 'Where the hell is he? Why don't we know?'

Ash stood, rising slowly from the chair. He began to walk, taking Harper gently by the arm. Outside, he closed the door behind him.

'Sir, I know you want him. We all do, I know you understand that. Every one of us is as frustrated as you.'

'Yes. You're right.' He nodded.

That small, familiar hesitation. 'We've known each other a long time. I hope you'll forgive me if I take the liberty of saying that taking it out on the men isn't going to help, sir.'

His words carried a sharper sting for being spoken so politely. He sighed.

'I'm sorry. Yes, they're doing everything they can.'

'I shouldn't have—' Ash began.

'No, no, you were right,' Harper told him with a wan, regretful smile. 'After almost thirty years working with me, you'd better be able to let me know when I'm out of line.' He placed a hand on the doorknob and took a deep breath.

'Gentlemen,' he announced to the detectives, waiting until they were all staring at him. 'I'm sorry. I was wrong. You didn't deserve that outburst. I know you're working all hours and trying everything you can to find Gibson. I appreciate it all, I really do. I selected you because you were the best and you've proved it time and again in this. Nobody could have done more.' He looked around; they were all staring down at their desks. 'Tell me what I can do to help you, and I will. We're going to find Gibson and put him in a cell. Thank you.'

He turned and left them to it. That was a short, sharp lesson to remember: rank didn't grant him the right to take out his frustration on others. When he was on the receiving end he'd griped about men who did it.

Let them work, he reminded himself.

There was plenty to keep him busy. The result of the sweep for deserters had been disappointing. Only twenty nabbed. That looked bad.

He picked up the next letter from the pile. One to all chief constables from Neville Chamberlain, head of the Department of National Service. It was set to become a ministry next month. God only knew why, Harper thought; the country didn't need more ministers. It needed people who could deal with the shortage of labour for the industries that could win this war.

More words with no powers to back them up. It would change nothing at all.

The morning wore away, bit by tiny bit, like chipping pebbles from a block of granite, until the four walls of his office seemed to be closing in on him. He needed to escape somewhere for a few minutes, to see something that wasn't an official piece of paper.

Before he had the chance to decide where to go, Miss Sharp tapped on the door and slipped through, carefully closing it behind herself.

'Sir Richard and Lady James are outside.' She kept her voice low, glancing over her shoulder in case they'd entered behind her.

The last thing he needed right now. 'What do they want?'

'To take you to luncheon.'

'What did you tell them?'

Her eyes narrowed. 'I know you refused their last invitation. I said I didn't know if you were busy.' A small pause. 'She's very glamorous, isn't she? That coat has to be pure sable and her dress must have cost a fortune.'

'He can afford it. Give them my apologies, say I'm tied up with work all day. The usual thing.'

'Very good. Do you want me to tip you the wink once they've gone?'

He smiled. 'Yes, please.'

It had come to this; he was cowering in his own office to avoid

people. Ridiculous. Even so, he waited until the coast was clear
before hurrying upstairs.

'Anything?' he asked Ash. He was alone, the men all gone.

'A possible sighting of Gibson this morning in Holbeck.'

It wasn't far from Beeston, on the way into town.

'What time?'

'A little after eight, sir. Dixon and Larkin are trying to discover
where he spent last night.'

'What about Walsh and Fenton?' Harper asked.

'They're trying to anticipate where he might go. I've put that
second man in place at Gledhow Hall.'

Gibson had shot a copper himself, but he needed Openshaw to
inflict any real damage. Openshaw was the reason he'd come
to Leeds. Could he try and spirit him away from the hospital?

'Come with me. We're going to find some dinner and talk about
this,' Harper said. 'And you can tell me what you've heard about
Sir Richard James.'

TWENTY-TWO

'That's better,' Harper said as he pushed the empty plate away
and took a swig of tea. 'Now, let me know what you've
learned about Richard James.'

Ash dabbed at his mouth with a serviette as he finished chewing.

'The way I understand it, sir, he's been around so much because
he's been negotiating a contract to supply soap to all the Leeds
council offices, including the schools.'

Something like that would be worth plenty of money; no wonder
he was here, buttering up the councillors, maybe slipping them
something in a plain envelope. It would be lucrative in the long run.

'Then what would he want with me?'

'You're in charge of the police, sir. That's very useful if your
business isn't all above board.'

'As simple as that?' It seemed too obvious.

'It appears that way. There are a couple of rumours of back-
handers. It's worth a fair bit, and he's going to need ways to bring
in money once the war is over.'

Harper gave him a sceptical look. 'Will it ever be over?'

'Bound to be, sir. We'll have the Yankees with us soon. That'll make all the difference. But when it's done, James will need to find an income somewhere.'

'He won't be having much help from me. He'll get the message sooner or later.'

'The problem with men like that is that the message never seems to find its way home, sir.'

True enough. He'd met others like that. Men who never heard the word no. On a much smaller scale, but equally certain they could have whatever they wanted. Several of them were in jail now.

'Gledhow Hall.' Time to change the subject. It seemed almost clean in comparison. 'Tell me how you intend to arrange things . . .'

'The doctor says you're on the mend,' Harper said to the man in the hospital bed. 'It went straight through the flesh of your thigh. Missed the bone and the artery.'

'That's what they tell me, sir.' Ken Townend had a round, ruddy face with watery, owl-like eyes hidden behind thick spectacles. He'd been lucky when Gibson had shot him; no lasting damage. 'Still hurts like the devil, though.'

'You're a brave man. You chased after him.'

'I just did what anyone else would, sir.'

He wished that was true. Most would keep their distance. It took guts to take a risk that way. 'All I can give you is my thanks and a commendation.'

Townend beamed with pleasure. 'That's very good of you, sir.' He put out his hand and Harper shook it.

'We'll be glad to have you back once you're well again. But make sure you're properly fit first.'

'I will, sir. And thank you for coming to see me. I hope you catch him soon.'

'Believe me, so do I.'

'We're getting closer.' Walsh's face was flushed with excitement.

'Where?'

'We've tracked him through Holbeck, sir, and we've discovered where he spent last night. It was a lodging house near the football ground.'

'I thought we'd already talked to them all.'

'We had, but he offered ten shillings if the man would keep his mouth shut.' His smile hardened. 'The proprietor is in custody now.'

'A good place for him. Where's Gibson?'

'We know he crossed the Neville Street bridge, sir. He was spotted cycling across. The message has gone out to every copper in the city centre. It should only be a matter of time now.'

His heart was racing with anticipation. They were so close. But there was still so much that might go wrong. 'I want a cordon of men round Gledhow Hall. Nothing except essentials in or out, and we search every lorry.'

'Yes, sir.'

The commandant would play hell with him, but he didn't care. His job was to keep Leeds safe and this was the best way of doing it.

'That's very good work, Inspector. Now let's finish the job.'

After the door closed, he lifted the telephone receiver and asked for Carlton Barracks.

'Your men are making progress,' Brigadier Cox said after Harper brought him up to date. 'What can I do to help?'

'Keep your troops alert,' Harper told him. 'Put some in those woods below Gledhow Hall, too.'

'Do you really think he'll try to get to Openshaw?'

'I do.'

It was all Gibson had, his whole reason for being here.

'Then I'll make sure of it. What if they spot him?'

He hesitated before answering, thinking of Townend in his hospital bed. 'Tell them to shoot. Gibson's deadly.'

He'd done all he could, made every preparation. He hoped he'd anticipated every eventuality. The only thing left was to wait. But that was the hardest thing. Harper kept working, checking the clock only to see that just five minutes had gone by. Again and again.

He felt the slow start of a headache behind his eyes, the pressure growing, and went to beg one of Miss Sharp's headache powders.

As she gave it to him, she pushed a small, plain box across the desk. 'This came for you a little while ago. That chauffeur brought it, the one who brought the invitation from Sir Richard James and his wife.'

Curious, he lifted the lid. A shiny gold tie pin with a small diamond. He showed it to her and heard her click her tongue in surprise.

'Send it back to them at the Metropole, will you? Say . . . I don't know, thank them but point out that my position means I'm unable to accept any gifts.'

'A pity.'

'No,' he told her. 'No, it's not. It's never good to be beholden to someone.'

Refusing invitations, returning gifts . . . it should be enough, but he felt sure this wouldn't be the end of things.

Dusk arrived, and no word on Gibson. He was out there, drawing closer to Gledhow Hall with every minute. Harper stood at the window, watching traffic pass in the growing darkness.

'There's not much more the men can do today,' Ash said.

Harper hadn't heard him come into the office. 'Send them home. They've earned a good night's sleep.'

'Already done it, sir. Everyone in bright and early tomorrow. We'll have him then.'

Would they? He wished he could be so sure.

'You go, too.'

'Very good, sir. Having me home will be a change for my Nancy.'

'Has she applied to be a clippie yet?' He remembered what the superintendent had said.

'She has. Starts next Monday.' Harper heard the astonishment in his voice. 'I never thought she'd really do it.'

'The world's changing.'

'It is that, sir. It is that.'

Another hour or two of work. The headache faded to a mild annoyance. He tried to think up a campaign to recruit more special constables. Maybe he could use Townend; after all, the man was a hero now.

'Not straight back to the Victoria,' Harper told Bingham as he settled in the car. 'Gledhow Hall first.'

The house looked eerie in the night. Ghosts should be wandering the halls, he thought as he waited for the commandant.

'What have you done to my hospital, Chief Constable? It feels like an armed camp. Several of my patients are upset. Corporal Openshaw is the worst of them.'

There was no compromise on Miss Cliff's face, nothing but fury at him for coming into her kingdom and changing things.

'My apologies,' he began. No chance of ending her fury, but he might manage to calm it a little with a full explanation.

'You should have consulted me first,' she said when he was done.

'When there's a man with a gun wandering around Leeds, time is one thing we don't have,' he said. 'And he's on his way here.'

'For the corporal.'

'Yes,' he said. 'If he manages to spirit him away, then it's a pound to a penny that more people will die. I can't allow that. I trust you'll understand.'

She gave a slow nod. Maybe not understanding, but acceptance. That was enough.

'I'll make sure all the doors and windows are locked.' She looked at the watch that hung from her apron. 'Now, I have my evening rounds to make. I'll wish you good night, Chief Constable.'

A dismissal with proper formality. At least he'd made her understand the danger that Gibson posed.

'Now we can go to the Victoria,' he said as he slid into the back seat. 'Finished for the evening.'

Half of him hoped that was true. He needed a night where this didn't crowd into his thoughts and dreams. But the rest of him craved a sighting of Gibson, the chance to finish this hunt.

He woke, feeling curiously refreshed after six hours of sleep. Ready and eager to face the day as he waited at the bottom of Roundhay Road for the car to pick him up. He'd just climbed into the vehicle, the door not even closed, when the shot rang out.

So loud that the noise seemed to fill the street. Harper didn't think, he just threw himself to the floor. A second shot and the window exploded, showering him with glass. Had he been hit? He didn't think so. No pain, no warm gush of blood.

'Are you all right?' he hissed.

'Fine, sir.' The motor was still running.

'Get us out of here. Pull round on to Manor Street.'

He held his breath, still cowered, pressed down against the floor. Bingham eased the car into gear. Harper waited. No third shot. They bounced and jerked over the cobbles, then stopped as the engine died.

'Ready to run?' His mouth was dry and the words rasped out. 'Go.' He grasped the door handle, took a deep breath, closed his eyes as he sprinted for the back gate of the Victoria. Only three yards, but it felt as if it took forever. He was out in the open, an exposed target.

He dragged down the handle, then he was through and pushing it to as Bingham dashed past him. No bullets. Nothing at all. Harper slid the bolt home and let himself breathe. They were safe here. The brick wall was too high to climb and topped with glass.

His legs felt like India rubber. He could barely stand. His hand shook wildly as he drew the ring of keys from his pocket and tried to fit one in the back door of the pub.

'Pour yourself a brandy,' he said. 'You probably need one.' Harper felt bitterly cold 'Better make it two. I'll telephone the duty officer.'

The stairs were like a mountain. Climbing them was an act of will, each step forced. He had to reach for the wall to steady himself.

Annabelle and Mary were wild-eyed, full of frantic questions as soon as he entered. Jaak, Johanna and Jef huddled in a corner, fearful. They'd heard guns before; they knew what it could mean.

'Da—'

'Nobody's hurt.' He picked up the telephone receiver. 'Millgarth Police Station,' he told the operator.

There were coppers buzzing all over Sheepscar. The pair from the tiny station on the corner of Chapeltown Road, a dozen more from A Division. Gibson was long gone, of course, pedalling around somewhere in Leeds. Heading north, he felt certain. Larkin and Dixon were in charge of the house-to-house. But it had happened early, before most people were out and about.

The shivers had finally abated. For a few minutes he'd felt frozen, even with the eiderdown over his shoulders. The tot of brandy helped, followed by a cup of hot, sweet tea. Finally, his hand remained steady when he extended it in front of him. His heart had stopped thumping a tattoo.

That didn't mean the fear had vanished. Lady Luck had been with him. He'd suffered nothing worse than a long gash on his cheek, cleaned up with the sharp sting of antiseptic solution.

'One second earlier, sir,' Ash said. He sat at a table in the bar, giving his orders as men ran to and fro. 'And if Gibson had been a better shot . . .'

'Believe me, I know.' He'd seen nothing. He hadn't even been looking. 'Have you tightened up security at Gledhow Hall?'

'Yes, sir. And I've alerted Brigadier Cox. He's sending more men over there.' Ash pursed his mouth and his moustache twitched. 'We couldn't have anticipated he'd try this, sir.'

'No.' They'd imagined that Gibson was focused on reaching Openshaw. Harper asked the question preying on his mind. 'Do you think he really intended to kill me?'

'He'd probably have been happy to succeed, sir. But I'm not sure we'll ever understand what's in his head.'

That was true. Gibson's brain . . . the doctors could have a go before they hanged him. If he survived that long.

'How did he know where to find me?'

'Common knowledge, sir,' Ash told him. 'A senior police officer who lives upstairs from a pub? You're probably the only one in the country. Famous for it.'

That must have been it. Harper glanced at the clock. Almost eight. Gossip about the shooting would have flown around the force. He needed to show his face at the town hall before any rumours grew out of hand.

With blood covering half his face, Annabelle hadn't known him. She'd kept coming up to him and asking who he was, what he was doing in her home. Nothing he could say convinced her that he was her husband. Finally Johanna had to take her into the bedroom to calm down while he cleaned himself up.

'Da—' Mary began.

'Gibson's moved on,' he said. 'He won't be back.' Too many coppers around, and this had never been his real destination, just one stop along the way.

'He tried to kill you.'

The words made fear freeze his body. It passed in a heartbeat, but the chill lingered. Everything could change so suddenly. From life to death, out of nowhere.

He hugged her, feeling Mary cling tight to him. It was understandable; she'd already lost Len, one man she cared about.

'I'm not dead yet and I intend on staying that way,' he told her.

TWENTY-THREE

'You're alive,' Miss Sharp said as he walked into her office. 'As large as life and twice as ugly. A slight delay this morning.'

'People are saying—' she began. 'Was anyone hurt?'

'No. Everyone's fine, although I daresay the gossips are already telling it differently. Any word from Gledhow Hall?'

'Nothing.'

He settled at his desk, trying to find the rhythm of routine. But every time, his mind slipped back to the blast of the gun and the shattering of glass and he began to shake again, and had to force his hand into stillness.

All that terror from two bullets. How did the men in the trenches stand it? Machine guns, heavy shells, day after day after day. The miracle was that they didn't all suffer from shell shock.

He had meetings scheduled: a group of councillors at eleven, concerned about truancy enforcement. Vicars, priests and rabbis at noon, with their fears about religious tensions. But he couldn't deal with them. Not today.

Harper rang for his car, shrugged on his overcoat and hat. His fingertips lingered as they stroked the cut on his cheek. Lucky, he thought. So very damned lucky.

'Postpone the meetings,' he told Miss Sharp.

'Where are you going?' she asked. 'What time will you be back?'

'Later,' he answered.

The replacement car was older, battered, a loud beast of a vehicle. It didn't glide, it bucked and bolted; Bingham had to caress and persuade it through the gears, and the brakes screeched as he stopped.

'We'll have your proper one back in a day or two, sir,' he promised. 'I hope we do, any road. As soon as they can clean it up and fit the new windows.'

Harper walked through the grounds. A steep hill down to an ornamental lake. Paths that wound through copses and bushes. Gledhow Hall was probably charming and decorative when everything was properly maintained. But with the war, the gardeners had gone, and wildness had quickly returned. Grass and weeds had become tangled, growing tall and thick. Shrubs that grew into one another. Stark winter tree trunks brooding over everything.

'You could hide an army in all this,' he said to one of the soldiers standing guard.

'Like as not, sir,' the man agreed. He was young, face so fresh and smooth he looked as though he'd barely started shaving. 'This chap we're looking for, if he has the slightest clue, will be able to stay hidden without a problem.'

'And get past you?' Harper asked.

'If he's careful, he has a good chance.' He realized his honesty and reddened. 'Sorry, sir. But it's true. We're trained, but we've never been out of England yet.'

Harper clapped the private on the shoulder. 'No, I'd rather you were open about it.'

In the house Harper gathered his men, reminding them that Gibson was dangerous. They'd have heard the news; they could see what had happened from the vivid red line on his cheek. He wanted them alert. After an hour or two of nothing it was all too easy to let down your guard.

Gibson would come today. He'd been working his way up here, unleashing his damage as he came. He *had* to come today. This place, Openshaw, was his goal.

The corporal was well guarded. He still had the run of the building, but there was always someone watching him.

The men were doing everything they could. Harper stood by an upstairs window, gazing down over the valley. Even ragged and neglected and in the middle of winter, it had a stark beauty. The lake at the bottom of the hill reflected the trees and the light.

Part of him wished he could sit here and wait for Gibson to arrive, to finally see his face as he was arrested.

He'd just finished a session with the chairman of Leeds City football club about policing their matches when Miss Sharp announced Superintendent Ash.

'Do you have something?' Harper asked.

'Not really. We found the two cartridges from when he shot at you, but that's it, sir. He must have scarpered straight after. One person saw him in the shadows and three or four spotted someone cycling away, but that's it.'

He sighed. What else would there be to find, anyway? 'Gledhow Hall seems secure.'

'It should be.' Ash's tone was hesitant.

Harper cocked his head. 'What is it?'

'I've been wondering how Gibson manages to disappear. You have to agree, sir, he's good at suddenly making himself invisible.'

'Yes.' That was true. Most of the time he was anonymous, unnoticeable.

'I talked to an inspector I know in Colchester, asked him to do more digging.'

'What did he find? You wouldn't be telling me if it were nothing.'

'Gibson was a boy scout, sir. Baden Powell's lot.'

'So were a lot of lads.'

'Not like this, sir. He was a proper standout. On his way to becoming a King's Scout before he joined the army. That's the best of the best. Excellent at woodcraft, according to his scoutmaster. Gibson knows how to live off the land and that kind of thing. Keen eyes, too, but we already knew that. He wouldn't have been a spotter otherwise.'

A boy scout. Who'd have credited it? Harper sat and thought. With skills like those, and his army experience, Gibson might well be able to avoid the patrols around Gledhow Hall.

'Any recommendations?' he asked.

'Make sure our men are alert,' Ash replied. 'Honestly, I don't know what else, sir.'

Neither did he. And that was the problem. He was the chief constable. He was supposed to have all the answers.

It was late in the day. Most of the clerks and typists had gone home, a procession of footsteps on the stairs. Miss Sharp had wished him goodnight before she trotted away.

Harper worked on. He knew he was reluctant to have the car take him home. Terrified that Gibson might appear again like a dark spirit and take another shot. One that didn't miss.

His rational mind knew that the man wouldn't return, exactly as he'd told Mary. Good sense was fine, but this was something different, something that ran deeper.

But there was more. The hope that the telephone would ring, bringing the news that Gibson was under arrest or dead. Maybe if he stayed at work, keeping himself busy, that would happen. As if it was a talisman.

All stupid. And sooner or later he'd need to face his fears and go back to the Victoria.

Without warning, the door opened and a bulky giant of a man in an expensive suit entered. Harper started to rise. His hand snaked toward the cosh he kept in his jacket pocket, then stopped. The only weapon he'd need here was his wits.

Alderman Charles Thompson. The leader of the council, a Tory who hated every socialist, a man who'd been a fixture around the town hall for many years. Too many, some believed.

'Chief Constable,' he said. It was as much of a greeting as he was likely to offer. 'I heard what happened this morning. I'm glad to see you're still on your hind legs and kicking.'

'That makes two of us, Alderman.'

Thompson squinted behind his spectacles. 'Have you found him yet?'

'We know where he's going, and we have men waiting for him.'

'That's a long-winded way of saying no.'

Thompson lived in Chapeltown, a grand house that stood not half a mile from Sheepscar and the Victoria. But for all its grandeur, it might as well have been a world away. His orbit revolved around politics and its skulduggery. He relished it.

Harper smiled. 'If you say so.'

'I do, Chief Constable. How are you settling into the job?'

'I'm doing my best. I daresay I won't be here for long.'

'No, like as not we'll appoint someone else when we get around to it,' Thompson admitted.

He'd been one of the driving forces behind the formation of the Leeds Pals regiment at the start of the war and he was fiercely proud of them. Since their near annihilation on the first day of the Somme in July, he'd seemed bowed by the weight of the world on his shoulders.

'This man you're hunting,' he continued. 'Is he a traitor? A saboteur, whatever you want to call him?'

'I thought he was,' Harper replied. 'Now I'm not so sure.' He gave a small shrug. 'I'm not certain what he is. And I don't know if I care. I just want him off the streets.'

'And dead?'

He knew it was a loaded question. No matter. 'Yes.'

'I remember when you were just an inspector,' Thompson told him.

'That seems like a long time ago.' It was. More than twenty years since he made superintendent.

'The past is always waiting to haunt you. You were friends with that union organizer, Maguire, weren't you? The socialist. Once your wife started giving speeches for the suffragists, I had you marked as a firebrand.'

'Maybe I still am, Alderman.'

But Thompson was shaking his head. 'Listen to yourself. You just said you'd be happy to see Gibson dead. I'd say you're right. But you're the one who's changed, not me.'

'Perhaps it's the world.'

'Aye, that too. You know what they say – men become more conservative as they grow older. You've become living proof of that.'

He didn't know how to answer. Wiser, perhaps, to keep his mouth shut.

'Keep it up, catch this man soon and you never know – maybe this post will fit you better than you think.' With a nod, Thompson turned on his heel and left. The door shut with a smooth, low click.

Well, well, well. In less than five minutes, Thompson had given him enough food for a year's thinking. Criticizing, then dangling the prospect of removing 'Acting' from the job title. Far too much to consider when he was sitting here.

He gripped the seat as the car approached the Victoria. Eyes trying to look everywhere for danger.

'Manor Street again.'

Fewer places to hide there.

'Everything's safe as far as I can see, sir,' Bingham said when he'd parked.

'Goodnight.' Harper scurried, bent over to make a smaller target. He didn't dare to breathe until he'd closed the back gate. His hand shook as he pushed home the bolt. It would be a while before he felt properly safe again. Not until they had Gibson.

Mary was gone, a patrol night. Annabelle was in a bright, merry mood. No memory of the night before, or of the gunshot, when she hadn't known him and had been so fearful. Perhaps it was all for the best. Now she asked him about the cut on his cheek as if she'd never seen it before.

'Just a bit of a scrap,' he said.

'You're the chief constable now,' she told him, brow pinched with worry. 'You should let other people do the fighting.'

'I will,' he promised her with a smile. Should he mention Thompson's hint? No, it was too vague, too easy to withdraw. Probably too confusing. He still wasn't certain he believed it himself.

TWENTY-FOUR

'Where the hell is he?'

Morning, and Harper stood with the squad, staring at a map pinned to the wall. There'd been no sign of Gibson. No attempt to make his way into Gledhow Hall. And all they could do was wait for him to appear.

'If we knew that, we'd have him behind bars, sir,' Larkin said.

Harper stared at the map, picturing every street and its hiding places. He'd hurried out of the back gate that morning, glancing around before dashing across the pavement to his car. His brain might know that there wouldn't be another shot, but his heart refused to believe it.

Until Gibson made his move, their best hope was pure luck. A bobby sharp enough to spot him and put two and two together.

'Make sure everyone knows he's still out there.'

Ash followed him down to his office.

'Any good suggestions?'

'Not a thing, sir. But you asked me to see what I could dig up on Sir Richard James.'

The man with the blue Rolls-Royce, who appeared so eager to be his friend. 'I thought it was soap for the council.'

'It is, sir. That's the beginning, anyway. A little bird told me that he's eager to become the sole supplier to other councils for their facilities. Offices, everything.'

Leeds was a big city; that would be a hefty contract with large profits. And if he was angling to supply several places, James had no shortage of ambition.

'I still don't see why he wants to be in my good books.'

Ash shrugged. 'We both know it's not going to happen here without some cash changing hands. A few councillors will put together nice little nest eggs out of this. He's either seeing if you're open to that, or he wants to claim you as a pal. That could count for a lot with some folk.'

It would certainly explain the invitations and the tiepin. He'd done right to follow his instincts and refuse everything. Maybe his successor would think differently, but that wouldn't be his problem.

'That's useful. Thank you.'

'I'm sure you're keeping your distance, sir.'

Harper grinned. 'Wouldn't touch him with a bargepole.' The smile disappeared. 'What are we going to do about Gibson? Can we flush him out at all?'

'Not that I can see. It's up to him at this point. All we can do is be ready to react quickly.'

'Are any of our men up at the hall armed?'

Ash shook his head. 'The soldiers Brigadier Cox sent have rifles, and they've had their training. That should be enough.'

He hoped it was. He didn't want any more innocents to die.

Alone again, he rang the infirmary. Townend had been discharged. On the mend, but it would be a while before he was back on duty. Harper wrote up the commendation, with a note for it to be placed in the man's file.

After a moment's hesitation, making sure the door was firmly closed, he picked up the telephone. He had a rare afternoon free of commitments. It was time to do what Mary had suggested. He needed to know what to expect with Annabelle so they could make a plan.

'Dr Hilton, please. It's Chief Constable Harper.'

'We have a sighting of him, sir.' Walsh's voice was scratchy on the other end of the line. Harper pressed the receiver closer to his ear. No need to ask who he meant.

'Where?'

'Harehills. A soldier on his way to guard duty at East Leeds Hospital spotted him and called out. Gibson pedalled away. It was definitely him. So far we've been able to track him to Roundhay Road, but we lost him in the back streets.'

His chest felt tight. Harehills, Roundhay Road, both so close to Gledhow Hall. He was making his move.

'Alert the men keeping watch on Openshaw,' Harper said. He tried to keep the eagerness and anticipation out of his voice. 'Make sure you let the brigadier know so he can inform his men.'

'Already done it, sir,' Walsh told him with dour satisfaction. 'If he tries to get close to the hall, he doesn't stand a chance.'

But how many times over the years had they felt certain of something, only to see their hopes fall apart in a moment?

'Keep people searching around Harehills,' Harper ordered. 'He's smart enough to keep moving, but let's not take any chances. Make sure they're careful. Remember what happened to Special Constable Townend.'

'Very good, sir.'

He sighed, took the pocket watch from his waistcoat and popped open the lid. Checked the time against the clock on the wall. Pulled on his overcoat and squared his hat on his head.

'I'll be back in an hour or so,' he told Miss Sharp.

She raised her eyebrows. 'What if someone's looking for you?' The woman was angling to discover where he was going.

He smiled at her. 'Then they won't be able to find me.'

He hurried back, only a short distance from Park Square, where every doctor in Leeds seemed to have his office. Hilton had asked plenty of questions; he answered each one honestly and fully. The doctor wanted to examine Annabelle, of course, not that she'd willingly come here. Still, he was willing to offer an opinion and some suggestions.

Harper knew he'd need time to consider everything he'd just heard. But time wasn't something he had at the moment. 'Anything?' he asked as he entered the squad room.

'Still playing the waiting game, sir,' Ash replied.

Dixon and Fenton sat at their desks, smoking, tense, not even trying to look busy. As soon as the word came, they'd be on their way.

'Where are the others?'

'Beating the bushes around Harehills and seeing if they can pick up Gibson's scent,' Ash said. 'Haven't heard from either of them yet.'

Harper's instinct was to wait up here with his men. Instead, he turned away; his presence would just make them uneasy. He'd risen too high to keep a close bond with them any more.

More papers and a late afternoon meeting with the head of the fire brigade. It was part of the police force, and he was asking for more men in case of a Zeppelin attack on Leeds.

'We're already stretched.' His fingers worried at each other in his lap as he spoke. 'I've got men working too many double shifts as it is. That means they're not alert if they have to attend a fire.

As you know, sir, that can lead to injuries and time off work, making everything worse. A vicious circle.'

'I'll see what I can do,' Harper promised. But he knew there was little hope. There simply weren't enough men available. The newer specials didn't meet the standards of the ones recruited at the start of the war. If this dragged on and on, everything in Leeds would fall apart. He didn't see how things could be any better in Germany. Over there, a chief constable in some town was probably sitting at his desk and wondering how to make his resources fit his needs. It was small comfort.

At seven he packed up and left, patting the town hall lions as he passed. His real car was waiting, glass and coachwork replaced, washed and gleaming in the dusk.

'Roundhay Road this time,' he told Bingham as they approached Sheepscar.

'Very good, sir,' he answered, but Harper could hear the note of caution in his voice.

He wasn't going to skulk and hide. He was scared, terrified, but he couldn't allow it to show. With a deep breath, he opened the door and strolled across to the Victoria. No shot. Only the constant background of factory noise that was the music of this place.

Morning, and still no ringing of the telephone bell with more word on Gibson. Harper was the first to rise, moving silently through the early tasks, and standing outside at six. Looking around nervously, although he knew the man wouldn't return.

The driver lifted the handbrake and started towards town, but Harper leaned forward and said: 'Gledhow Hall.'

Still full dark as they parked outside the main entrance. As he stood in the blackness, his eyes and ears began to adjust. Even with his poor hearing he could pick out birdsong and the movement of animals through the grass. Some of the things Openshaw had mentioned when they'd talked. Faint stars still hanging in the sky. Small slashes of light from the building where the blackouts didn't fit properly.

The door was locked, an armed soldier guarding the other side. He had to show his warrant card.

Two soldiers and three coppers inside the hospital, every one of them suspicious until he identified himself. Good. He wanted them on their toes. As he came back down the main staircase, Commandant Cliff emerged from her office.

Her uniform was exact, the apron starched a perfect, crisp white. Not a hair out of place under her cap. 'Are you satisfied with what you've done to my hospital, Chief Constable?' Her voice rang out, sharp and displeased.

If she wanted to challenge him, he was in the mood to give as good as he got.

'I'd say we've already saved a life or two, Commandant. So yes, I'm satisfied. But not as much as I will be when we capture the man who's lurking somewhere out there.'

'I trust that will be soon.'

'So do I,' he told her. 'After that, you'll be able to return to your routine. Meanwhile, I'm grateful for your cooperation.'

Harper stared at the woman until she finally turned and stalked away.

He was close to the front door, when a uniformed constable came running through the building.

'Thank God you're still here, sir. We've just had a call to warn us. There's something happening at the Blackburn works down on Roundhay Road. They wanted to let us know we might receive some casualties, being near and that.'

'What is it? Do you know?'

'No, sir. But I thought I should tell you.'

'Good thinking. I want everyone here on full alert, understood?'

He hurried to the car and felt a spasm of terror run through his body. The Blackburn factory was less than half a mile away. It was in the Olympia Works, building aircraft in what had once been a skating rink. It was important for the war effort, a perfect target for sabotage. An ideal distraction, too. Something to keep people occupied.

Gibson was behind it. Not a shred of doubt in his mind. While everyone was attending to the Blackburn crisis, he could creep closer to the hall.

The car jounced and bumped down Gledhow Wood Road. Two fire engines were already at the works, putting out the blaze and making certain it didn't spring up again.

'How did it happen? When?' His gaze moved between the fire brigade inspector and the factory manager.

'One of my men noticed it about half an hour ago,' the manager began. 'We're trained to deal with a fire. Used a hose on it while we called the fire brigade. We'd just started to get it under control when another one sprang up on the other side of the building.'

A second? Christ, Gibson had been thorough.

'We arrived in time to deal with that, sir,' the inspector continued. 'Put it out sharpish while another crew took over here and made sure everything was extinguished. A few more minutes and we should be on our way.'

'Anybody hurt?' Harper asked, relieved when both men shook their heads. 'How bad is the damage?'

'Negligible,' the manager answered. 'We'll need to clean up and make some small repairs to the structure. But it's nothing bad and it won't affect production at all. We were lucky it was spotted early, though. It could have been nasty.' He glanced back over his shoulder where men moved, busy and intent on their work. 'As it was, we only had to stop for about ten minutes.'

The firemen were coiling up their hoses and packing their equipment into the engine.

'What caused it?' Harper asked the inspector.

'Arson, sir. Both blazes. No doubt at all about that.'

'I want a full report on my desk today.'

For a moment he wondered if he should go back to Gledhow Hall. No, if Gibson was making an attempt to enter, he'd simply be in the way. There was nothing he could do to help.

'Can I use your telephone?' he asked the manager.

'I heard you were at Olympia Works, sir,' Ash said. He sounded muffled and distant.

'It's a feint. Lucky it was caught early. But I want more uniforms at Gledhow Hall now. Tell Brigadier Cox. He can send more men.'

'We'll have the place chock-a-block, sir.'

'Good.'

Gibson was close. He could smell him in the air. Come out and show yourself, Harper thought. Let's put an end to this.

'You know, this morning makes me think of what happened at the clothing depot,' Ash said. He sat back in his chair, rubbing at his moustache.

'*If* that one was real,' Harper reminded him. 'I thought we'd decided it was nothing.'

'We did, sir. I certainly had my doubts about it. But maybe I spoke too soon.'

'Could Gibson have been responsible for the clothing depot?'

'It's possible,' Ash answered after a second. 'We know security there was like a sieve, the way people went in and out. No checks. But if he did it, he was scared off before he could do any damage.'

'Or he had cold feet,' Harper said. 'It was his first time.'

'The first that we know about.'

'The only other thing was the explosion at Barnbow, and the inquiry was satisfied that was an accident. The site was secure and properly guarded. If it was him, the clothing depot was his first attempt in Leeds and something happened to stop him.'

'It would make sense, sir. After a fashion, anyway.'

Harper stayed silent for a long time, letting his mind follow all the avenues of thought.

'The way I see it, there's one thing arguing against all this. Gibson came up here to use Openshaw. He had no other reason to travel halfway across the country. Would he risk that by doing something on his own when he might be caught?' Suddenly, he sat up straight in the chair. 'We never searched Openshaw's room. He and Gibson must have exchanged letters.'

Ash lunged for the telephone. Thirty seconds later he was issuing instructions to one of the coppers at Gledhow Hall.

'He'll ring us back as soon as he finds anything.' The superintendent grimaced. 'I'm sorry, sir. I should have thought of that.'

'It doesn't matter now. We know where Gibson's going.'

They were passing the time, waiting. Another five minutes of silence and Harper rose to his feet and walked down the stairs to his office.

'You've had a flurry of telephone calls,' Miss Sharp told him, 'and the post is on your desk.'

Back to drowning in the routine.

'What are you doing for your dinner?'

'Nothing, Da.' He could hear her surprise. 'Why, do you want to treat me?'

'I went to see your mother's doctor yesterday, the way you suggested.'

'What did he—'

'We'll have to eat at the town hall.' There would be time for questions later. 'I need to stay close.'

'Gibson?'

She'd know all about it from the patrol. 'We're right behind him.'

A moment, and she said: 'I'll be there a little after noon if that's all right.'

'Perfect. The canteen here isn't up to much, but it's handy. If anything changes, I'll let you know.'

As the hands of the clock moved to twelve, nothing had altered. They were still waiting. Harper stood by the window, hands thrust in his pockets, watching the traffic grind past on Great George Street. Boys pushing their heavy barrows, nags hauling carts, lorries and cars stopped and moving.

It felt like the story of his life.

Then a tap on the door and Mary was standing there, dowdy in her widow's weeds.

The canteen was busy, but they found a table in the corner and ordered. Miss Sharp knew where to find him when something happened. If it happened. Gibson was taking his time, toying with them, playing his game and keeping everyone on edge. Waiting for his moment.

'What did the doctor say about me mam?' Mary asked. He knew she was brimming with questions, but she'd been patient, waiting until they were on the sticky toffee pudding with its warm, thick custard.

He stared at her. 'It's not good news.'

'It was never going to be, Da. *How* bad?'

'He wants to examine her. But from everything I told him, he suspects she might decline quite quickly.'

She moved her spoon around the bowl. 'Decline? What does he mean by that?'

'Her good days will become far fewer. She'll become more confused and spend more time in the past. Or she might be silent, off somewhere.' He paused for a moment. 'There are going to be more times when she doesn't know us.'

Mary nodded as if it was what she expected to hear. 'What about physically?'

Harper was slow to reply, choosing his words very carefully. 'She's still young; she's not sixty yet. It's possible her body could keep going for a while. But in Dr Hilton's experience, health often goes downhill along with the mental capacity.' He sighed. 'That more or less sums it up.'

'Then what can we do for her? How can we look after her? The Palmaers won't be here forever. It's looking more and more like the Yanks will enter the war.'

Like everyone else, Harper had heard the rumours – and something more, a vague secret whisper out of the War Office about an intercepted telegram that could turn the Americans into an ally.

'Even if they do, the fighting still won't end overnight,' he warned her. 'But once it does . . . we can afford someone to live in and look after her. Your mother's made money, I have a good salary. We're quite well to do,' he said, as if the notion astonished him.

'What about the pub?'

'We'll sell it and move somewhere smaller.'

Mary stared at him. 'All of us?'

'Of course,' he assured her. 'All of us.'

'How long?' Mary asked and he knew exactly what she meant. How many more years would his wife stay alive?

'He wasn't willing to give me a number.'

That wasn't strictly true. Wilton had sat back in his chair, frowning as he rubbed his chin, and told him he might expect the worst in five or six years. And well before that, Annabelle would be in a bad state. But how could he tell Mary news like that? Simply knowing it was a heavy enough weight to bear.

Harper felt as if he was in a tiny boat, bobbing on the ocean with two storms approaching. There was Gibson, but that would be short, sharp and violent. And over quickly. Then there was Annabelle. That one would linger and cut him to ribbons.

TWENTY-FIVE

Why was Gibson biding his time? He had to be waiting for something, but what was it? Harper had expected him at Gledhow Hall as the fires burned at Olympia Works. Instead, he'd vanished again.

No sightings of him in the area. All the men remained on full alert, but how long could that last?

He stretched in his chair, arching his back and feeling the tension in his body. He was like a stretched wire. What he needed was a hot bath with some Epsom salts to ease his muscles. When this was over, he promised himself. Once things calmed down a little.

The telephone rang and his hand shot out to pick it up. Superintendent Collins from Armley. A bad accident out there between a tram and a lorry. Three dead, maybe more. He needed some extra men for a few hours, and a string of ambulances. Harper made another call and everything was set in motion.

There was no question; he needed to go out there and see it for himself. If anything happened with Gibson, Ash could handle it. There were enough men up at the hall, almost a small army.

It was more than two hours before he returned, quiet and sobered by the blood and the mess. Men were hauling away the vehicles. They were pulled apart with shrieks of metal. A butcher from up the road was sprinkling sawdust to soak up the blood from the cobbles. The bodies had been taken by the time he arrived, along with the worst of the wounded. Volunteers from St John's Ambulance were patching up the ones who remained.

Witnesses claimed the lorry had come down the hill, unable to stop, and careened full tilt into the tram. Everything he saw fitted that. Newspaper reporters roved around, interviewing anyone they could find. Harper shook his head when one approached him with a question.

Finally he made his way back to the waiting car. Too much blood and pain.

'Town hall,' he ordered. 'But for God's sake, let's be careful.'

'Nothing yet, sir,' Ash said before Harper could speak.

'Where the hell is he?'

'Still around. I'd put my salary on that.'

'Then why's he waiting?'

'He wants to catch us off our guard, sir. And the longer he waits, the better his chance.'

'How long a shift do our men put in at Gledhow Hall?'

'Twelve hours.'

'Make it six,' Harper said. 'I know it'll be more difficult, but it will keep them fresh and alert.'

'Very good, sir.'

He paced around the room, trying to imagine what else they could do. 'There's no choice but to wait, is there?'

'None. Unless we're very lucky.'

'We'd better not bank on that. Let's just be certain we're ready when he does come.' He glanced out of the window. Dusk was growing, the city turning darker. 'Night would be a good time for him.'

When Bingham parked in front of the Victoria on Roundhay Road, Harper opened the door, stood tall and strode to the door of the pub as if he didn't have a care in the world. But he felt as if he had a target in the middle of his back, only relaxing as the door closed behind him.

Another bad day for Annabelle. Once again she thought he was Harry Atkinson, remembering things the two of them had done. Trips to the seaside and into the country. Times when she'd been happy.

Annabelle had loved her first husband; that was what he'd told Johanna. Now he could see just how deep that bond had been. The pain she must have felt when he died. He'd been a lot older than her, Harper knew that much. A few decades. But it was obvious that it hadn't mattered a jot.

How could their marriage ever compare to that? He listened as she kept talking. Her face was rapt, caught up in events that had happened more than thirty years before, so alive in her mind they might as well have taken place yesterday.

Suddenly her voice faltered and stopped and she stared straight ahead at the wall. It only lasted for a few seconds before she was back, talking again as if nothing had interrupted her and he was Harry. Harper looked at Johanna. She shook her head; this was new to her, too.

Just the single instance, but it was something to watch for in the future. It would be back, he felt sure of that. Another symptom to add to the list.

In bed, she snuggled against him, affectionate and eager. But who did she think was here with her? Tom Harper or Harry Atkinson?

*   *   *

Mary stood over the bed, shaking him awake. 'Telephone, Da. You slept right through it.'

He stumbled into the living room, blinking and yawning. Something big had happened. They'd caught Gibson. It was the only reason to ring in the middle of the night.

'Harper.' His voice was thick and heavy.

'We've had an incident at Gledhow Hall, sir,' the duty sergeant said. 'They said to inform you. One of the patients up there—'

'Which one?'

'Someone called Corporal Openshaw, sir. He put his fist through the window in his room and sliced open his wrist.'

Jesus.

'How is he? Is he still there?'

'Evidently he lost a lot of blood. They've transferred him to the infirmary.'

'Send a car for me.'

Before he dressed, Harper called the hall.

'It was a right mess, sir,' the constable on duty told him. 'He'd pushed the chest of drawers behind the door before he did it. First we knew was that smash of glass. Then we had to force our way in.'

'How long did it take?'

'I'm not sure, sir. A minute, perhaps. But the room was covered in blood. The nurses got to work, trying to patch him up. The infirmary is more a precaution than anything else.'

'Stay alert. Gibson won't know what's happened. He's going to arrive sooner or later.'

'Yes, sir.'

The infirmary was a strange place in the small hours. Lights burned bright in the corridors. The soft moaning of people in pain, unable to rest. The smell of carbolic trying to overpower the stench of disease and decay.

Openshaw had been put in a private room, away from the ward, with a constable on guard outside. Harper spoke to the sister in charge.

'There wasn't much for us to do. They'd bandaged him well. We're keeping him in as a precaution, really. He's sedated. It's up to the doctors, of course, but I think he'll require some specialized care. There are some facilities where they do wonders with people who've been shell-shocked.'

'He was in one and improving,' he said. 'That's why he ended up in Leeds.'

'I see.' She glanced at the closed door and sighed. 'Sounds like it's back to square one for him, poor chap.'

More than that. If Openshaw ever realized what he'd done in this country, the people he'd killed and wounded here, who knew how it might affect him? Was that what had made him try to kill himself? A sudden understanding that he'd done what Gibson wanted of him? Was that his way of trying to stop it?

Too deep. Far too deep for him.

The clock in the central court read a little after three. Dark as the grave outside. It was a very short walk to the town hall. He wasn't ready to start his work day yet, but he was too wide awake to go home and try for a couple of hours of sleep.

'Gledhow Hall,' he told the driver.

The room was cold, bitter air coming in through the broken window. Openshaw had punched a hole through the glass, then sliced his arms again and again with one of the shards. The constable was right. It looked like a bloodbath. Everything would have to go.

As he came back down the stairs, Commandant Cliff was waiting. The middle of the night and she still looked fresh in her uniform. When did she sleep?

'I blame you and your men for what happened to the corporal,' she said. 'He needed to be outside. It allowed him to breathe properly.'

'I'm sorry he felt the need to do that,' Harper told her. 'But I told you my reasons and I don't regret them.'

'Corporal Openshaw won't return,' the commandant said. 'I'm certain of that. He needs more than we can offer here. That means you can withdraw your men.'

'There's a man out there who doesn't know what's happened. He thinks Jimmy Openshaw is still here and he wants to free him. Until we catch him, the men stay.' Before she could open her mouth to argue, he continued, 'I know this is your hospital. But Leeds is my city. I hope you can understand that.'

She was beaten, but her expression showed she couldn't accept it with good grace. Harper didn't care. His job was to try and keep Leeds safe.

A walk outside, bundled deep in his overcoat. As he looked up at the clear sky, his breath steamed. But all the stars on show . . . it was majestic. A reminder that people were so small, not even a speck of dust in the universe.

Yet right here, things still moved on and they had to find Gibson.

The café in the market was open, serving the traders who'd set up early. Hot food, a couple of mugs of strong tea and he felt ready to face the rest of the day. Hours and hours ahead of him.

The entire squad was in the office, buzzing with the details of Openshaw's attempt to kill himself.

'It doesn't make a scrap of difference to us,' Harper reminded them. 'Gibson doesn't have this news.'

'As far as we know, sir,' Ash warned.

'How would he hear?'

'People from the hall might gossip . . . plenty of ways, sir.'

It was possible; it just seemed unlikely. Still, for want of a few words, it would be stupid to dismiss it.

'Tell the men up there to go round and question all the staff. See if anyone's been asking them about Openshaw. If they have, we need to know when, who it was, what they asked. Everything.'

Back in his own office, he phoned the doctor who'd been treating Jimmy Openshaw.

'Have you been to see him at the infirmary, Dr Bishop?'

'I intend to visit later today, Chief Constable. I'm meeting the physician who's looking after him there. I have to tell you, I don't think that would have happened if he'd been free to roam the grounds.'

'Maybe not,' Harper replied. 'But I can guarantee you that a few more people would be dead in Leeds. That's not a price I'm willing to have this city pay, Doctor.'

'I think—'

'Is your patient going to need the kind of treatment he can't receive here?'

'There's a strong possibility he will,' Bishop said. His voice was coloured with caution, in that way doctors and lawyers had, everything shaded and weighted to avoid a straight answer. 'It's impossible to say until I've examined him.'

'Where would you send him?'

'If it's necessary' – the doctor laid a soft emphasis on the word
– 'then it would probably be the facility in Scotland where he
was a patient.' Bishop sighed. 'He was making progress here,
too.'

Harper thought of the man he'd seen, sitting in the cold, smoking
cigarette after cigarette, quite removed from everyday life. If that
was progress, how had he been before?

'I'd appreciate a quick decision. A lot depends on it.'

'Very well.'

'And if you'd let me know what you intend.'

'I'll send a message,' the man promised.

From there, the morning vanished in a blur of meetings and
correspondence, of waiting on tenterhooks for word about Gibson.
Anything at all to help them catch him.

'Nothing, sir,' Ash said after Harper had climbed the stairs to the
squad's office. 'There was one orderly who said someone had been
asking him questions in a shop. It sounds like Gibson. But that was
before Openshaw tried to kill himself.'

'What was he looking for?'

'Ways into the hall without being seen. No need to worry, sir.
The orderly didn't tell him anyway. Said the place was guarded as
well as the Mint.'

Thank God for that at least. But he doubted it had discouraged
Gibson. He was out there, biding his time and looking for his
opportunity. Not knowing his quarry wasn't even in that hospital
any longer.

At least, he hoped the man didn't know. Prayed. Harper had
contacted all the newspaper editors and asked them to block any
mention of what had happened to Openshaw. It wouldn't have been
more than a small item, but silence was safer.

They hadn't seen anything of him. What the hell was he waiting
for? Harper wondered. A sign? The right moment?

The ringing of the telephone cut through his thoughts.

'Larkin and Fenton have gone through Openshaw's room, sir,'
Ash said. 'Top to bottom, while they're cleaning the place. They
found some notes he'd written.' He paused for a moment. 'More
like poems, really, although nothing rhymes in them. Disturbing
reading. We think they're recent.'

'What do they say?'

'He talks about guilt a lot. Blood and death. I'm not an expert, but it sounds to me as if he realized what Gibson had made him do. That might be why he tried to commit suicide last night. Knowing it was all too much for him.'

It wouldn't be the first time that knowledge and memory had made someone do that. Shell shock and then this. Poor man.

'We might need them for a court case.'

'They're grim reading.'

'I daresay. Nothing more on Gibson?'

'We're scouring everywhere, sir. Asking in all the rooming houses, but he seems to have gone to ground. Mind you, it's like we said – with that boy scout background and army training, he'll be quite handy at making a camp for himself.'

And impossible to find. They had to wait until he made his move, then hope they reacted quickly enough. He replaced the receiver and rubbed his chin. What would Gibson do next?

A tap on the door and Miss Sharp appeared.

'This came in the second post,' she said, holding out a letter. 'It sounds like she knows you, and this might be important.'

Typewritten, with a woman's looping signature at the bottom of the page.

Dear Chief Constable Harper,

I daresay you won't remember me, as we only talked briefly when you were conducting your investigations into the incident at the Clothing Depot on Swinegate. I'm Gladys Naylor, the secretary to Mr Hardy who runs the depot. I trained at your daughter's secretarial school, but I don't expect that to ring any bells.

The last two evenings, as I left work, I've noticed a man just around the corner. He stands there as if he's waiting for something, but he's out of view of the guards on the door. Yesterday I went into a shop so I could observe what he was doing. He kept peering at the depot entrance, then finally disappeared into an area behind the building where he was waiting, and reappeared with a rucksack that had something like a wrapped fishing pole sticking out of the top.

I realize it's probably nothing, but with all that's going on I felt you should be aware.

I remain yours sincerely,

(Miss) Gladys Naylor

He dashed up the stairs and burst into the office.

'Walsh, Larkin. I want you down at the clothing depot now.' He took a breath. 'Go and see the armourer. Draw a pistol each and some ammunition.'

'Sir?' Walsh asked, as if he could scarcely believe the order.

'It sounds like Gibson's been lurking down there. Around the corner. Search the area. If he draws his rifle, fire. But only if you can do it safely.'

It was all they needed to hear. Harper passed the letter to Ash.

'Is this young lady reliable, sir?'

'I only talked to her for a few seconds, but she seemed sensible enough. They'll still be at work down there. Do you fancy a stroll?'

TWENTY-SIX

Sunday, but she was working. Like so many other places the clothing depot was going seven days a week.

'Can you describe the man you saw, Miss Naylor?' Harper asked. They were standing in the manager's office.

'Very short hair,' she replied. 'Almost right against the scalp as if he'd just had it cut. His expression was . . . furtive, really. When I walked past him and looked at him, he wouldn't meet my eyes. Glanced away.'

He looked at Ash; the superintendent gave a small nod. It was Gibson, not that they'd ever really doubted it. The woman had been precise in her statement.

'What about his clothes?'

'He was wearing a rather battered overcoat and a scarf. He had a cap, but it was in his hands. The bare head was one reason I first noticed him.'

Of course. Almost every man wore a cap or a hat as habit. Not to do it was to stand out.

'Did you notice his shoes at all?' Ash said.

'Worn and dirty,' the woman answered. 'Honestly, at first I wondered if he was some sort of tramp.'

'What made you change your mind?'

'I'm not sure. There was something about him.' She thought for a moment. 'He seemed so intent.'

'Intent?'

'Peering around the corner to see the entrance to the depot here.' She turned to Harper. 'Is he dangerous?'

'You're safe enough, don't worry about that. What made you stop and watch him?'

'It was the second evening, when I saw him again. Since he looked suspicious, I thought I'd watch him for a few minutes.'

'You said he had a haversack.' Ash picked up the conversation.

'That's right.' She nodded. 'It was out of sight in the ginnel. He vanished and came back out with it on his shoulders. There was something wrapped that stuck out quite a way from it.'

'How long was he standing there that you saw?'

'Between five and ten minutes.' She held up her arm with its wristwatch.

'Which way did he go when he left?'

'Off towards Briggate.'

'Did he have a bicycle with him?'

The question took her by surprise. 'No, not that I saw. He was on foot.'

'You've been very helpful, Miss Naylor,' Harper told her and saw the blush rise up her face. 'We're grateful, believe me. Especially since you're very observant.'

'Thank you, Chief Constable. If there's anything else . . .'

'Then we'll be in touch. Thank you again.'

'Why?' Ash asked once she'd gone. 'What does Gibson want here?'

'I don't know. But it makes that first incident look more likely, doesn't it?' Harper said. A wild thought came. 'Do you think he wants to finish off what he started? A big fire here would certainly keep us busy. It would give him the chance to break into Gledhow Hall.'

But even as he spoke he knew it made no sense. It was too far away, a good three miles. He was trying to see inside Gibson's mind. And that was a place so dark and full of twists and corners he might never find his way out again. All the reasons could wait until they had the man in a cell.

'We'd better see if Walsh and Larkin have him yet,' Ash said. He opened a leather case, took out two Webley revolvers and handed one to Harper. 'I thought we'd better be prepared, too, sir.'

The gun felt heavy and awkward in his hand. He'd never liked weapons: a truncheon or the small cosh had always been enough for him, the way they should be for any copper. But times were changing; Gibson was armed and very, very dangerous. It was better to be careful.

He took a breath. 'Let's hope this is the end of it, shall we?'

Harper kept the pistol out of sight, buried in an overcoat pocket, his hand tight around the grip. It was already evening, workers streamed along the pavements as they headed to the trams and home.

He looked around, taking in everything. No sign of any man watching the entrance. They followed the road, pausing to peer down every ginnel they passed. Still nothing.

Harper felt too calm. His pulse should have been speeding, heart thumping as if someone was banging a drum, but there was nothing more than tension. Anticipation. And in the end, they reached Briggate without any sign of Gibson. Without a word, they turned and began to stroll back.

The sign high on the brick building read *Charles Walker & Co. Limited, Mill Furnishers*, the words picked out in white paint. Above it, a clock, all topped off proudly with *Established 1887*. Solid, firm, lasting. Now they were carrying on war work inside the walls, machines buzzing and hammering as Harper passed, the sounds beating against his poor ear.

Suddenly Ash began to run, haring off full pelt down Sovereign Street. All he could do was follow, dragging the gun from his pocket as he moved. A woman screamed.

Finally Ash slowed, then stopped, bent over with hands resting on his knees as he tried to catch his breath.

'Where did he go?'

'Over the Neville Street Bridge, sir.' A few words, then he inhaled again. 'He was well ahead of us when he saw me and took off. He'll have vanished into Holbeck now.'

They stayed for a minute, two men who were really too old to be chasing through the streets. Past their prime. There'd been a time when they could have given Gibson a good run, but those days had long since vanished.

'How would he know you were a copper?' Harper asked on the way back to the depot.

'Maybe he's seen me before, sir.'

'Did he have the haversack?'

'On his back, sir. And he was running like the hounds of hell were after him.'

Harper gave a grim smile. 'We were.'

At least they were if they'd been able to catch him. Gibson had a charmed life. He escaped bloody everything. He seemed to slide through everything almost unseen. Without Miss Naylor's good eyes they'd never have known he'd been down here.

'One thing, sir. He won't come back to the depot again.'

'No,' Harper agreed. 'But what was he doing here in the first place? What did he want? Let's have some men go through the place top to bottom. Anything that doesn't fit, I want to know.'

'I'll have a few uniforms start on it.'

'No. I want plain clothes.' They'd been promoted because they were sharper. 'And I want a thorough job.'

Walsh and Larkin were waiting by the doors. They'd been all around the streets but never spotted Gibson. Now the bastard had managed to escape again.

Harper felt like he was banging his head against a brick wall.

'He was by the clothing depot?' Brigadier Cox said in disbelief. 'My men never noticed him?'

'The only person who really noticed him was a secretary,' Harper said. 'She thought he looked suspicious and let us know.'

'What did he want there?'

'We're going over the depot inch by inch to see what we can find.' Harper ran a hand through his hair, noticing how thin it felt these days. 'Truth to tell, I'm blowed if I know what that can be.'

'What do you want me to do?' Cox asked.

'What you've been doing, sir,' Ash replied. The three of them sat together in Harper's office, the curtains drawn to keep out the night outside. 'We still believe he intends to go to Gledhow Hall.'

Cox nodded. 'What's happening with Corporal Openshaw?'

'He's at the infirmary,' Harper said. 'According to his doctor, he should be physically fit enough in a couple of days to go back to the place in Scotland where he'd been treated before for shell shock.'

'Craiglockhart.' Cox nodded. 'I went up there once. Visiting one of my chaps who was a patient. You wouldn't believe how bad some of the men are.'

'He'll be going by ambulance. I'd like a couple of your men to travel up with him,' Harper said.

'You don't think Gibson would try . . .?'

'No, sir,' Ash told him. 'He probably doesn't even know what's happened to Openshaw. We're simply trying to be prepared for every possibility.'

Harper saw Cox staring at him. 'How long before you arrest him, Tom?'

He let a few seconds pass before he answered. Nothing glib, no easy words. Just the truth. The man had soldiers out there, waiting to confront Gibson. He deserved to know.

'I really don't believe it can be long,' he said. 'But I don't know. I don't have a clue what's going on in Gibson's mind. He was over by Elland Road, nowhere near Gledhow Hall, then he was at the Olympia Works, which are almost next door to the hospital. Then he turns up at the clothing depot, just down the street from here. I can't make head nor tail of what he's trying to do, besides lead us a merry dance.'

'My men will be ready,' Cox promised.

'I hope so. One thing's certain: whatever he does, it's going to take us by surprise. He's been leading us by the nose.'

'At least no one else has died since you cut him off from Openshaw.'

'Yet,' Harper warned. 'Yet. I'm not going to breathe easy until we've got the handcuffs on him.'

'Or he's dead,' Cox said.

'Yes.' He let the word expand until it seemed to fill the room. 'Or he's dead.'

His head was pounding, a hammer banging against the inside of his skull. Every jolt, each tiny bump of the car went straight through him.

'Can you pull over?' he asked. 'I'd like to walk.'

'Sorry, sir,' Bingham told him. 'After what happened the other day, my orders are to stick with you until you're home.'

What? He didn't understand. 'Orders? Whose orders? I'm the chief constable, for God's sake.'

The man kept his eyes on the road. 'Superintendent Ash, sir.' A hesitation. 'He's made sure I'm armed, too. A revolver. Just in case.'

'When did that start?'

'Right after that man took the shot at you, sir.'

He wasn't ready to be mollycoddled and treated as if he couldn't look after himself. He'd been terrified after Gibson tried to kill him. Anyone would have been. It had faded – not gone, it was still bobbing around at the back of his mind. But it didn't fill his thoughts now. More than anything, he was glad that Annabelle forgot things so quickly. Not Mary, though. He couldn't miss the worry in her eyes every time he looked at her face.

A quiet evening. A constant undercurrent of noise from the bar downstairs that had been part of his life for decades now. Annabelle and Johanna busy with a jigsaw puzzle while he caught up with the *Evening Post*. Domestic, mundane. Satisfying, he thought as he spooned tea into the pot for a final cup.

'We're almost out,' he called.

'We go shopping tomorrow,' Johanna replied. 'We buy more then if there is any.'

He'd just placed the tray on the table when the telephone rang. His heart jumped. They'd caught Gibson. He held his breath and hoped.

'Harper.'

'Yes, sir.' The duty sergeant's voice was as flat and expressionless as ever. 'You wanted word about that ma—'

'Is he under arrest?'

'No, sir. He gunned down one of ours a few minutes ago.'

He tried to swallow but his throat was like a desert. 'How bad is he?'

'She, sir. One of the Voluntary Patrol girls. Up near the stadium in Headingley.'

Christ. Mary was on duty tonight. He glanced at the mirror. Annabelle was paying attention to the jigsaw pieces, not even listening to the call. Thank God for that.

'How bad?' he repeated.

'Not sure, sir. She's on her way to hospital.'

'Who is it?' He could barely bring himself to ask the question.

'I don't know, sir. I don't—'

'I want a car here. As soon as you can.'

'Very good, sir.'

A kiss for his wife, into his overcoat and waiting outside on the pavement. He shuffled from foot to foot. If he kept moving, the worst might not catch up with him. Trying not to imagine how bad it might be, but unable to keep it out of his head.

Mary shot, bleeding, lying on the pavement, on the table in the operating theatre.

He had the door open before the vehicle had come to a stop.

'Headingley,' he said. 'As fast as you can.'

There were scraps of traffic on the road, but the driver wove in and out, making time without ever seeming to go too fast.

Harper pressed his hands against the leather of the seats, scarcely seeing the streets pass. The bulk of the Webley weighed down his pocket.

St Michael's Lane, on the scrubby earth embankment behind the rugby ground. Six constables in their capes, bulls-eye torches lighting up a group of young women standing around a bench.

The moon was reflected in a pool of blood on the pavement. He felt bile rising into his throat and forced it back down.

Another woman sat apart, huddled over with her knees up, head in her hands. She had the Voluntary Patrol armband on her sleeve. Before Harper could reach her, Ash appeared out of the darkness and took hold of his arm.

'I came out as soon as I heard,' he said softly. 'It's not your Mary, sir.'

The relief flooded through him. She was safe. Thank God for that. Half a second and the guilt arrived. If it wasn't her, some other woman had been shot.

'Who?' The word came out as a croak.

'A woman called Jean Bascombe,' Ash told him. 'Married, in her thirties.'

'How bad?'

'Seems he caught her full blast with the first shot. Just came close, pulled the rifle from under his coat and fired. Less than five yards. They didn't have any chance to react. He tried to shoot again, but it jammed.' He nodded towards the girl. 'Just as well for her.'

'Gibson.'

'Not a scrap of doubt, sir.'

Harper looked around. Why this? Why *here*, for Christ's sake? That didn't make any sense. It was a good five miles from Gledhow Hall. This . . . it was pure slaughter. No rhyme or reason. 'You know what to do,' he said.

He squatted by the young woman, not saying a word until she raised her head to peer cautiously at him.

'I'm sorry, I don't know your name.'

'Miss Taylor,' she answered. 'Caroline Taylor.'

Even here she kept to the politeness she been taught when she was a child. She looked to be in her middle twenties, about the same age as Mary.

'I'm Chief Constable Harper.'

'I'm sorry, sir. I didn't recognize you.' She started to sit upright.

He laid his hand gently on her arm. 'No need.'

He spent ten minutes coaxing the words from her. How she and Mrs Bascombe had just talked to the girls at the bench, telling them to stop loitering and go home. They'd finished, strolling away, heads down as they chatted, when the man appeared from nowhere and brought out the gun.

'When he aimed it at me, I was sure I was going to die.' Her voice was oddly calm. 'The girls were screaming their heads off. Jean was already on the ground. Then it was silent, just for a moment. I heard him pull the trigger and then there was nothing. He tried again. After that, he ran off again. I tried to do what I could for Jean and I was blowing on my whistle.' She paused. 'As soon as the constables came, I started to cry. I felt so helpless. I'm sorry, sir.'

'It's fine,' he assured her. 'I'll find someone to take you home.'

She looked at him, questioning. 'But what about my statement?'

'In the morning,' Harper told her. 'That's soon enough.'

Ash had everything organized. A quick word to arrange transport for Miss Taylor. A doctor first, then home.

He stood by the car door. His breathing was back to normal, pulse down to where it should be. Mary hadn't been hurt. He could take comfort in that. But meanwhile, Gibson was still out there with his rifle. And there was Mrs Bascombe.

'Infirmary,' he told the driver.

The woman was stable. That was all the surgeon would say after Harper had waited an hour for him to come out of the operating theatre. He wasn't about to promise she'd recover completely, refused to say she might die. It didn't matter how much he pressed, the doctor remained evasive.

'The injuries could have been much worse, Chief Constable.' The man chose his words with care. 'I will tell you that much. None of the major organs were damaged.'

'But?'

'There's still so much that might happen. That's as much as I'm willing to say. It's late and I've been on my feet since seven this morning. Goodnight, Chief Constable.'

He was left alone in the corridor. Off in one of the wards someone screamed for a moment. Harper turned on his heel and left.

It was late, the pub dark when the car dropped him off outside the Victoria. Harper was just pulling out his keys when he felt someone close and turned. Oh, Christ, it was Gibson. Frantic, he fumbled with the lock, heart racing hoping he could reach safety in time.

'Da?'

He stopped, suddenly able to breathe again. Mary, home from patrol, safe and well.

'You'd better sit down,' he said once they were inside.

She gave him a frightened look. 'Why? What's happened. Is it something with my mam?'

'No. It's Jean Bascombe from the patrol. She's been shot.'

'But . . .' She sat, bewildered. 'I just saw her at the start of shift. How . . .?'

He explained. Her face turned a dead, pale white. She stared into space, and he knew what she was thinking: there but for the grace of God . . .

Behind the bar, he poured a small measure of brandy into a glass and watched as she drank. The colour began to return to her face.

'How is she?' she said, her face full of dread. 'I mean . . .'

'The surgeon wouldn't say. But from the way he was talking, she'll survive.'

They were speaking in urgent whispers, trying not to wake Annabelle.

'I should go to the hospital.'

'There's nothing you can do,' Harper told her. 'Chief Inspector Collins arrived before I left. Get some sleep first, then go tomorrow.'

'What about Caroline?'

'She was lucky.' As he explained, he saw the tears begin to roll down her cheeks. Harper passed her his handkerchief, watching as she swiped them away with wide, clumsy strokes. Exactly the way she'd done it when she was little, as if she couldn't wait to be rid of them.

'It was Gibson?' she asked.

'Yes. Miss Taylor described him.'

'Why?' She searched his face. 'Why would he do that?'

'I don't know.' That was all he could tell her. He didn't have an answer. Destruction? Confusion? He'd thought about it as the car returned from the hospital. Maybe they'd understand after they caught him.

TWENTY-SEVEN

Before eight o'clock, Harper strode out of the town hall, down the steps to Great George Street. It was a warmer day, with the first hint that winter wouldn't last forever.

He passed an invalided soldier. The man was hobbling around on crutches, with one leg missing above the knee, A cigarette dangled from his mouth and there was a look of fierce concentration on his face as he forced himself on.

Hard to believe that he was one of the lucky ones. He was still alive.

Mrs Bascombe was recovering on the women's surgical ward, behind screens and still sedated. Her husband was sitting on a chair in the corridor, a mousy little man in a faded pinstripe suit and carefully polished black shoes.

'I'm sorry,' Harper told him.

'She's going to be fine,' the man said. 'That's what the doctor told me. But it's going to take time.'

He had a high voice, so everything sounded like a whine. His worry seemed to fill the air. More than worry: fear.

'If there's anything we can do, please get in touch with my office.'

He'd known the ward sister since he'd been a detective sergeant. She made her nurses jump and obey, but she cared for her patients as if they were family.

'Just as well it was a bullet. If it had been shotgun pellets, she might well have died. It caught her above the hip. Plenty of fatty tissue and very little to damage.'

'I suppose that's something,' Harper said.

'It is. Believe me. We have so much packed under the skin that it's more like a miracle. Is her husband still outside?'

'Yes.'

'Can you do me a favour and ask him to go home? She'll be out for a while yet, and woozy when she comes to. Visiting's at two, he can come back then.'

Bascombe was reluctant to leave, but Harper stood his ground until the man walked softly away.

Openshaw was awake, sitting in a chair in his room. Mesh covered the inside of the window; no chance for him to give a repeat performance. His hands and wrists were heavily bandaged. The man didn't even glance up as Harper entered. He barely seemed aware of his surroundings.

'He'll be ready to travel tomorrow,' Dr Bishop said, and shook his head. 'He'd been making progress at Gledhow Hall, too. Now we're almost back to square one.'

He thought of the withdrawn, isolated man he'd seen, sitting and staring over the valley. Progress?

Miss Sharp came to her feet as he entered her office.

'The superintendent wants you. It's Gibson.'

He turned, dashing up the stairs as his footsteps echoed around the building. Harper patted the pocket of his overcoat. The revolver was still there, a comforting weight in his pocket.

'Where?'

'Spotted in Harehills, sir.' He was pulling on his coat and placing his old bowler hat on his head. He took out the gun and checked the bullets in the cylinder. 'We lost him, but our man doesn't think Gibson spotted him.'

'Heading towards Gledhow Hall?'

'Yes, sir. There's a car downstairs.'

'I'm coming with you.'

Ash could handle it all, he had no doubt about that. But this was the most important case in Leeds in years. Yet it didn't officially exist, and it would remain secret for decades to come. Tell that to the dead and the wounded.

But they were close to the end. He could feel it bubbling up inside him. Not long now. He was ready.

* * *

Harper didn't speak as the car sped up Roundhay Road. The churning of his own thoughts was quite enough. His throat was dry. They turned just before the Olympia Works, climbing steeply up Gledhow Wood Road, a straggle of stone buildings close to the top of the hill.

Then they were at the gatehouse to the hall. A pair of wary soldiers, rifles drawn, waved them down and checked their warrant cards.

'Any action?' Harper asked.

'No, sir,' the private replied. He was an older man, perhaps thirty-five, with deep-set eyes and a grizzled face. 'But I've just got a feeling, if you know what I mean. A niggle up my spine. Used to get it on the line when a raid was coming, too.'

'Pay attention to it. I think you're right.'

'I'll do that sir.' The man grinned as he saluted. Half his teeth were gone, the rest a deep, dirty brown.

They pulled up on the gravel in front of the building. Harper climbed out and breathed. Clean, clear air out here. The scent of earth and plants, loam and life. But there was an air of expectancy. The soldier standing outside the main door watched them carefully.

Gibson was coming. They all seemed to sense it.

'Sir?' Ash called, and he dragged himself away.

As he turned, a chill passed through him. No reason at all; there was no breeze, the day wasn't chilly. From nowhere, a phrase his mother used slipped into his mind: *Someone's walking over your grave.*

Christ, he hoped that wasn't true.

They stood upstairs, in Openshaw's old room. It smelled of paint and putty. New, shining glass in the window, fresh distemper on the walls to cover the blood. New linoleum on the floor, its pattern still sharp. It felt as if the man had never been here. Every trace of him had been erased. By evening there would be another patient in this bed, sitting in this chair. For now it was a good place to keep watch. High enough to offer a view of the valley, with the lake glistening at the bottom.

Five minutes, and they couldn't see a thing stirring. The hillside was a tangle of bushes and branches and tall grass. Paths cut through it all where hundreds of feet had left their tracks.

'Nothing,' Ash said.

'He's coming.' He knew it, as certain as tomorrow. Gibson was on his way.

'We might as well go back down, sir. The army has professionals keeping watch. They'll spot him long before we do.'

Commandant Cliff's door was closed, he noticed as they passed. But he had no doubt she was in her office, disapproving of all the men tramping around her hospital.

The patients had all been gently ushered inside, bemused men in their blue jackets with white facings, looking at him with hopeless eyes.

Ten minutes and the first shout went up. Harper picked out a faint sound at the edge of his hearing; Ash was already moving.

'Which way?' Harper asked.

'Down the hill, sir. Towards the lake.'

They stopped at the edge of the terrace, pistols drawn. It would be dangerous to go further. They'd be flailing through the undergrowth, at risk of crashing into the waiting soldiers. Let the men do their jobs, he thought. A little patience and they'd have Gibson.

He felt the weight of the gun in his hand and looked down at it in surprise, not sure how it had ended up there. He had no memory of pulling it from his pocket.

Another sound, from a different direction. The report of a rifle. Where was he?

'What's he doing?'

'Can't tell, sir. It might be the soldiers popping off at shadows.'

Harper tried to swallow. His throat felt dry as a desert.

Another sound. A third direction.

'What—' Ash began, but something scurrying through the grass stopped him. Harper caught sight of a bushy tail. A fox, sprinting towards safety.

Harper had barely moved, but he was breathing as hard as if he'd just finished the hundred yards dash.

'The army men are jumpy,' Ash said. He peered into the distance. 'That's the only explanation. Gibson can't be in three places at once.'

Another shout, then a volley of shots from the bottom of the valley, close to the lake. He could see smoke start to drift upwards, but nothing more.

Ash took a pace forward, but Harper pulled him back.

'We're more use here.' In case Gibson made his way through the defences.

More shots. But no cries of victory and nobody yelling out in pain. They were firing, but they weren't hitting him. He was still coming.

Harper's hand was sweaty, the Webley sliding a little in his grip. He wiped his palm on his coat, never taking his eyes off the valley.

A few seconds of silence stretched out. It became a minute, two, five. They stood on the terrace, still watching, not exchanging a word.

Had Gibson been chased away? Had he retreated? No. He was still in the woods. It had taken him long enough to come this far, he wasn't about to go back now. This was his do or die mission. Gibson believed Openshaw was still a patient in the hall and he was coming to free him.

'Come with me.'

He led the way back into the building, taking the stairs at a fast clip, then along the landing to Openshaw's room.

'We'll wait inside.'

Ash raised his eyebrows as he lowered his bulk on to the chair. 'It's all going to happen out there, sir.'

'I hope it will,' Harper said. 'And there are plenty of younger men who are a damned sight better prepared to deal with it than us. We're the last line. If he makes it into the hospital and up here, we'll be the ones waiting for him.'

'If you say so, sir.' He sounded doubtful. Resentful. He wanted to be close to the action.

'I do.'

With the door closed, there was nothing to do but sit and wait. No more shooting from outside. Not even a yell, from the little he could hear. Every time he imagined he heard a sound, Harper looked up, only for Ash to shake his head.

Ten minutes passed . . . a quarter of an hour.

'He's gone, sir.' The superintendent started to rise from his chair. 'He must have.'

'He's still around.' He'd never felt more certain of anything in his life. 'And he's coming closer. Just be ready.'

His heartbeat was steady. His pulse even, not too quick. He was prepared. Harper lifted the revolver and checked the ammunition once again. A bullet in every chamber and the safety catch was off.

Ash stared straight ahead, not looking at anything at all. He knew the man was listening, alert for the slightest noise that could mean trouble.

Then it came, muffled and distant. Two blasts from a rifle. A gap, the sudden absence of sound, then a third and someone cried out again and again. Eventually, over a minute that seemed to last an hour, it faded to nothing.

Harper didn't move. There was nothing he could do to help. He hoped Gibson wouldn't break through and make it into the hall. But if he did, he'd find a surprise.

'We're cowering in here, sir.'

'No, we're not.' He didn't have the slightest doubt. 'We're doing exactly the right thing.'

Another shot, this one closer, louder. They hadn't killed Gibson yet. God only knew what possessed the man, but it was keeping him alive. Seconds passed, each one longer than the last.

Something inside the hall. A noise he didn't recognize. A soft gurgle.

Ash sat upright. The pistol seemed small in his large hand. He'd be directly in the line of fire when the door opened.

'Move.' Harper hissed the word, but the man didn't budge an inch. He raised the pistol, prepared.

Someone was out there, but Harper's hearing was too poor to pick out any sound. He swallowed and stood. He was hidden from sight, over in the corner and against the wall.

Suddenly, the handle turned and the door crashed open.

'Jimmy. I—'

Two shots, almost together. From the corner of his eye, he saw Ash slump to the ground. Without even thinking, Harper fired into the door. Four bullets, one right after the other. Then he heard the footsteps tearing down the hall and the stairs.

Chase? Stay? It wasn't even a question.

He knelt by Ash, ripping the buttons off his coat to open it. The bullet had caught him in the stomach, blood seeping out, a stain across his clothes and on to the floor. He was unconscious. Every breath came wheezing and painful. But he was alive. Thank Christ for that.

Out on the landing, Harper bellowed for a nurse. Somewhere in the distance he heard rifles firing.

'Up here!' he yelled again. 'We need a nurse up here.'

Commandant Cliff came running up the stairs, a first aid kit in her arms, another nurse following her. They pushed past him and set to work. Not a word wasted, hands moving quickly and surely.

Miss Cliff turned her head. 'Leave us to do our job, Chief Constable. You go and do yours.'

He stared down at Ash's face. No sign of anything. 'Is he going to live?'

'I don't allow my patients to die.' Her voice was so firm, so sure, that he had to believe her as he turned away.

He had to put it out of his mind. Only one thing could matter: catching Gibson.

Take his revenge.

A thin trail of blood snaked across the floor and he followed it all the way to the front door. He'd wounded the man. But how badly?

Just inside the door, Harper reloaded the revolver. The cartridges stank of cordite. He fumbled with them, dropping some on the tiles, picking them up with fingers that didn't want to obey him, then fitting them in the chamber. He clicked the cylinder home.

Ready.

The army sergeant on the terrace brought up his rifle as soon as he heard Harper's footsteps.

'Police.' He raised his arms. 'Where did he go?'

He pointed towards the lake. 'Down there somewhere.'

Harper took a breath, scared to ask the question. But he needed to know. 'Has he killed anyone?'

The man shook his head slowly, never shifting his gaze away from the woods. 'Not yet, thank God. We're just bloody lucky the bastard can't shoot straight.' He realized what he'd said. 'Sorry, sir.'

'No need,' Harper told him.

'He still managed to wound three of my lads. The medics are looking after them.'

Harper glanced back towards the hall. 'He got one of mine, too. Is he still armed?'

'He is.'

A nod to the soldier and he began to walk. The ground was dry, hard and unforgiving under the soles of his feet.

'Watch yourself,' the soldier called. 'My men are still down there. A few of yours, too. Right now they're likely to shoot first.'

He gave a wave and carried on, one step after another.

The hill was steeper than he'd expected. Twice he almost slipped, grabbing for low branches to steady himself. A perfect target for anyone wanting to fire. He moved from tree to tree, looking for cover and trying to keep quiet. But that was a hopeless task. He might as well have sent up a flare to show his position.

Finally Harper reached the path. The water lay a few yards away, still and grey. Before he could catch his breath, a soldier appeared beside him.

'Copper?' he asked. The sneer on his face showed he wasn't impressed.

'Yes.'

'He's gone that way.' He pointed along the valley. 'We have men at the far end, he's not going to get out. We're here to stop him if he tries to double back. You'd do best to stay here with us and wait.'

Harper smiled. 'I daresay you're right.'

'We've got tea in a billycan,' he offered.

He shook his head and carried on walking.

The woods were quiet. The trees were spread apart, trunks tall and straight. Roots extended like veins bulging up through the ground. Suddenly something moved at the edge of his sight. He turned, raising the revolver and starting to squeeze the trigger.

Only a squirrel. For Christ's sake.

Harper stopped. He felt clammy sweat on his forehead. His heart was beating so fast he felt it might explode.

Look at yourself, he thought. Revenge? You're knocking on the door of sixty and you still want to prove yourself, to show that you're a man. Grow up. You're not a youngster any more. You've got a wife at home who's going to need you more and more. A daughter who's already lost one man from her life. You don't need to prove a single damned thing. There's already a sign with Acting Chief Constable and your name underneath on a door in the town hall. Don't be a bloody idiot. Go back. Have a mug of tea from that billy. Follow the ambulance to the infirmary and keep vigil on Ash. He means a damned sight more to you than Gibson.

Yes.

The shot hit the ground a good five yards away, sending up a wild spray of dirt. A flurry of birds squawked and rose up from the branches with a racket of wings.

It hadn't landed near enough to do any damage. But far too close for comfort. For a split second he was too stunned to react. Then the terror arrived. The urge to survive. Hunched over, trying to make himself small, Harper dashed for the cover of a bush, holding his breath and expecting a second bullet any moment.

Nothing came.

Christ, he'd been stupid to come out here. To imagine he was a big enough man to bring Gibson down. Now he was going to pay for his arrogance.

He studied the landscape. The man must have fired from a clump of undergrowth about fifty yards ahead. Too far for a pistol, but he still took aim and pulled the trigger.

Harper dropped to the ground and crawled ten yards through the tall grass to the safety of a broad tree trunk. He was breathing so loud they must have been able to hear it in the city centre.

Gibson fired a round at the place where he'd been. Wild, high, whining through the branches.

Still panting, Harper glanced around, quickly taking stock of the cover. Not as much as he'd like. Gibson had the best of it, well hidden from sight.

A small building stood in the distance. Squat, surrounded by a wall of dressed stone. He remembered seeing it on the map. A well or a spa of some—

The rifle cracked again. Without thinking, he ducked his head and tried to burrow into the ground. But he was safe. Gibson was still firing where he'd been.

A crackle of leaves. The man was running. No, not a run. Harper could see him now. Gibson was hobbling fast and favouring his left leg. That must have been where Harper had wounded him in the hall. It felt like another age. Ash . . .

Gibson had slung the rifle over his back, his body hunched down. Harper raised the revolver and took aim.

No hope of hitting him. Still worth a bullet to scare him. Gibson sped up, half-tripping over a tree root before he recovered his balance and limped on.

Very cautiously, Harper began to follow. Not a straight path, but scuttling from cover to cover. Every second in the open, his heart was in his mouth. With each step he anticipated the report of Gibson's gun.

But all his weak ears could hear were the sounds of the wood and his own footsteps.

He crouched behind an oak, feeling the rough bark under his palm and wishing he had a canteen of water as a volley of shots exploded.

Gibson must have tried to break out at the end of the valley and the guards had opened fire.

He watched, utterly still. Eyes alert for the smallest movement. For a long, slow minute there was nothing.

Then Gibson was there. He was dragging his leg across the ground, grimacing with the effort and clutching his left arm. Desperate, the man looked around and lurched towards the well.

Once he was inside, he would be secure. The wall was the height of a man. Only one way in or out.

Harper lifted the Webley. It was steady in his hand, seemed to weigh nothing. He sighted along the barrel. He'd need the devil's own luck to hit from this range. Scaring Gibson would be enough.

Slow pressure on the trigger. Breathing out, the way he'd been taught. Then the recoil, his wrist jarring.

Gibson tumbled to the ground and crawled through the doorway into the well. Out of sight. And safe. For now, at least.

Harper sat, his back against a tree trunk, and closed his eyes for a second. The moment passed. He dug in his jacket pocket until he found his police whistle, brushed the dirt from it and started to blow.

Cox was directing the troops. Gibson didn't have a hope in hell of escape.

Harper gulped down water from a private's canteen as though he hadn't drunk in a week. From his own squad, Walsh and Larkin had arrived.

'What—' Harper began, but Walsh was already speaking.

'The super's having emergency surgery, sir. The bullet tore up his stomach. We're here, Fenton's waiting at the office and Dixon's over at the infirmary.'

I should be there, too, Harper thought. Down in the waiting room, saying prayers and hoping.

'You go, sir,' Walsh told him. 'The car's waiting up at the hall. We can finish this. It shouldn't take long now.'

'Gibson's penned in, Tom,' the brigadier agreed.

'He's right, sir. All over bar the shouting.'

They were right. Harper knew it. Time to go to the infirmary. But before he left, there was one final thing. He needed to do this, to try and end it without any more blood. He took two paces forward and drew in a deep breath.

'This is Chief Constable Harper. You don't have any way out of here. Put down the rifle and give up. No one will shoot. I'll give you my word on that. I'll make sure you have whatever medical help you need and you'll receive a fair trial.'

He'd made his offer. It was the best he could do.

Harper waited, staring at the doorway. All shadow and darkness. Nothing moving. Five seconds passed, then ten. No reply.

At least he'd tried. If Gibson wanted to die, that was his choice. He turned away.

Then a voice.

'I'll give myself up.' He sounded exhausted, as if living was too much for him. 'But I want you to come in here. I want to talk to you alone before I come out.'

Brigadier Cox was shaking his head.

Walsh stared. 'Don't, sir.'

'Throw your weapon out,' Harper shouted. 'Then I'll come in.'

The sound of a rifle bolt being drawn back, and the soldiers all took aim on the doorway. The Lee Enfield arced through the air and bounced twice on the ground, a short echo of metal where the barrel struck a rock.

'We'll go in and get him now,' Cox said, raising his hand to signal to his men.

Harper shook his head. 'He did what he promised. Now I have to keep my word.'

'Sir—' Walsh began, but Harper cut him off.

'Five minutes.'

'I don't like it, sir.'

'Neither do I, Tom,' the brigadier agreed. 'Gibson's sly. I wouldn't trust him an inch.'

'I'll give him a chance.' The Webley was in his hand. 'I have this if he tries anything. Five minutes.' He gave a cheerless smile. 'If I'm not out by then, come in and shoot him.'

He walked, eyes on the doorway, finger on the trigger. Alert for the smallest movement.

It was a small room. Flagstone floor, scattered with dead leaves. An empty fireplace in the corner. Light filtered down where slates were missing from the roof.

But no Gibson.

'Out here.'

A door to the side led to a pool with steps going down into the dark, slimy water. Out in the open air, protected by the wall. A stone path surrounded the pool. Gibson stood there, no more than six feet away, cradling his cap in his hands.

He looked too ordinary to have caused all the damage and death, Harper thought. Pale skin, in need of a shave. His eyes were a faint, distant blue, his hair blond stubble on his scalp.

Burrs and rips on his overcoat, knees covered with dirt where he'd stumbled and fallen. Boots dusty and worn. Blood on his trouser leg.

Gibson nodded at the gun. 'Going to shoot me now?'

'Not unless I have to.'

'I threw out the rifle, just like you asked.'

'Why do you want in here?' Harper asked.

'To make sure I stay safe.' Gibson's voice had a soft, surprising warmth. 'I don't want them shooting me when I go out.'

'You'll stand trial.'

'I never shot anyone. That was Jimmy.'

'With you directing him. Telling him where to aim. The spotter and the sniper. Openshaw trusted you. He had no idea what he was doing.'

Gibson shrugged. 'Prove that.'

'He must have realized. He tried to kill himself.'

'Did he?' The man sounded suddenly hopeful. 'Did he manage it?' 'No.'

'Pity. If he'd succeeded, all the pain would be gone now.'

'Why did you do it?'

This was the question he'd come to ask, the only answer he wanted.

'You haven't been out there, have you?' For a moment, he could see the contempt broad on Gibson's face.

'Look at me,' Harper said. 'I'm too old.'

'Count yourself lucky. We rotted in those trenches. Water up to our ankles every day so you get a fungus on your feet. Lice every-where. When the Hun starts a barrage, it seems like the world was going to blow apart.'

'You were buried by a shell.'

'Me and Jimmy and Fergus.' Something changed in the way he spoke. Flatter. Colder. Bitter. 'They sent us to try and take out a couple of their snipers who'd been doing some damage. We'd just got settled in when our side started lobbing shells at their line. It was pointless us being there. No German was going to show his head when that was going on. The usual cock-up. Then one came down so close that it tore Fergus apart, poor bastard. Me and Jimmy were buried in the mud. Could hardly breathe. I kept hold of his hand. We thought we were gone.'

'But they dug you out.'

He snorted. 'Eventually. We were both covered in mud and in Fergus. He was in our hair, on our skin. I've never been able to scrub him off. Not completely. Jimmy . . . did you talk to him at all?'

'I tried.'

A nod. 'It affected him worse than me. They sent him off to try and treat him. I was the only one he'd trust.'

'And what about you?'

'Me?' Gibson snorted. 'I never let things show. I made them think I was getting better.'

'Now you're taking your revenge.'

'Why not?' He shrugged. 'The army didn't give a toss about us. The people over here don't bloody care what it's like for the Tommies. Give them a taste of their own medicine.'

'You used Openshaw.'

'He was just happy to be with me and take one of our little outings together. He didn't know what he was doing.'

'You made him into a murderer.'

A shake of the head. 'We were already murderers. The army trained us for it. It was what we did. I picked out the targets. Jimmy and Fergus killed them.'

Harper saw Gibson coming closer. A small shuffle of the feet, narrowing the distance inch by inch. Hands still hidden by that cap.

Four feet away now. Too close for comfort. He edged backwards until he stood in the doorway to the pool, the room behind him.

'What about the clothing depot? Right at the beginning. The newspaper and the matches.'

The man frowned. 'That wasn't me. I started the fires at the Olympia Works, but that's all.'

Maybe they'd never know the truth of it, Harper thought. Perhaps there was no truth to know, just someone's imagination.

'I told them I'd give you five minutes,' he said. 'You've had that. It's time to go now.'

Gibson shook his head. 'I'm not going anywhere.' He dropped the cap, showing the bright metal blade of a knife. 'It's not a bayonet, but it can still kill you. Chief Constable murdered: you won't be able keep that out of the papers.'

Harper raised the pistol. His arm was steady. It was impossible to miss from here.

'Go on.' Gibson taunted him, raising his arms wide. 'It's easy to do. Get rid of me. I don't care, I'm dead either way. You never know, you might get a taste for it.'

'We're leaving. You're going to stand trial.'

'No.'

'My superintendent is in surgery right now – the man you shot less than an hour ago. Three others are dead. Then there are the wounded. It was your idea. You orchestrated it all. And you're going to take responsibility.'

Gibson smiled. 'No, I'm not.'

He lunged forward. Harper pulled the trigger once, twice, and saw the blood burst out of Gibson's chest. He fell sideways, splashing into the water.

Dead before he landed. A red stain billowing around him.

Harper stared down at the body. Gibson had got exactly the death he wanted.

He was aware of people. Cox, with his pistol drawn, gently lifting the Webley from his grasp. Walsh, taking him by the arm and leading him outside, where the air didn't stink of cordite.

Somewhere high above, a bird sang and another replied. There was life out here. Harper closed his eyes for a moment. No, he'd never acquire a taste for killing. He'd had to do it before and he hoped he'd never be forced to do it again.

'Send word back to the hall,' he ordered. 'The bobbies can go back to their regular duties. And ask the driver to pick me up on Roundhay Road. It's closer than climbing all the way back up there.'

TWENTY-EIGHT

Dixon sat staring at the floor, elbows resting on his knees as he smoked a Capstan. He glanced up as Harper entered; out of habit he tried to hide his cigarette.

'Any word?'

'Still in there, sir.' A door led through to the operating theatres.

On the chair beside him, Nancy Ash stared up at him hopefully. She was small and round, with grey hair and frightened eyes.

Harper took her hands. 'I'm sure he'll be fine. You know he's made of iron.'

He tried to give an encouraging smile, but she didn't believe it.

'What happened with Gibson, sir?' Dixon asked.

'No need to worry about him now.'

He didn't want to say more. It would be all over the force tomorrow, probably all manner of bloody stories. Sitting in the back of the car as the driver sped through Harehills, he'd pulled out his pocket watch. Not even two o'clock. He felt as if the day had lasted forever while also passing in a blur. How was that possible?

He was drained. Nothing left. He sat and leaned his head back against the wall. Cool, solid. All he really wanted was to go home and sleep for twelve hours.

'I can get you a cup of tea, sir,' Dixon said. 'You look parched.'

'That would go down a treat,' Harper agreed. 'Something to eat, too, if they have it. Nancy?'

She shook her head. No wish to talk, lost in her own prayers, making bargains with God for her husband's life.

After a while, he paced the room, pausing to peer at the door, willing the surgeon to appear with good news. But there was only the sound of his own footsteps and the echo of Gibson falling into the pool at the well. The way the patch of red spread across the surface of the well and the report of the pistol filled his brain. He'd killed a man. It was that or die, he knew. But he'd seen the light leave Gibson's eyes. He'd need to live with that.

Every muscle ached as he moved. He could smell the gunpowder on himself, see the dirt smeared on his suit. His nerves were screaming for somewhere quiet. But he had to be here. He was responsible for all this. It was his vigil to keep.

Harper saved the city the cost of a trial and a hanging. This way it was easier to keep everything secret. That was how the council would view things. Gibson would have dangled from the end of a rope in Armley gaol, but justice would have come from a judge and jury, not from the barrel of a gun.

They'd been sitting for almost an hour when the surgeon bustled out, taking off his spectacles and rubbing his eyes.

Harper was already on his feet, Dixon beside him. Suddenly he was alert again – all the weariness had dropped away. But the doctor ignored them, going over to Mrs Ash.

'He's going to live.'

The terror fell from her face and she looked ten years younger. 'How . . .?' she began.

'Your husband will be recovering for a long time.' He spoke slowly, as if he was addressing a child. 'What kind of work does he do?'

'He's a police superintendent,' Harper said.

The surgeon nodded and spoke to Nancy Ash again. 'There's no question of him continuing in that. He's going to need months of care at home once he's out of here. I'm sure you'll be able to manage that.'

Harper thought of her, starting her job as a bus conductress. All that independence was snatched away from her now.

'Yes,' she replied. 'Of course.'

'You might as well go home for now. It'll be a while before he comes round and then he'll need plenty of rest before he has any visitors. You can see him tomorrow.'

A small bow and he hurried away again. Harper followed into the corridor.

'The superintendent . . .'

'Who are you?' The surgeon looked him up and down, not impressed by what he saw. Patches of dirt on his clothes, the smell of cordite clinging to his coat. A face so weary his skin was probably like parchment.

'I'm the chief constable.'

'I see. Well, you heard what I said. He can't do a policeman's work any more. He was lucky. We've learned so many surgical techniques since this war began. Without them, I'm not sure we'd have been able to save him.'

'How bad will he be?'

'He'll still be able to talk and think perfectly normally, if that's what you mean,' the surgeon answered. 'Everything is fine there. He's always going to be short of breath, and he'll need a stick to get around slowly. Now, if you'll excuse me . . .'

And he was gone.

Harper stood, letting the sounds and scents of the hospital rise around him.

*   *   *

It was done. Ash was going to live. Now he could go home, after a stop at the office. He wasn't even through the door before Miss Sharp said, 'I've been ringing everywhere to try and find you.'

'Why? What's happened?'

'Your daughter's been trying to get hold of you.'

His pulse started racing. Something had happened to Annabelle. It had to be. He felt the world slip away from under him.

'When did she ring?'

'Started at noon. Five times since then. I tried you at Gledhow Hall but they didn't—'

'Where was she?'

'Home, she said.'

Harper heard it ring and ring, urging someone to pick up. *Come on.* He could scarcely breathe, hardly stand.

Let her be all right. Please God, let her be all right.

'Da?' Mary's voice was frantic.

'What's happened to your mother?'

'She's gone missing.' Her voice was so tense, so brittle it might crack. 'Johanna says it happened about half past eleven. We've been looking everywhere.'

'I'm on my way.' He replaced the receiver and took a deep breath, feeling his heart slamming against his chest.

'I need my car,' he told Miss Sharp. 'Immediately.'

'Is there anything I can do?'

'Keep telephoning the infirmary to find out how Superintendent Ash is.'

'What . . .' she began, but he was already hurrying down the stairs, cutting around clerks who dawdled, willing everyone out of the way.

It took too long for Bingham to arrive. Time enough to imagine everything bad that could have happened to Annabelle.

He pulled the door open before the vehicle had come to a stop. 'The Victoria. Fast as you can manage.'

'We've been all over Sheepscar.' Mary paced around the living room, picking up small objects – a bird feather, a decorated china jar – then putting them down again. 'Johanna was in the kitchen, making a cup of tea. She's done it a thousand times before. When she came out, my mam was gone. Took her coat and hat from the hook.'

'How far have you looked?' Harper asked. He was wound too

tight, feeling as if his nerves were on top of his skin and the world was rubbing against them.

'All the way down to Skinner Lane and up past Roseville Road. Johanna went searching. When she couldn't find her, she tried to ring you. You weren't there, so she telephoned me.' She looked up, not even trying to blink back the tears. 'I don't know where else she could be.'

His mind tried to conjure up places she might go.

'Who's out now?'

'Johanna and Jaak. Those two bobbies from the little sub-station across the road. Mr Harris from Manor Street and his son. They asked me to stay here and pass on messages and be around in case she came back of her own accord. I don't know what to do, Da.'

He drew her close, feeling her shudder and cry, her fists banging against his back as she let out her fears. For a minute, the competent, brisk young woman was a little girl again.

'I don't think your mother's going to come walking through that door by herself,' he said when she'd pulled away, wiped her eyes and blown her nose.

'No,' Mary agreed.

Harper picked up a photograph of Annabelle and pushed it into his pocket. 'Come with me.'

She was still pulling on her coat and crushing her hat down on her head as he opened the car door.

'Do you know Leather Street?' he asked the driver.

'I do, sir. Up on the Bank.'

'There. And wait for me.'

It was a gamble. But Annabelle had grown up there. And lately, when she'd vanished inside herself, she'd sometimes gone back there. Old neighbours, childhood Saturday nights, mistaking him for her father. Maybe her feet had carried her over that way.

If Annabelle had still been in Sheepscar, they'd have found her. Too many people there knew her face. They'd have taken her in or helped her back to the pub. Word would have passed.

Mary gazed out of the window, fists clenched tight. She was hoping one of the faces they passed belonged to her mother.

Motor cars were an unusual sight up on the Bank. As they pulled to a stop, boys and girls crowded around. They should all have been in school, but who was going to force them? Their parents were in the forces, or working all hours just to keep them alive.

All around, the decaying, hopeless smell of poverty. The children were hungry. Hollow cheeks, legs bandy from rickets. Sallow faces.

But they were here, and he could use them. Harper took out the picture of Annabelle and held it up so they could all see it.

'Have you seen this lady?'

They craned their necks. Most of them shook their heads. A couple smirked and started to say something until they saw his face.

'Anyone?' He was beginning to feel desperate. Had he judged it wrong? Had Annabelle gone somewhere else? Was she was lost in Leeds?

A girl at the back of the group was staring intently at the photograph. She was ragged, the pattern long faded on her cotton dress. No stockings even in the winter weather.

Mary had already noticed her. She edged around and whispered in her ear. A couple of seconds and they were talking. The girl pointed up the hill as she spoke. Mary slipped the girl a half-crown, probably more money than she'd ever held in her life. His daughter looked at him and began to run.

'If you spot this woman, tell me immediately,' Harper told the children. 'There's a reward.'

He hurried after Mary. Not a chance of keeping up. She was too young, too fit, and after the morning he was hollowed out. The report of the Webley kept echoing through his mind. Only love and fear were keeping him upright.

It was a bleak area. Houses black with soot. Weeds poking up through the cracks on paving stones. Cobbles missing in the roads. Glancing down the hill he could see the roof of the old Black Dog Mill. Annabelle's mother had worked there; that was what she'd said. Maybe . . .

He turned off down Bow Street, showed the photograph to the women gossiping on the doorsteps. None of them had seen his wife.

The panic was tightening his grip. Under the skin, his stomach was clenched. His head ached.

No Annabelle by the mill. He scrambled up the hill, as fast as he could, back to Leather Street, then rushing along Tab Street towards St Mary's.

She was sitting on the steps outside the big wooden door, gazing up at the sky with wonder. Safe, as far as he could see. She was wearing a black woollen coat, the dark blue hat she loved with its wide brim, handbag clutched primly in her lap.

As soon as he saw her, he slowed, trying to calm his breathing. Strolling with his hands in his pockets as he approached. She turned her head as he approached and gave a bright, childish smile.

'I thought I'd meet you coming home from work, Da.'

For a moment he believed his heart would break. But he'd found her and she was unharmed. That was all that really mattered. Harper reached out a hand, helping her to stand. They ambled along the pavement.

'What did you do today?' he asked.

'After school me and Mary went to her house, then down by the gardens to watch them digging. She wanted to go and make daisy chains, but I told her there weren't any daisies yet.'

'You're right. Later in the year,' he said.

They swung their arms as they walked. She was completely content. On Leather Street he turned towards the car. Mary was standing, hands on her hips, watching them.

'Look! Me mam's here, too!' Annabelle sounded delighted.

She was wary of the car at first, but as soon as it moved off she was staring out of the windows, a little child eagerly pointing out this street and that.

By the time they parked behind the Victoria she'd settled a little.

'Go in through the back,' Harper said to Mary. She led her mother through the tall gate and into the yard. He waited until they'd gone and leaned into the car to talk to Bingham.

'I'd appreciate it if you didn't say anything about this.'

The man's face was serious. 'Not a word, sir. I promise. It happened to my aunt. I'm sorry it's . . .' He couldn't find the words to complete the sentence. But how could you? Harper thought. Not when it was someone still as young as Annabelle.

'We'll manage. But I'd prefer it to stay private.'

'You can count on me, sir.'

'Thank you.'

Mary was bustling around. Coats and hats on the pegs. Annabelle looked around the parlour as if she was a visitor who'd never been here before. At some point this might happen and her mind would never return. It would all be a mystery to her, all new. But not today, please. He couldn't take anything more today.

The daughter was being the mother, disappearing into the kitchen to make a pot of tea. Harper sat beside his wife, took out the photograph of her and placed it in her hands.

'It's a good likeness of me mother,' she said. Her fingertips traced the outline of the face and hair. 'Have you shown it to her yet? She'll be over the moon when she sees it.'

'Sees what?' Mary asked as she appeared with a tray.

'This picture of you. Whoever did it really caught you.'

He had to walk away. He wanted to be there, to hear her voice, to see her face. But not like this. Not now. On top of everything else that had happened, it was too much. The slightest pull and he might snap.

The Palmaers saved him. They burst through the door. Johanna spotted Annabelle and rushed to her, full of apologies and questions.

Jaak stood, large, solid. 'We are sorry.'

'No harm done,' Harper told him. A glance back over his shoulder. The women were tending to his wife. 'I have to go.'

Morning. He'd slept deep and long, Annabelle beside him in the bed. He could have rested longer; a week off might help. But there was no chance of that. He'd have to press on, the same as everyone else.

'Was everything all right?' Miss Sharp asked. She studied his face.

'For now,' he answered after a second. 'Have you rung the infirmary today?'

'All they would tell me was that he's in a bad way, but he's resting.' She shook her head slightly, as if she couldn't believe it all. 'Inspector Walsh told me what happened.'

'Yes.' He couldn't summon up more than that. Ash with the wound in his belly. Gibson's body falling into the water . . .

She'd started to go through the list she'd written on a pad. 'Councillor Walton from the watch committee wants to speak to you. So does Councillor Thompson.'

'They'll have to wait.'

'Brigadier Cox rang.'

'I need to go upstairs. I'll try him from there. Anything else?'

'Nothing important.'

The workmen in their buff shop coats were already removing the tables and chairs and filing cabinets from the squad room. A few more minutes and it would return to being the chief constable's office.

Walsh and Fenton were packing files into a wooden tea chest.

'Anything more about the super, sir?'

'Holding his own.' He sat behind the desk, Ash's place since it all began. His now. He'd need to become used to that, at least until they found someone permanent as chief constable. 'You'll need my statement.'

'When you're ready, sir,' Fenton told him. 'There's no rush.'

'Later today,' Harper said.

Five minutes and they'd gone. A few more and everything was back the way it had been.

Harper ran a hand through his hair and picked up the telephone. 'Carlton Barracks, please.'

A simple conversation, just dotting the i's and crossing the t's. He turned off the electric light and closed the door. Tomorrow would be soon enough to start up here.

Harper looked at the plate by the door and ran a hand over his name. Acting Chief Constable. Who'd have ever thought that?

He heard the voice as he approached Miss Sharp's office. A man, pleasant but insistent. He didn't want to see anyone from outside. It didn't matter who they were.

Especially this one. Sir Richard James gave his slick smile as soon as he saw Harper.

'I heard what happened, Chief Constable. I just wanted to offer my congratulations.'

He came forward, hand extended. Harper ignored it.

'That's very kind of you, but we have work to do here. And there's something else. You might not be aware of it, sir, but attempting to bribe a police officer is an offence that can put you in jail.'

'I—' James began.

'Given that, you can see why we'll be keeping an eye on you in the future.'

It was all he needed to say, staring until the man stalked away, slamming the door behind him.

Miss Sharp raised her eyebrows. 'You've just made an enemy who has some very important contacts. Are you sure that's wise?'

She was probably right. At the moment, though, he was beyond caring. 'At least I can live with myself. Have the driver pick me up at the infirmary in an hour, will you? And starting tomorrow, we're upstairs.'

She smiled. 'Very good . . . Chief Constable.'

No change. No doctor or nurse who was willing to say much. Simply wait and see. He'd stood here often enough before with lives in the balance. This was different. Ash was more than another copper. He was . . . as close to a friend as anything else. They'd always understood each other. Something like that struck deep. And there wasn't a damned thing he could do to help. He was here in this waiting room, completely impotent. Ash would survive. At least there was that.

All he had was hope. And that had been in precious short supply these last few years.

'How was she today?'

'Quiet, Johanna said.' Mary leaned back against the sink in the kitchen, cradling a mug of tea, looking as exhausted as he felt. 'She didn't remember anything about yesterday.'

'Maybe that's a blessing.'

Mary turned her head, staring out of the window. 'I mentioned Leather Street, just to see. She looked at me and said, "I worked half my life to leave that place. Why would I want to go back?"'

He sighed. 'There's going to be more of this, and worse.'

'A plan,' she said. 'And we need it very soon, Da.'

TWENTY-NINE

June 1917

A warm day for a ceremony. Even worse when he was crammed into a uniform, the cap tight against his forehead. Tom Harper was sweating and trying not to let it show. Today of all days, he needed to look calm and collected.

Thank God it was a good day for Annabelle. Mary had taken the day off work to bring her, and the two of them sat beside him.

Annabelle squeezed his hand, leaned in and whispered, 'I'm right proud of you.'

He beamed. It was the highest praise he could ask for.

A nod from the Lord Mayor and he climbed the three stairs to the dais, standing to attention as he looked down at everyone. His wife, his daughter, with the Voluntary Patrol armband on her coat. Inspector Walsh, about to become a superintendent, even if he didn't know it yet. Ash, with his wife. He was still using crutches, unable to walk far without a break, but he was alive. Retired on a full pension. The only one missing was Billy Reed, but he'd been gone for nine years. Dead of a heart attack in Whitby.

The mayor brought him back to the here and now. 'Mr Harper, you've been acting as the chief constable of Leeds since the sad, untimely death of Robert Parker. The watch committee has undertaken a search for the best person to take on the role permanently and concluded that he was already in the job.' A pause to let the councillors mutter their agreement. 'Therefore, we're here today to officially invest you as chief constable of the city of Leeds.'

Applause. Some cheers from the ranks who'd manage to sneak in at the back.

Harper looked down at the floor for a moment, unfolded the piece of paper in his hand and put on his spectacles.

'Thank you, Your Worship. I never expected this honour. Not even in a temporary manner, let alone permanent. But the real credit goes to the men on the force and' – he turned towards his daughter – 'the women who volunteer. They do the work, and without them this city would be in a bad way. I give them my thanks, and also to those on the watch committee for deciding I was the right candidate. Finally, to my wife, for her love and support across the years.'

More applause. He stood and accepted it, then held out his hand before nodding to one of the councillors, who passed him a small scroll.

'My very first duty as chief constable is to present this. It's a commendation for bravery above and beyond what we expect from our men. I want to give it to retired Superintendent Frederick Ash for all he did in helping to apprehend a very dangerous criminal.'

No need to Ash to come up there. Harper walked over and handed it to him with a long handshake.

'Thank you, sir.'

'You've earned it. Many times over.'

Done, apart from the buffet afterwards. Talk of the war and how soon it might end now that America was involved and pouring troops into Europe. Still plenty of blood and death ahead, and a long struggle. But it felt as if they'd turned a corner.

But none of that brought back the dead. The loss still haunted Mary's eyes. The photograph of Len standing proud in his uniform sat on her dressing table. How many other women were going through the same?

And then there was the truth hidden in the name of war. The women who'd died at Barnbow whose families would never know what really happened. The relatives of the people Gibson had killed. Even Gibson himself; his parents had been told he'd died in an accident.

Time to leave all that behind.

'They put on a good do here, don't they?' Annabelle said. 'You wouldn't think there were any food shortages from this spread.' She had a piece of cake in one hand, a fancy in the other, and a face full of pleasure.

She hadn't disappeared again since that day in February when she'd wandered over to the Bank. She had no memory of doing it. But they kept a closer eye on her now. Johanna locked the door of the living quarters above the pub so she couldn't walk away.

Harper and Mary had come up with a plan. So far it was working. But things would grow worse, and Annabelle would need more and more care.

'Making a greedy guts of yourself?' he asked with a grin.

'Taking advantage while it's here.' She nudged him. 'Go and talk to Ash. He looks like he wants a word.'

It was strange to see the big man on crutches. He'd lost weight, his face thinner and more serious. Nancy Ash stood at his side, watching him closely.

'Congratulations, sir. It's the right man in the job. Nice that they decided to confirm it.'

'Thank Councillor Thompson.' He looked around. Charles Thompson hovered in the far corner, raising his glass in a toast as Harper caught his eye. 'He approved of the way we handled the Gibson case.'

'You could do worse than have him behind you, sir.'

'So I hear.' But he'd rather not end up beholden to anyone.

Thompson was the powerhouse on the council, eager to make Leeds as large as possible as he pushed to annex the surrounding villages and suburbs. Whatever he wanted usually happened. And he'd been the one to tell the watch committee that Harper should be chief constable.

The question was what he'd ask for in return.

Walsh ambled over, an almost empty glass in his hand. 'Congratulations, sir. I hope you'll have some sympathy for us out there working.'

'Not a chance, Superintendent.'

At first he didn't seem to notice. Then his eyes widened, filled with disbelief. 'Sir?'

'You're in charge of A Division now.' It hadn't had a proper commander since Ash retired. 'I'm going to expect a lot from you and the men at Millgarth.'

'Yes, sir. Of course.' He was blushing with pride. 'Thank you.'

He stayed a few minutes longer, circulating, making small talk, with half an eye on Annabelle and Mary. When his daughter gave him the nod, he made his farewells and escorted the women down to his car.

'I'll tell you what, Tom Harper,' Annabelle said. 'If I'd known you were going to rise this high, I wouldn't have waited so long to marry you.'

'Strange days.' He stared up at the town hall. Blackened, bruised by the years. The spotter nest up at the top. 'Home?'

'Yes.' Annabelle sighed. 'I've loved this, but I'm exhausted. I get tired so easily these days.'

'It doesn't matter.' He kissed her cheek. 'It really doesn't matter.'

AFTERWORD

A writer might have the idea and put the words on the page. But no writer works alone. I'm grateful to everyone at Severn House for the work they do, and no one more than my editor Sara Porter, whose eye for detail has saved me from many of my own errors. Kate Lyall Grant, when she was there, Joanne Grant . . . the list is long.

Lynne Patrick has edited my work since the very first novel. That partnership has become an enduring friendship. She understands what I do and I trust her completely.

To the real Palmaers who inspired the ones here: thanks.

To all the librarians and the booksellers: I'm grateful for all your work. We don't say it to you enough. And to all of you who read my books, thank you. It means so much to have you come along with Tom and Annabelle and Mary, and we're not done yet.

Finally, to Penny Lomas. Her support, her wise criticisms and her love keep me going, more than I ever imagined.